Praise for Dwain L. Herndon's previous book
When the Birds Stop Singing

"When an author can bring you seamlessly to another time it is truly a gift to the reader. Dwain L. Herndon does just that in his book *When the Birds Stop Singing*. I read approximately 25 books a year and it is definitely in my top five for 2014. The story takes place in rural Kentucky during the age of Prohibition. When you read this book you get to face everything: young love, intrigue, racism, secrets, murder, small town politics, and northern views—southern views regarding how we saw each other then. The characters are very well developed and the area is so well described you can almost hear the whippoorwills. When I had to put the book down I was excited to return to it as the mystery unfolded. Best of all, I couldn't predict the outcome, and that's rare! Congratulations, Mr. Herndon, this one is a winner."

– Elbie Ancona, former New Yorker now living in Atlanta

"This book turned out to be most riveting. It's very good with meaningful, well-developed characters and a plot that makes you anxious to turn to the next page. I truly enjoyed the book. It's a good read. I recommend it to anyone who enjoys a good page turner."

– Patricia Gates, suburban Atlanta

"*When the Birds Stop Singing* is an appealing story set in rural Kentucky during Prohibition. Mr. Herndon has brought to life well-developed characters from another era. His protagonist, Nick Kincaid, defies his father and follows his dream to become a teacher by leaving Chicago and moving to Kentucky. This carefully crafted story keeps the reader turning pages. Who was the killer? Whose baby was found in the woodbin? Who is trying to take over the whiskey business? Does Nick ever get his girl? The characters are engaging and the plot keeps shifting with ever turn of a page. I truly enjoyed the book."

– Mary Bowman, Lilburn, Georgia

Praise for Dwain L. Herndon's book
Beyond the Next Hill

"*Beyond the Next Hill* is a remarkable story of redemption, love, and the desire for one man to put to rest the ghosts of his past. Tyler Bracken comes across as real, down-to-earth, the kind of man who has made too many mistakes and knows it. When given the chance to right some of those wrongs, it's riveting to watch the character make the choices he does, some wise, some not. That's what makes Tyler (along with the rest of the characters) so compelling to this reader.

"Written in a very readable prose with vivid descriptions of both the characters and the area of Kentucky where the story is set, you will find this story hard to put down. It's gritty and emotional, a truly excellent debut novel."

> – Jana Oliver, award-winning author of the
> *Time Rover Series* and the *Demon Trapper Series*

"If you've ever hoped for a second chance in life, this book is for you. Tyler Bracken, the hero in the story, is a little rough around the edges, a little crude, and swings more temper than a boxer with an attitude. But underneath it all is a caring heart that's just waiting for a reason to come out.

"Dwain L. Herndon paints the small Kentucky town with all the warmth and kick of Southern whiskey. You can't help but fall in love with the characters. Forthright Molly, rebellious Luke, warmhearted Lindy, and my personal favorite, the sheriff. But it's not all down home appeal as the story unfolds the elements of an unexpected crime and people wrongly accused. Get ready to curl up with the book and just keep reading. I loved this story!"

> – Nanette Littlestone, award-winning author and
> publisher of *F.A.I.T.H. – Finding Answers in the Heart*

"I could not put this book down! I loved every beautifully crafted word in *Beyond the Next Hill*. The author's ability to turn a catchy phrase put vivid pictures in my head and made my experience more like watching a film than read a book. His characters are both realistic and enduring. I was engaged from the first sentence to the last."

> – Colleen Walsh Fong, Ezine.com expert and
> author of the touchscreen *Easy Weekly Meals* series

Somewhere a Pinch of Love

Dwain L. Herndon

WORDS OF PASSION • ATLANTA

Published by Words of Passion, Duluth, GA 30097.

Editor: Nanette Littlestone
Cover: Ginnifer Herndon
Interior Design: Nanette Littlestone and Peter Hildebrandt

ISBN: 978-0-9960709-9-7

To my children Kimberly, Myles, and Devin Herndon

Acknowledgments

Special thanks to Words of Passion author and publisher Nanette Littlestone. I'm fortunate to have her as a friend, as well as the editor and publisher of *Somewhere a Pinch of Love*. Thanks also go to my friends, Colleen Walsh Fong and C.J. Atticus. Their input and suggestions are always appreciated.

Many thanks to my talented daughter-in-law, Ginnifer Herndon, who designed the book cover. She catches the spirit of the book.

PART ONE

1

CHICAGO, ILLINOIS
MAY 4, 1960

I awoke to loud voices outside the motel room door. Mama and her new boyfriend were in a fight again. I couldn't understand what was said until Johnny shouted for her to choose one. It was my birthday. I thought it had to do with choosing a birthday gift until she called him a son-of-a-bitch. She slipped back inside and leaned against the door for a moment, and then grabbed her handbag and began digging for loose coins. Those found and the ones stolen from Johnny's pocket while he showered filled an ashtray.

"Wake up, Rudy." She jerked the sheet aside and shoved the ashtray toward me. "Here's some change. Get a soda and candy bar from the vendin' machines outside the main office when you get hungry. Don't talk to nobody, and hurry and get back inside." She

1

took a sealed envelope from her purse. "If a cop comes lookin' for me or Johnny, give him this. Don't open it."

Johnny pounded the door and shouted, "Come on, Margaret, make a choice and get your ass moving."

"Mama, it's May 4th. Look, I marked it on the calendar. Am I still having a birthday? You said we'd celebrate."

She reached across me and yanked my younger brother out of bed and onto the floor. With Benny half asleep, she dragged him, stumbling out the door.

Something wasn't right. Mama had me look after Benny when she went away with a man for a few days, but this time she'd said nothing.

A motor cranked. I rolled out of bed and raced outside as the car shot across the parking lot and onto the street. I ran screaming for Mama to take me with her. She never looked back.

I dropped to my knees and began to cry, more scared than I'd ever been, more than when the old man grabbed me in the alley. I'd kicked him hard and he'd let go. But I couldn't make Mama take me with her.

I ran back into the room and pushed the deadbolt into place. She took Benny. What had I done to make Mama not want me too?

I crawled into the closet and didn't move when the motel manager came for the rent later that day. I cried so much my eyes were swollen the next morning. As scared as I felt, I couldn't hide forever. Mama wasn't coming back. When the manager came again to collect the rent, I opened the door. He stepped inside, looked around. "Okay, kid, where's your mom? Did she leave the rent money?"

Too scared to speak, I stuck the letter for the police toward him.

He pushed long, oily hair away from his eyes and tore into the envelope. "Where's the rent money?" he growled.

I backed away and said nothing.

He read the letter and looked down at me. "Sorry, kid, life's a bitch some days. How old are you?"

"Eight. It's my birthday. Mama said we'd celebrate, but now I don't know."

He reached for my hand. "Come with me."

I backed away and asked where he wanted to take me. Mama said never to go off with men who promised you things.

"Kid, your mom's not coming back. This note is to the police. You'll be sent to your grandmother. She lives in the Kentucky mountains." He held up the letter. "Got her name, phone number, and address right here."

Tears pushed past my eyelids and rolled onto my cheeks. "Doesn't Mama want me anymore?"

He looked away. "I hear Kentucky is a real pretty place. You'll be living in real high mountains. I bet that will be fun."

"I don't think so. Mama's mama is my only grandma. Mama hasn't seen her in years and called her bad names all the time. She doesn't like her one bit."

The man handed me his handkerchief. "Wipe your eyes. Everything's going to be all right. I'll take you across the street to the diner for a hot meal before talking to the police."

"Will they put me in jail?"

"No, they won't do that. That's for bad guys. I can tell you're a good guy. You'll be sent to your grandmother."

"But I've never even seen her."

"Where is your dad? What about him?"

3

"Mama said I never had one."

2

BARBOURVILLE, KENTUCKY
MAY 1960

The sun feathered the trees across the mountains and shadows had crawled across the valley when the bus rolled to a stop in front of a small grocery store. Its white and blue clapboard exterior was in need of paint. A small woman with bird-like legs and bushy white hair sat on a bench beneath a Greyhound sign. She wore a baseball cap, denim pants, and a faded, blue-checked shirt.

She rose and stood with her arms crossed as her eyes moved from window to window until settling on me. That had to be my unhappy grandma. The Chicago policeman had described her to his partner as a pain in the butt after talking with her on the phone. I think he was right. Her mouth turned down at the corners like an upside-down smile, and her blue eyes flashed like she was afraid of something. I stepped off the bus and smiled real big.

"You've gotta be Margaret's kid," she growled.

I pointed to the name tag pinned to my shirt that read "Rudy Kelly, Barbourville, Kentucky." She grabbed my arm and jerked me toward an old, rusty, multi-colored truck that offered no clue to its original color. After tossing the paper bag that held my belongings into the truck bed, she told me to get my ass inside.

We started up the mountain. I waited for her to say something, but she never said a word, though she cut her eyes toward me several times. After I'd decided she wasn't going to talk, she blurted, "You don' talk much, do you?"

"No, ma'am."

"People call me Will Jean. It ain't my real name. Willa Jean was my name before I changed it years back. You can call me Grandma if you want. Course it wouldn't hurt nothin' if you wanted to call me Will Jean."

"Will is a man's name."

"You can see I ain't no man and don't want to be one. A name is what you want it to be. I've been callin' your mama a few choice names for sending you here. She ain't no good puttin' you off on me. God's gonna punish her ass for it, you wait and see."

"I don't like you saying bad things about my mama."

"She's what she is, kid. No good! She left yo' ass high and dry, didn't she? She's been chasin' a black bear all her life."

"Mama doesn't like bears. We went to the zoo once. She doesn't like them."

"It's just a sayin' mountain folks use. It means a person is always doin' somethin' to get 'em in trouble. Nobody is stupid enough to chase a bear, are they?"

"No, ma'am."

"Her daddy was a loser too. I hope you ain't like him or your mama, 'cause if you are, your skinny ass goes out the door. I ain't puttin' up with shit from you. You got that?"

I didn't answer back. Mama was right about her. On TV, all grandmas loved their grandchildren. My real-life grandma didn't love me. I didn't think she even liked me.

Her house was built with logs and roughhewn sawmill boards. It stood on a sloping hillside, surrounded by tall trees. Steps led up to the porch that ran the length of the house. I followed her into a large room where log beams spanned an open ceiling. A massive stone fireplace stood at the end of the room. Two electric stoves were side by side by the fireplace. I couldn't figure why she'd need two stoves, but I thought it was better not to ask.

She pitched the paper bag that held my things to me and pointed toward a hallway. "You stay in the second door down."

Unsure about what to do next, I slipped into a rocker beside the fireplace. This wasn't the welcome I'd expected. She was strange . . . talked funny and seemed not to like anything. I decided the less I said from now on was for the best.

The next morning, she pounded on the door and yelled for me to get up. I rolled out of bed and reached for my pants. They were gone. I'd left them on the floor beside the bed. I dropped to my knees thinking they could have been kicked underneath. It was then that I noticed the pants and shirt hung neatly pressed over the back of a chair. Why would she do that? She didn't even like me. My grandma was strange for sure.

She pointed to a chair at the table. I sat and stared wide-eyed at my plate. Food was piled a mile high, enough to last a week:

homemade biscuits, ham gravy, fried potatoes, eggs, sausage, black-berry jam, and two glasses of milk.

"Eat up," she growled.

I'd had only candy bars on the bus. I was hungry and stuffed myself. When I finished, I pushed my plate aside and she yelled, "Boy, you can't be finished. Some little mountain girl half your size will beat the crap out of a skinny ass kid like you."

I didn't like her thinking a girl could beat me up. No girl could, but I kept quiet. She talked funny. She must be part crazy like Mama always claimed.

"You're startin' to school this mornin'," she announced. "That will keep you out of my hair for the day. There's a pan of warm water on the stove. Take it to the back room and wash your private parts. If it takes too long, you're gonna grow warts on your hands, you hear?"

I felt my face grow red. How could she know about that?

She insisted on combing my hair. Said it was long enough for me to pass as a girl. I didn't like that either, but it got worse when she asked me if I'd ever looked up a little girl's dress.

I told her no, loud and clear. What was wrong with this grandma? I had no reason to look up a girl's dress. But now that she'd asked, I wondered what I'd see.

She told me to wait on the porch until she cleaned the kitchen and then we'd leave for school. I dangled my feet from the end of the porch and watched the sunrise. It was the prettiest sight I'd ever seen in my whole life. At first the sky glowed above the mountain top, and then it spread like a peacock's tail feathers, becoming a rainbow of colors. The sun soon climbed over the tree tops and spread beams of light across the valley. Just seeing it was reason enough to believe there was a God like the Chicago street preacher told me.

Will Jean came out the screen door wearing what looked like men's clothes, but I wasn't about to say anything. She grabbed a hickory walking cane that leaned against the wall by the door and motioned for me to follow.

We started down a long graveled lane that connected to a narrow blacktop road. She tapped the cane against the ground with each step. I asked why she had the cane. She looked at me and rolled her eyes. "That's a dumb-ass question if I've ever heard one. It's to pull me back up the mountain. Anybody knows that."

Her answer made no sense. Nothing about her did, especially her thinking a girl could beat me up and that my hair made me look like one.

I liked the mountain right away. Birds were singing or talking to each other as we went down the path. As the sun moved higher in the sky the mountainsides changed colors. One side turned golden and the one across the valley remained shades of brown and green. This was the prettiest place I'd ever been. I loved the mountains, but I couldn't say the same about Grandma. She was too strange to love yet. I decided to call her Will Jean until I had reason to want her as my grandma.

A shallow river at the edge of town required us to use the swinging bridge. It was about three feet wide and made of boards suspended on cables stretched across the river. I moved back and forth with each step. It was fun to walk on and I began to jump around. The bridge swayed from side to side even more. I began to laugh until Will Jean nearly lost her footing. "Stop it, you little shithead." She yelled and whacked at me with the cane.

9

Kids sitting on the school steps cleared a path to the front door in a hurry as we drew near. I understood why. Will Jean's jaws were pulled tight and her eyes were going from side to side as if trying to decide which kid to eat first. Her expression never changed when we marched into my homeroom and faced a tall, thin man with brown hair and a warm smile. He rose from behind a desk.

"Rudy Thomas Kelly is this boy's name. If you ever whoop his ass, I'll whoop yours." With that said, Will Jean left me standing there. I turned red and didn't know what to say.

The young teacher's mouth hung open as he watched her go. He turned to me and chuckled. "Is that your granny?"

I nodded. "She's kind of different."

He chuckled again. "She doesn't mince words, does she? Shall I call you Rudy or Thomas?"

"Mama called me Rudy."

He smiled. "You look like a Rudy. If I remember correctly, Rudy in old English means *wolf*. Did you know that?"

"No, sir."

"I'm Mr. Wells, your homeroom teacher."

He sounded like Will Jean when he talked, but he smiled. She hadn't done that yet. I wasn't sure she knew how.

"I assume you live with your granny. Where are your parents?"

"I never had a daddy. Mama took my younger brother but didn't want me."

He grimaced. "You look like a fine young man. I can't imagine anyone not wanting you. Maybe she knew you were strong and could make it without her better than your brother."

"I don't think so. I did something to make her not want me."

"No, Rudy, what happened is not your fault."

"It feels like it's my fault. How do I make it stop?"

"It will take time. Look, Rudy, should you need to talk about a problem in or outside of school, you can come to me. Okay?"

I nodded.

He pointed to a seat beside the window. "That's your desk."

I liked it right away. "I can see blue sky past the top of the mountain."

"That's Bear Mountain. I go camping there often."

"Why is it called Bear Mountain?"

"A lot of bears live up there."

The bell rang and the hall filled with running feet and voices that fell silent as a swarm of kids streamed into the room. A girl with yellow curls sat in front of me. She smiled and said "Hi" as she took her seat. I couldn't find my tongue, so I smiled back real big, so big she could see most all my teeth. A Chicago teacher told me I had a wide mouth and good teeth, so I should smile more.

The day started with addition and numbers, followed by spelling, and then came the part I liked best, a story about the Cherokee Indians who once lived in the area. Mr. Wells said there was a park not far away. He listed the names of native animals that lived there and said that some could be dangerous. Many of the dangerous ones lived within a few miles of our homes.

At recess girls giggled and looked me over like I was in a zoo. I didn't like the ones telling me I was cute. But it was good to know that none of those wanted to beat me up. I couldn't understand why some giggled and asked questions after I told them I didn't want to talk.

During recess, we were taking turns on the slide when a girl wearing a short dress smiled real big and pushed in front of me. She started up the ladder with ruffled underwear only inches from my face. I took a quick peek without thinking. The tall boy behind me laughed and said, "You looked at Nadine's fancy drawers."

"Did not," I said.

"You did too," the kid behind him said.

"What's holding up the line?" Mr. Wells called as he hurried across the playground.

"Nothing," the tall boy answered and whispered for me to move on.

He later admitted he'd watched a neighbor lady take a bath in a washtub on her back porch. I didn't have the nerve to tell him he was going straight to hell and wondered if I might be going myself for wondering what she looked like.

I thought about Mama a few times during the day, but not enough to make me want to cry until Mr. Wells read a story about a lost pony. The writer had put words together in the story that made me sad when the pony couldn't find his mama and happy enough to cry when he found her. I felt like that lost pony.

After school, I hung around and played ball with the two brothers I'd met on the slide. They were from the orphanage at the edge of town. Their mama didn't want to give them up, but there were too many kids to care for after their daddy was hurt in a mining accident.

We played until the sun moved behind the tree line and dark shadows moved up the mountainside. I wished I had started for home sooner and took off for home at a fast run. No birds were singing and the woods on each side of the narrow road were dark. I imagined the dangerous animals that Mr. Wells had listed on the blackboard waited behind the next bush.

12

I pushed up the mountain, straining to go faster. My shirt was wet and my legs ached by the time I reached the house. Will Jean waited on the front steps with eyes flashing waves of anger. She demanded to know where I'd been.

"To school," I answered, gasping air while wiping sweat with the bottom of my shirt.

"Don't lie. It let out hours ago."

"I played ball with some guys for a while."

"With me worryin' my ass off, afraid somebody had took you."

"I'm sorry."

"I never wanted you in the first place. You're headin' for an ass whoopin' if this is the way you're gonna be." She turned and disappeared inside.

Hurt and angry, I dropped down on the steps. Mama never cared where I played unless she wanted me to keep Benny so she could go clubbing. It made me nearly cry to know that no one wanted me. Not mama, not Will Jean. What had I done? The screen door opened behind me and Will Jean stuck her head out. I jumped to my feet, expecting her to send me packing like she'd threatened.

"Get to the table if you're aimin' to eat."

I hurried inside and took my chair at the table. I couldn't believe my eyes. The plate of food in front of me included two chicken legs, sliced tomatoes, fried yellow corn, green beans, buttered squash, and a bowl of fresh blueberries, swimming in heavy cream.

I looked up at her, thinking this couldn't be for me. She planned to snatch the plate away after the first bite.

"There's more on the stove," she snapped. With that said, she resumed cleaning the kitchen.

13

I couldn't believe she wanted me to eat all that food. Was she trying to fatten me up? I'd heard mountain people sometimes did strange things. Could she be a witch with plans to eat me?

After my last bite, she jerked my empty plate away and pitched my school books down in front of me. "If you have lessons to get, get 'em."

Hoping not to make her mad at me, I thanked her for dinner and told her it was the best meal I'd ever had.

She rolled her eyes. "Don't you know nothin' from nothin'? It ain't dinner. It's called supper. Dinner you eat at dinnertime."

Was she trying to make me crazy? What time was dinner time? What was the difference between supper and dinner? I decided to just say nothing and do my homework. She sat in her chair by the fireplace and knitted while listening to a country western station.

I finished my homework and saw that her eyes were closed. Her fingers continued to make each stitch. Was she dead or asleep? She was breathing. To knit in her sleep was proof I had a strange grandma . . . maybe even a crazy one.

It made sense to lock my door that night, but it was unlocked the next morning. The woman must know about magic. I was sure she'd used magic after I found my pants and shirt pressed and hanging on the chair back the next morning.

From that day forward her routine never changed. She cooked, washed and pressed my clothes, but how she talked to me and what she did for me was like dealing with two people. I soon decided she wasn't a witch, but she was strange for sure.

3

Weeks passed and the hot meals kept coming, along with hurtful threats and constant criticism. I tried to do what she wanted, but there was no pleasing her. It hurt to know that I wasn't wanted, but it made me angry to be reminded. Not a day passed without her telling me I was no good like my mama and as useless as my daddy, whoever he was.

School was the best part of my day. Mr. Wells was my teacher and friend, if I understood how a grownup friend should act. One afternoon, as the class poured out the door, he called for me to wait up. He smiled and pointed to a chair across the desk.

"Rudy, you're doing well with your studies. This month you've read more books from the library than any other student in school."

"It's fun to read."

"Yes, it is. What else do you do to have fun?"

"I play ball with my friends at recess and sometimes after school."

"That's here at school. What do you do for fun at home?"

Will Jean wouldn't allow friends over, so the answer was nothing. But I didn't want to say that. My mind raced to come up with an answer, but there was none. I shrugged and said, "I mostly look at the mountains."

"You like the mountains, huh?"

"Yes, sir, but they're kind of scary. Will Jean told me to stay near the house so a bear couldn't kill me."

"I'm sure she never meant to scare you. Bears will leave you alone if you'll do the same with them. The exception is when a bear is hurt or has cubs nearby. That rule is true with most wild animals protecting their young."

"Will Jean said a bear could eat me up like I was never born."

"Bears don't eat people. Perhaps she was teasing. I've lived in the mountains all my life, and I respect an animal's space. My dad took me camping when I was about your age. Would you like to go camping sometime?"

"Maybe."

"Maybe indicates a condition."

"Will Jean might not let me go if bears could kill me."

"If you were with me the bear would have to kill me first."

I couldn't believe what he'd just said. To protect me like that meant he was really my friend.

"If you went camping with me, it would be my responsibility to keep you safe. Find out if your granny will permit you to go. I'll speak with her if you like."

I felt a lump in my throat. If I had a hundred dozen wishes, I'd use them all to make Mr. Wells my daddy.

I hurried home after school and found Will Jean out back taking clothes off the line. I helped while trying to gather enough courage to ask about camping with Mr. Wells. She was her usual self, growled at me when I let the end of a sheet touch the ground and found fault with the way I folded towels. There was no use waiting, so I finally blurted that Mr. Wells had invited me to go camping.

She acted like she never heard and kept pulling clothes from the line and dropping the wooden pins in a tin bucket. I waited, anxious for an answer. When I had listened to the pins hit the bucket for what seemed forever, I was ready to kick the bucket across the yard when she said, "I reckon it would be all right for you to go. You need to be around a man so as not to turn into a girl."

Why would she say that? We weren't even made the same. No way could I turn into a girl. But she'd said I could go and that's what I wanted to hear.

The camping trip took place two weeks later. While going up the trail, Mr. Wells told me not to expect favors in the classroom just because we went camping together. He also said I could call him Leon when camping, but it must be Mr. Wells at school.

After two hours of walking we reached the campsite. The teacher part took over as Mr. Wells explained camping rules. I was not to be out of his sight, not even when I used the bathroom. I wasn't sure I liked that rule, but I said nothing.

"Okay, Tiger, the first order of business is to prepare the camp for the night. It gets cool after sundown. There's driftwood washed up along the creek. You gather it for a fire and I'll set up the tent."

Happy that he'd called me Tiger and eager to please, I raced alongside the rushing stream and gathered driftwood, sometimes dragging pieces too large to carry. I made trip after trip, though Mr. Wells had me in his sight at all times. I was sure dads did that when camping with their sons. It felt good to have Mr. Wells care about me like I was his son.

The camp was ready for the night with plenty of daylight left. We settled down on a rock next to the stream and cast our lines. He whispered, "It'll be deer jerky and beans for supper if neither of us snags a trout."

"Why are you whispering?" I whispered back.

"Don't want to scare the fish."

"Can they understand what you just said?"

Mr. Wells laughed. "Who knows?"

"If they heard us planning to eat them for supper, it'd be a dumb fish to bite."

He laughed again. "You're a bright kid, Rudy. "

I was pleased to hear him say I was bright but more pleased when I caught a trout weighing about two pounds. He complimented me on bringing it in, but he did most of the work. I was anxious to tell my friends at school. They would be impressed, but not Will Jean. She found something wrong with everything I did.

I shut my eyes when he split the fish belly open but peeked when he scraped the insides into a paper bag.

He smiled. "It's gross, but it's the law of nature at work. You should never kill an animal unless it's for food or to protect yourself. My dad taught me that."

"Did he teach you to save the bad parts in a bag?"

He laughed. "No, but he taught me to respect the rules all good campers follow. And that's what we're doing by burying the bag, so it can't draw hungry animals here. Some might be unfriendly. Your assignment is to dig a hole twelve-to-eighteen inches deep to bury the bag. I'll get kindling for a fire."

The soft soil was easy digging and it took only minutes to open a good-sized hole. Mr. Wells called for me to come quick. I dropped the shovel and raced to join him in an open area at the edge of the campsite. He pointed toward two birds in an air battle. "That's a red-tailed chicken hawk giving chase."

"He's a bully if you ask me. I don't like him fighting with the little guy."

Mr. Wells chuckled. "They're not fighting. It's an attack. The hawk is after food, perhaps to feed her young."

"You mean the hawk is going to eat the little bird?"

"Yeah, just like you and I are going to eat the fish you caught. Both are perfect examples of how nature works. That hawk could be after baby chicks in your granny's backyard."

"That would make her steaming mad."

"I'm sure it would. Come, I can show you something else that might be of interest."

I followed him a quarter mile up an incline to a higher elevation. He handed me the binoculars from around his neck and told me to focus on a naked rock with dark green foliage around it, and then move up near the top.

"Do you see anything?"

"Yeah, it's an eagle. I've seen pictures before."

"That pair comes here each year to raise their young. I've watched them for five or six years. You're seeing the female. She tidies the nest while the male is off gathering more sticks."

"Is it like they're married?"

He laughed. "Something like that, except the female thinks nothing about cheating on him."

"What would she do to cheat?"

19

"Well, uh. That's a conversation . . . maybe I can explain it this way. I have a girlfriend. We're getting married this fall. I would never cheat on her by going out with another girl."

"Oh, I see. Mama's boyfriend went out with other girls. He cheated all the time. They had fights and I'd take Benny outside when they got loud or hit each other."

"That was a good thing to do. You're a terrific young man, Rudy. I'm really glad that we've become friends."

"Thanks," I muttered. To hear him say we were friends made me feel like crying, but there was no way I'd do that. Only babies cry.

"Okay, Tiger, let's cook our fish. I'll race you back. My legs are longer and I'll give you fifty feet. Get set and count to three."

I ran ahead for what I thought was fifty feet, then hollered, "The last one in camp is a rotten egg."

"You're on," he called.

I took off at full speed, but sensed that Mr. Wells was gaining. I checked and saw that he was getting closer. When I turned back, two baby bears in a wrestling match rolled onto the path in front of me. I tried to stop and slipped on loose gravel, colliding with the cubs. They went screaming back into the woods.

Mr. Wells was beside me in a flash and jerked me to my feet. I tried to run, but he pulled me against him. "Don't move," he whispered. "You're going to be fine. I'll take care of you. If the sow heard her cubs cry she needs to locate them before we move."

After a moment of silence, bushes parted about thirty feet up the trail and the mother bear shot out of the underbrush and charged toward us. Mr. Wells began shouting and waving his hands about his head. The bear kept coming.

"Oh, my God! No, no." He pulled me against him, locked both arms around me and turned his back toward the oncoming bear.

A jolt of pain ran the length of my leg. I cried out, "It hurts."

"He's coming out of it," a strange voice said.

A leathery hand smoothed my hair back. "Ain't no need to whine, boy. You're in the hospital being doctored."

"My leg hurts."

"Course it does," Will Jean said. "It's cut deep."

"What happened?"

"You hurt it. Doc sewed it up. Only a dumb-ass kid like you would run from a bear." A pain hit again. "Why are you makin' such a face?"

"It hurts real bad."

"Suck it up, boy, unless you want Doc to give you some more dope."

A man leaned forward. "Rudy, I'm Dr. Miller. You'll be fine. I can give you something if your leg hurts."

"It hurts real bad."

"You're carryin' on like a sissy ass kid. Now stop whinin'."

"I had the worst dream. It was a camping trip. It was fun until . . ." The horror of the attack flashed in front of me. I screamed, "Mr. Wells, where is he?" I thrashed with both arms and tried to crawl out of bed. Will Jean pushed me back. I struggled against her, but she held on tight. "Quick, give him a shot of that dope again," she said.

The sting of a needle warmed like a blanket as it swept over me. Days and nights merged. Footsteps came and went. Voices faded in and out for hours, maybe days. I wasn't sure how long before I heard voices again, faint at first, and then Will Jean's voice grew louder.

"Doc, stop the damn dope and let him wake up. He's gonna get to likin' it too much."

"Not yet, Will Jean. The boy's body needs rest to recover. His leg's infected. That's what caused the fever. The terror he witnessed from three days in the woods can't be dismissed. He's had reason to be irrational, to babble about fish not being buried, and his daddy's face gone."

"He ain't never had a daddy."

"All boys need a male in their lives. Maybe Leon was the kind of man he wanted for a father. Sheriff John's theory is that Rudy tried to run. Leon confronted the bear to save the boy. He was the kind of man to put his life on the line for a kid." He leaned close and I felt his breath. "The injection is working."

Days later the fever broke. I awoke to voices in the hallway and heard someone comment on the large turnout for Mr. Wells' funeral.

I began screaming. Nurses came running and held me down, but I couldn't stop screaming. "Mr. Wells is dead. There's no one to like me now."

Bouts of crying continued for weeks each time I thought about Mr. Wells. My infected leg remained stubborn, and so did the pain that came mostly at night. It would sometimes send me to the porch in tears until a little white pill kicked in. As days passed, I thought nothing of sneaking a few from the bottle to get me through the day. Will Jean discovered them in my pants pocket and marched me in to see the doctor.

The new pills left me flat. No energy. Lifeless. I wanted to sleep all the time, but Will Jean wasn't having it. She pulled me out of bed and lined up chores. I cried and protested to no avail. Each day I hobbled around, fed chickens, watered cows, shucked corn, and weeded the garden . . . something all the time. She preached constantly that a little work would create good blood flow and heal the leg. I'm not sure if she was right or wrong, but by the time school started that fall the wound had healed. I took up running to strengthen the leg as the doctor advised. Not only did it help the leg, I grew in bulk and height, no longer the skinny little kid.

4

I awoke to hear Will Jean cursing politicians on TV. It was my birthday. I reached for a card on the night stand that my teacher had given me. She'd written that I was such a special student and it was a pleasure to have me in her class. I raised up and listened after Will Jean called some politician a lousy, lying son-of-a-bitch. This time, she was cursing out the democrats who had ended a two-day protest in favor of gun control by having a sit-in on the floor of Congress.

I slipped into pressed jeans and a tee shirt that hung on a chair back. It'd been five years since Mama pushed me off on Will Jean. My relationship with her had worsened. I was older and it was difficult not to fight back. I hung out in the mountains as much as possible just to avoid her.

Birthdays had never served me well. I always thought about the day Mama left. I wondered what she was doing. I hoped she thought of me on my birthday, but I doubted it.

A string of curses came from the other room. Will Jean was giving the president hell. I found her watching the news and drinking coffee. I tossed the birthday card down on the TV tray beside her coffee. "My homeroom teacher gave me a birthday card. She wrote that I was her best student. You want to see it?"

"Why would I? That teacher don't care shit about your birthday and I don't either."

I stared at her for a moment and walked away. "Happy birthday, Rudy," I muttered, and gave her the finger.

"That sorry-ass Johnson and his Great Society. A piss poor president, I'd say. He's gonna take my taxes and give them to some lazy ass who won't work. You just wait, it'll be the death of this country. Everybody will be wantin' somethin' free."

Knowing that it would piss her off, I poked at her by saying, "He's just trying to help the poor."

"Poor, my ass. I'm poor and nobody gives me nothin'. I don't want nobody givin' me nothin'. I just want the government to stay out of my business."

I dropped down at the table and began to eat. "Then write the president and tell him what you think."

"Let me tell you what I think about you. You need to get your ass home the minute school turns out. There's always chores to do. I never know what you're doin' or when you'll get home."

"I've told you I run the trails after school. It relaxes me . . . makes me feel good."

"You can't be runnin' all the time. Don't try to fool me. You been layin' out with some little slut after school?"

"I wish," I muttered.

She jerked around. "What did you say?"

"I said, I'm thirteen and not familiar with sluts yet."

"Don't get smart with me. I've watched your eyes follow a pretty girl."

"I don't go for pretty guys."

"What do you mean by that?"

"Nothing. Just a joke. I'm going to school." I started for the door.

"Wait. You ain't eat hardly nothin'."

"Not hungry. The conversation made me lose my appetite."

I had forgotten that students who qualified to represent the school in track and field would be announced today. Our school was competing with a neighboring school in a Health and Fitness Day. It was done to emphasize the need for exercise among young people.

I sensed that I had done well in the qualification rounds, though I had never clocked myself as a runner. When the coach leaned close to the microphone and asked me to stand, I was surprised. Excitement followed when he announced that I had clocked under eleven seconds in the one hundred meters, the best time in the competition and outstanding for a runner in the twelve to thirteen age group.

Thundering applause followed, and later came congrats and back slapping from some of the guys. The attention felt strange, but good. It put a value on me, set me apart from all the other guys in the school. I liked the feeling since I'd never valued myself much. I felt a little special for the first time, but after giving it some thought

I decided everyone had something special about them if they could only decide what.

From that day forward, I stopped being the unnoticed, quiet kid and became known as the guy who ran the fastest one hundred.

Helms, the track coach at the high school, heard about my time and invited me to try out for next year's freshman team. He proved to be a man of few words. I introduced myself and he pointed toward the track and told me to let him see me run.

He pulled a stop watch from his pocket. I took off and pushed hard, certain that my time was good. I was all smiles and approached him, expecting a compliment, but only got, "Let me see you run hard next time."

I hit the track again and pushed myself to the limit and was gasping for air at the end of the run. Again, he made no comment about my time, nor did his expression offer a hint as to his opinion of me. He stated that his boys trained after school all week and on Saturday morning.

"But, sir, tomorrow is Saturday and I can't make it."

"Why not?"

"I don't have money for shoes, but I could pick up cans and bottles over the weekend and have shoes on Monday."

"Your parents can't help?"

"It's just Will Jean . . . my grandma."

"I see. Homer Kellerman owns the local newspaper. He supports our athletic program by helping boys who need financial help. I'll talk with him. Leave your shoe size at my office."

On Saturday morning Mr. Kellerman waited with gear for myself and two other guys. I liked him right away. He was laid back . . . real cool. I was surprised that he wanted to know all about me, what I wanted to become, and what my dreams were in life. He knew my grade standings and seemed pleased, which surprised me. He must have talked to my homeroom teacher. I wondered if he followed the academic progress of all the guys or just the ones who needed financial help.

My life changed during the following weeks. I had new friends and was invited into their circle. It was good to be one of the guys. The horse play, teasing, and stiff competition gave me a high. I could hold my own as a runner with any of them.

I hated to see Saturday morning practice terminated at the end of the school year, but I continued my friendship with some of the track members. We ran all that summer and made the high school track team for the next three years. I'd picked up a number of first and second place awards at meets. All through high school there was talk that colleges would be offering scholarships my senior year if I continued to train hard and improve myself.

5

I was seventeen at the end of my junior year and had gotten past the confusing age of puberty. My voice was deeper. Gone were the preteen pimples. The beard on my face, once as fine as peach fuzz, had become dark stubble. The first few pubic hairs monitored impatiently a few years back had spread sufficiently to put a swagger in my walk. My body was in prime shape, and the flat-chested girls of grade school had also undergone a change. Some caught my eye that never drew my attention before. The downside—I was a virgin without a car.

With a possible scholarship on the line I continued to train daily, but in spite of the good things happening in my life a fight with Will Jean often left me depressed for days, during which time I walked the mountain trails alone. Anything to stay away from her. The answer was to keep busy, to have some kind of distraction. Running and reading became mine. I was soon up to ten miles a day on mountain trails. It was during such a run one morning when I met

Kathy Olson. She was a tall, slender blonde with a bronze tan. Her family, who owned a cabin in the mountains, came for a two-week stay before leaving for Europe.

We waded the shallow streams together and swam in spring-fed pools, along with horse-play and gentle teasing. I picked wild flowers for her and sometimes let her beat me in a race. It was with her that I first felt the magic of two bodies touching and learned about making out in a serious way. It never went beyond touching and heated kisses. I think we both were afraid to go further. I knew I was.

Toward the end of the second week, I decided it was going to happen unless she said no. After thumbing through every magazine in the drugstore, I gathered the courage to approach Mr. Ellis. I whispered what I needed. He smiled and asked in a loud voice if he should put the condom on Will Jean's account.

"No, no," I whispered and dug in my pocket for money.

He laughed. "Just teasing. If you're going to do it, always use something."

I blushed and pitched a five-dollar bill on the counter.

"Keep your money. First time is free. Babies aren't."

I thanked him and slipped the condom in my wallet, but it was never used. Kathy left for home a day earlier than planned. Will Jean found it in my wallet and threw it away. One would think I'd become the worst pervert on earth. I heard a nonstop lecture about the sins of the flesh for weeks.

That summer temperatures had newscasters talking about record heat. I did my chores at daybreak and headed up a mountain trail with a backpack filled with newspapers, books, and a handful of deer jerky. I explored all that nature offered, sometimes pausing to watch a bird construct her nest, or to monitor activities by Mr. Well's eagles back for their tenth year. I often took a dip to cool off and ended my day by writing poetry or reading under a tree beside a bubbling stream.

Over the years, my homeroom teacher, Mr. Baker, continued to be my mentor and prepared me for college by suggesting I read two Pulitzer Prize-winners: *The Making of the President, 1960* and *Strange New World*. I began to look beyond myself and form opinions about the world around me, to make political and moral judgments. The ongoing debate about the war gave life to discussions about activism versus passive resistance. Such discussions triggered my interest in the afterlife. The idea had drifted in and out of my mind since Mr. Wells was killed. A reference to a lake of fire to punish the wicked was found in the Christian religion, and even went back to the Egyptians. An image of such a place was also found in Rome around 200 AD.

My interest in current events had also increased, thanks to Mr. Baker. The year was tumultuous in a number of ways. The Vietcong's massive offensive had a majority of Americans in doubt about winning the war. Then Dr. King's assassination was followed by widespread race riots. It seemed the world had gone crazy. Even my little community here in the mountains wasn't spared the madness. CBS covered the protests against the war and ran a daily casualty count of dead Americans.

One afternoon in late July I sat on the end of the porch to catch a breeze while reading when the sound of an automobile brought me to my feet. A blue 1960 Chevy came up the long driveway. We never had visitors. The screen door opened and Will Jean slipped onto the porch behind me. When the man climbed out of the car she made an audible sound. It wasn't a cry, more like the whine of an animal.

The stranger wore an army uniform. He smiled as he came forward. "Hello, Mama."

Will Jean didn't speak. I checked to see if she still stood behind me. She finally asked what in the hell he was doing here.

"I'm here to see you, Mama. It's been a long time."

"It has, yes it has. Fourteen years, seven months, and eight days. You'll share the boy's room. He'll most likely sleep on the porch because of the heat." She disappeared inside.

The stranger shook his head and chuckled. He focused large brown eyes on me and looked me up and down. He had short dark hair in an army cut and stood six one or two, about my height.

"Who are you?" he asked.

"I'm Rudy. She's my grandmother."

"Then you must be Margaret's kid. "

I nodded.

"I'm your Uncle Bob."

I'd heard about him. Womanizing alone had ended two or three of his marriages according to Will Jean.

"What about it, kid, may I bunk with you?" He took a pack of Lucky Strikes from his shirt pocket and offered me one.

I nodded and said no to the cigarette. I felt bad that he'd gotten such a cold reception from Will Jean, but it didn't seem to bother him. I was trying to decide if I should make an excuse for her when he asked if Willy Shoemaker was alive and did he still sell whiskey.

I shrugged. It was yes on both counts, but mountain folks never talked about who made whiskey.

"I'll check it out," he said. "Where are you in school?"

"My senior year is coming up this fall."

"Education can be the difference in having a life," he said.

"That's what everyone tells me."

He smiled. "I'll be back before Mama finishes supper, 'cause she's about to cook a big one, unless she's changed. I doubt she has." He lowered his voice to nearly a whisper. "I stopped in town for gas and got real friendly with a little blonde that works in the restaurant next door. I told her I'd be back. She was fine lookin', had a great butt. I'm gonna score with her. Don't you find that you sleep better after sex?"

I chuckled like a half-wit and turned red down to my toenails. It couldn't have been more obvious had virgin been written across my chest. He knew. I could tell by the way he smiled.

Uncle Bob returned on time. I wondered if he'd arranged a date with the blonde, but I didn't have the nerve to ask. He was right about Will Jean's cooking. The table overflowed with food.

"Mama, everything looks good," he said, as we took our seats.

"If you'd let me know you was comin' I'd of had a decent meal."

He winked. "Looks good to me."

We ate in silence. I couldn't think of anything to say. Uncle Bob tried to make conversation, but never succeeded in getting much of a response. Even when he complimented Will Jean about the egg custard pie, she pretended not to remember that it was his favorite.

He rose and patted his stomach. "I haven't had a meal as good as this since I was home last."

I shifted my eyes around to Will Jean and caught a slight change of expression. Though she made no comment, I liked to think she would have smiled if her expression had run its course.

35

"I've got a little business in town," he said with another wink. "It shouldn't take more than an hour or two."

He must have hooked up with the girl after all. I felt excited, which made no sense. He was the one getting some. He faced me and winked again. "You want to come along? She could have a friend."

Before I could open my mouth, Will Jean snapped, "The boy ain't goin'." She turned back toward the stove.

Uncle Bob shrugged and whispered, "I'll get you laid yet."

I turned red. My Uncle Bob was going to make sure I had sex. My best friend was doing it like a rabbit if I could believe him. I was lagging behind most guys my age.

I was awake when Uncle Bob returned from his date and slipped into bed as quiet as a burglar. I moved over to give him room. I'd never shared a bed with anyone other than Benny and we both were kids.

"I didn't mean to wake you," he whispered.

"No problem," I answered. One sniff told me he'd found Mr. Shoemaker alive and still in business. I turned my back and moved to the edge of the bed, expecting to get little sleep for fear of falling off. Then a greater worry popped into my head. What if I dreamed about the girls in the magazines hidden in the barn? Uncle Bob would punch me out if I had that kind of dream. I moved to the porch, but couldn't get comfortable. Nothing but tossing and turning until the sun came over Bear Mountain and hit me in the face. I wanted more sleep, but the smell from breakfast pulled me inside. "Mornin', Will Jean."

"What are you so happy about?" she snapped.

"Nothing, I guess," I muttered.

36

"You ain't runnin' with him while he's here."

"He's cool just like I want to be."

"You stay away from him. He's got his daddy's bad blood."

"What do you mean by that?"

"Nothin' you need to know. Go call him to breakfast."

I pushed the bedroom door open. Uncle Bob lay in the middle of the bed sound asleep. He was buck naked. I realized how well I'd slept in the deck chair. Careful not to make a sound, I closed the door, knocked a few times, and announced breakfast in a loud voice.

"Morning everybody," Uncle Bob said as he charged into the kitchen with his usual enthusiasm. He reached to hug Will Jean, who stood at the stove stirring gravy.

She pulled away. "Leave go of me. I ain't got time for such carryin' on."

Rejection scaled Uncle Bob's face for an instant before disappearing behind another smile. It struck me that his smiles hid real feelings. He turned to me and winked. "Hey, kid, how about we go fishing today?"

He must have noticed my hesitation and quickly added, "We don't have to go."

"No, I'll go."

Will Jean cut her eyes toward me, and then continued raking sausage gravy from an iron skillet into a bowl. "You two get to the table if you're eatin'."

We slipped onto our seats. Uncle Bob surveyed the table and said, "My, what a spread. Nobody can cook like you, Mama. I've been to a lot of places, believe me. I know. I remember that you love

37

fish. Me and the kid are going to catch a mess for supper tonight. How does that sound?"

"Got no problem with it."

"Rudy, I hope you know where to find the best fishing holes. The places I went to years ago could be gone. The mountains change as fast as the weather."

"Rudy don't fish," Will Jean snapped.

He looked at Will Jean, then back at me. "You don't like to fish? Why?"

"The boy ain't been fishin' since seein' the bear kill his teacher," she said.

"What happened, kid?"

"I can't remember."

"It was that bad, huh?" He squeezed my shoulder. "It's natural not to remember. I've met soldiers who saw a buddy's body explode in front of them. They blocked it out, couldn't recall much, but never stopped feeling what they had seen."

"I've tried . . . just can't remember."

"Don't worry about it. We don't have to fish. Let's walk the trails, enjoy the mountains, and then we can decide. There used to be a place where a waterfall spilled into a pool. It was great for diving and would be a great place to take your girl if it's still there."

Will Jean turned from the stove. "He don't have no girl. Don't need no girl. You want him to turn out like you?"

The hurt rushed across his face before he dropped his head. After a moment, he muttered, "No, Mama. I wouldn't want anyone to turn out like me." He took his fork and raked the food around on his plate as if putting it in some kind of order. "Rudy, my girl was named Irene. I did love that girl. I didn't give a damn about any of my wives. It was just Irene. As much as I tried, I could never get her out of my head. Irene was my soul mate."

"You was a damn fool messin' up with her," Will Jean said.

"That I was, Mama. You taught me how to be a damn fool early on in life, but I didn't know it until going to Nam. Does Irene still run the beauty parlor over in Corbin?"

"Stay away from her. You got no business there."

He rose abruptly. "It seems I don't have business anywhere anymore, Mama. Not sure I ever did." The room went silent. He stared at her for a moment, then turned to me. "Meet you outside, kid. Is the fishing gear still kept in the smokehouse?"

He headed out the back door without waiting for an answer. Will Jean took a step as if to follow but grabbed a dishtowel and started cleaning the stove.

I stared at his plate of untouched food. "What happened with Uncle Bob and Irene?" I asked.

"He did what men do. Knocked her up and left town. That's all you need to know."

Uncle Bob was quiet and deep in thought as we started up the trail. He never glanced at distant mountains or noticed the wildlife that scampered about. I felt sure he was thinking about Irene. But to me, it made no sense to marry all those times and not love any of his wives.

We were on the trail for about an hour when he suggested a break. We dropped our gear and sat on a rock with a clear view of the valley. He stuck a Lucky Strike in his mouth and cupped his hands against the wind to light it. "These things will kill you," he muttered. "Don't ever start."

I'd read enough research to know he was right. I could have told him that cigarettes were the reason he was breathing hard.

"How did you end up here with Mama?" he asked.

"My mama took my brother but didn't want me."

"Sorry, Rudy. I remember a time when Margaret was a sweet girl."

"She got over it."

Uncle Bob glanced at me, and then looked out across the valley for a moment. "I know what it's like to feel . . . unwanted. It takes your soul a little at a time if you let it. I'm sorry for what's happened to you. But get past it. It'll screw up your life and you'll be just like me and your mama."

"No big deal. Not being wanted isn't the worst thing in the world."

"Yes, it is," he shot back. "It eats at you. Never stops no matter how old you get." He picked up a rock and threw it hard. It crashed a distance down the mountain. I realized its crash landing was symbolic of Uncle Bob's life. He faced me and smiled. "At your age, I assume getting laid is a high priority."

Not knowing how to answer, I giggled like a school girl.

"You don't have a man to talk with, do you?"

"Just friends and Mr. Baker, but I couldn't talk to him about sex."

"And you can't depend on your friend's advice either. Most would be bullshit, either exaggerated or untrue. You're what, seventeen? That means you think about sex every fifteen seconds and engage in it once or twice a day."

I felt my face turn redder than a cockscomb.

He smiled. "Don't forget, I was your age once and had to deal with Mama too. I did a lot of lovemaking to a couple of magazines hidden in the hayloft back then. Mama is a one-woman police force hell-bent on keeping you a virgin, and your love life will go nowhere without a car. Here's the plan. Mama will think we went to a ballgame, but we're going a couple of mountains over to a place where I used to go and get you laid."

I smiled as my mind turned the tattered pages of my magazines, going from brunettes, to redheads, to blondes.

"Always use something." he said. "You do keep a rubber with you, right?"

"Not anymore."

"Oh, you've used it? I thought this would be your first time."

"It will be. Will Jean threw that one away."

He struggled not to laugh. "Sorry, kid. That's so damn funny I can see her doing that."

I didn't see the humor but said nothing.

"What you're thinking and feeling is natural. It's what every seventeen-year-old boy thinks about, except Will Jean is weird about sex. You're a good-looking kid. It just hasn't happened yet. No money and no car usually equal no sex. Does that fit you?"

I nodded. Uncle Bob was right on. My buddy had access to the family car. I'd often doubled with him, but our agreement was that he'd take me and my date to our homes an hour before his date's curfew. I got nothing more than to make out in the back seat during the drive from the movie to my date's house.

"Keep in mind, everything from birth to dying has a first time, kid." He checked his watch. "Are you ready to push on for a while?"

41

I nodded. We gathered up our gear and moved forward. Other than gravel crunching under our boots, silence settled in until I got the nerve to ask if his first time had been with Irene.

"Yeah, for both of us." He smiled. "You want to know my formula for making love to a woman?"

I nodded.

"A selfish lover is never a good one. Concentrate on making it good for her and she'll make it good for you." He glanced at me. "This ends all talk about Irene. Don't mention her name again, okay?" He turned and hurried up the trail.

The climb became steeper. Perspiration popped. Uncle Bob was breathing hard again. His face was drawn into the kind of frown that goes with anger.

"Are you okay?" I asked.

His expression dissolved into a quick smile. "The wildflowers we passed back there reminded me of your mama. She was nuts about flowers. Kept a bouquet in her room from the first bloom in spring until they were gone in the fall. Even picked flowers for neighbors." He chuckled. "Once she decorated the horse's stalls and made flower ropes as necklaces for the cows. They ate them and she cried. I don't know what happened, but she changed. Wouldn't go near a flower. It had to do with Mama. They had a fight."

"What about?"

"I don't know. I was some distance away hoeing the garden. Mama called Margaret a stupid girl real loud and slapped her hard. Margaret ran toward the house, crying. Soon after that she left without saying goodbye. She showed up a year or so later. Her and Mama kept getting into fights. And she only stayed a couple of days. You must have been about two years old."

"Then my sperm donor could have been a local man."

"A local man could be your *daddy*, Rudy. When you're older you'll realize that everyone has scars and has caused scars in their youth. You feel bitter toward your mom. I see frustration building in you toward your grandma. Listen to me, kid. There's such a thing as forgiveness even though I've failed at it. Bitterness hurts you, not the person you feel bitter toward. When I went into the service, I was angry at everyone. My last words to Mama was for her to bury me on top of this mountain if I was killed, so birds could shit on my grave like she'd done to me all my life. The war has taught me that life is not an accident. I had choices I never made or never kept."

"I never had a choice about Mama leaving me in a friggin' motel."

"You have choices now. You're not a kid any longer. You can survive Will Jean if you set your mind to it. Too much happened to make her want to be a woman or a mother. I heard she was gang-raped as a young girl. Some folks called her bad names. But Mama never cared what people thought. I'm told my old man beat her, treated her like dirt."

"She's unhappy about everything."

"It's my opinion that the way people are treated can shape the way they act. They become scared to feel anything. Mama's scared to be loved and you'll never hear the word love come from her lips. What she feels is in that pressed shirt and pants ready each morning or in pots and pans that constantly bubble on the stove."

Will Jean remained in my thoughts for the rest of the afternoon. How could I say how she should feel? Feelings got twisted and people did odd things. I'd decided that Uncle Bob suffered from a terrible sadness that grew out of his childhood. My suspicion was confirmed when he took me to the special place where he and Irene had fallen in love. It was the pool where I nearly had sex with Kathy Olson that summer.

I soon realized that going there was not a good idea. A mood change occurred immediately. He sat dazed and stared at the water. No effort was made to hide the tears that dampened his cheeks.

Approaching darkness forced me to tell him that we had to start for home. Without answering, he stripped off and dove into the pool. Time passed. Bubbles brought me to my feet. Could he have hit a rock? I kicked off my boots and shed my shirt to go after him, but he surfaced, coughing and gasping. "Oh, my God," I muttered. He'd planned to never come up. I jumped into the water and grabbed his arm. "Come on, Uncle Bob, we've got to go home now!"

He must have heard the panic in my voice and didn't resist, but I never pulled in a good breath of air until he was dressed and we were headed down the trail.

When we arrived at the house, he climbed into the car and drove away.

Will Jean stepped out the door. "Where's he goin'?" she growled.

"I don't know."

"To get drunk, I 'spect. Come and eat. I've cooked up some stuff. He's no good like his daddy."

"Stop it!" I shouted.

"You watch it, boy, or I'll cuff the side of your head. What's wrong with you?"

"Please, just . . . leave Uncle Bob alone tonight. He loves you, don't you know?"

"Don't talk about love to me."

"I want to love you too, but you won't let me."

She charged toward me with a hand raised. I braced for the blow that never came. She stood with her hand poised in midair for a brief second, then let it fall and shot back into the house.

What had I done? Words that were welcomed by most people only frightened her.

6

The next few days were tense for everyone. Will Jean cooked and cleaned more than usual, sometimes repeating the same job. I spent time in the library and visited with my mentors, Mr. and Mrs. Baker. They bombarded me with college brochures and scholarship applications, along with a gentle warning for me not to wait to apply.

On Saturday Uncle Bob remained in bed as the mantle clock struck twelve. I began to doubt that sex would happen today. I wasn't ready to call it hopeless and took the bar of Ivory soap to the creek and took a bath just in case. To use Will Jean's homemade lye soap for such an occasion didn't seem right.

Uncle Bob was awake and in an upbeat mood when I returned to the house. Perhaps his binge of the last few days had ended.

"Kid, you're going to enjoy the game tonight," he stated loud enough for Will Jean to hear and then invited her to go.

"Hell, no," she barked. "I ain't wastin' my time at no ball game."

He winked at me. "We're going to have fun, kid."

Uncle Bob's upbeat mood changed as the afternoon wore on. We sat on the porch in silence until he rose and left without a word. I watched the car go down the lane, and with it went my chance to get laid. I changed out of my good pants and blue shirt into jeans and a tee shirt. The light scent of Ivory soap drifted past and reminded me I was not having sex today, but at least I smelled good. I headed to the stables to check out my magazines, thinking I should have bought a new one instead of spending money on cologne and Ivory soap.

Darkness was creeping up the mountainside when I heard Uncle Bob's car. He stopped near the door. "Are you ready to go, kid?"

"In two seconds," I shouted and dashed inside to change. After a quick sniff of my armpits I dashed on a handful of cologne, slipped back into my clean pressed clothes, and then raced to the car.

"Hope you're loaded for action," Uncle Bob teased as I climbed in beside him. He turned toward me and sniffed. "Damn, kid, you smell like an over-worked whore." I didn't respond, though I'd realized the cologne was a little strong, but there was nothing that could be done now.

Little was said during the drive. He stopped at a package store outside of town for what I assumed to be a pint based on the brown bag. He sipped from it more than I wanted during the trip around mountain roads. The thought of rolling hundreds of feet down the mountainside kept me on edge.

A second stop was made for cigarettes. He was becoming less steady on his feet. My fantasy about having sex was replaced by a fear of never experiencing sex.

Once over the mountains, I felt both tense and excited. I would no longer be a virgin after tonight. A hefty lady with blonde curls, named Marlene, showed us into a small room filled with overstuffed sofas. A TV fastened on the wall with a swivel arm was showing the kind of movie I'd heard about but never seen. The women in the film looked fantastic and my jeans grew tight. I eased down on the sofa with my eyes glued to the action on the screen.

The conversation out in the hall between Uncle Bob and the blonde mentioned something about a clean bill of health and too much money. Two ladies popped into the room. The short, fat one led the way. She turned to the woman she called Josie and asked if she wanted the kid or the older dude. It took a moment to realize they were talking about us. They were nothing like the magazine girls. Both looked to be three times my age or more. I turned to look for Uncle Bob who was still talking in the hallway. The short one, with rolls of blubber plopped down beside me and got a handful of nothing when she grabbed my crotch.

"Baby, you're a little tense. Bet I can change that."

I jumped to my feet. "No, I don't think so."

"I bet I can." She lifted her tee shirt as she rose. Her breasts hung nearly to her belly button.

I shot into the hallway. Uncle Bob hollered, "Hey, where are you going?" I continued out the front door without answering and climbed into the car. The thought of being with that lady for my first time wasn't going to happen.

Uncle Bob came stumbling after me. "What's wrong, kid?"

"I can't do it. It would be like screwing a grandma."

Uncle Bob dropped his head. 'I'm sorry kid, I didn't think about the age thing. They were lookers twenty years ago."

Before we left the city limits the car weaved back and forth across the center line. Uncle Bob was too drunk to drive. The thought of him driving back over mountain roads scared me nearly as much as being left with those two women.

The only delaying tactic that came to mind was to fill him full of black coffee. "I haven't eaten all day," I said, which wasn't the truth.

"Damn, kid, why didn't you say something before if you were hungry?"

"I didn't notice until now."

We stopped at a little café at the edge of town that smelled of home cooking. Most everything on their menu was deep fried.

Uncle Bob hadn't mentioned what happened at Marlene's place. That bothered me a little, but not as much as losing an erection. I wanted him to tell me that was normal under the circumstances. It'd never happened before, even when a pretty girl triggered a fantasy in a public place. I couldn't have done that woman with a gun pointed at my head. But what if Uncle Bob thought I was gay?

Uncle Bob touched my arm. "Rudy, you told the waitress you wanted pie. Tell her what kind."

"Oh, I'm sorry. Make it one of each kind." I knew I could put away two pieces with no trouble. Eating real slow would give more time for coffee to sober him up.

The waitress gave me a strange look after Uncle Bob ordered only coffee. "Kid, you've got a hell of a sweet tooth," he said.

"Yeah, I love pie."

He smiled. "So, neither of Marlene's two broads turned you on?"

"I guess not." Did he think they should have after the way they looked?

He laughed. "What do you mean you guess not? You shot out of there like a bullet."

"What if I did? It's my business."

He frowned. "Sure, it is. What's going on? You're getting all riled up or I'm drunker than I thought."

"I'm not gay."

He looked confused and started to speak, but our order arrived. The tray held eight assorted slices of pie and two mugs of coffee. I looked from the pie to the waitress and then to Uncle Bob. He stared at the tray. "My God, are you eating a whole damn pie?"

I offered a weak smile. "I love pie."

"Enjoy," the waitress said.

Uncle Bob waited until she left, and then leaned across the table. "What's this about gay?"

"I'm not gay. I like girls. It just didn't work tonight."

"Kid, I don't think you're gay. An erection depends on a lot of things."

"I lost it. That's never happened before."

He chuckled. "Maybe it's never been challenged like it was tonight. They were duds. I screwed up bringing you here. Believe me, they were knockouts twenty years ago. You need to learn about sex with someone your own age, someone you respect and care about." His voice took on a sad note as he added, "But don't knock her up and run out on her."

I waited for him to continue. He didn't and I asked, "Is that what you did?"

He nodded.

"I thought you loved Irene."

"I did, but I was scared."

"Of what?"

51

"I don't know. I got on a bus and left. I felt guilty as hell . . . still do. It's never gone away. I came back a couple of years later. I was dead as far as Irene was concerned. She couldn't forgive me. I joined the army and tried to start over. It never worked." He paused. "My life's gone downhill since the day I got on that bus all those years ago. Kid, I'm not on leave like I told you. I got kicked out of the service." He stared out the window for a moment and faced me again. "I'm a drunk. Rehab after rehab never worked. I'm worth nothing to anyone, not even the army."

"That's not true. You're not a drunk and you are worth something. You didn't touch a drop the first week you were home."

"I made up for it later, right?" He reached across the table, tilted my face up, and looked into my eyes. "You have so much to learn and you've been dealt a stacked deck. Don't let your mama or Will Jean play the winning hand or you'll end up like me. Get out of this place, go find a girl, and have babies. I think that would teach you about real love. It's too late for me, but not you."

"It's never too late."

"Bullshit. You're dreaming."

"It's not bad to dream."

He chuckled. "You're right, kid. What's bad is forgetting how." He chuckled again. "Do me a favor."

"What? Anything."

"This afternoon, when I left the house, I drove over to Corbin and made you a co-beneficiary on an insurance policy."

Insurance dealt with death. That frightened me. He must have seen my expression and added, "Having insurance is just smart to have, okay? It's only for ten thousand. If something happens to me, you get half and I'm depending on you to make sure the other half goes to my daughter."

"Nothing is going to happen to you. You're not even forty yet."

He ignored me. "My daughter took Irene's maiden name. I went to her school this afternoon. She's beautiful. Looks like her mother." His voice crumbled. "She said she hated me. I understand why, but it takes a little of my soul each time I think about it."

"She didn't mean it. I've thought I hated Will Jean."

"She meant it. I could see it in her eyes." He pitched a twenty on the table as he rose. "Time for talk is over. Eat your pie, kid. I'll be in the car."

I watched him go. He was in trouble and needed someone to do grownup talk. I didn't know how. I wanted it to be the booze talking, but I knew it was more than that.

I nibbled at the pie and became even more frightened. Mr. Baker once told me that somewhere there was a solution to every problem as long as one could maintain a sliver of hope. Uncle Bob had run out of hope and I didn't know how to give him more.

He was asleep in the back seat when I reached the car. An empty pint lay on the seat. He'd been drinking more and was in no condition to drive now, nor would he be tonight. It would be up to me.

The drive home proved trouble free except for a few minutes of concern when a state patrol car fell in behind us and followed a couple of miles during a no passing zone. Mr. Baker had given me driving lessons, but I didn't have a car and never applied for a license.

I was sure the noise in getting Uncle Bob to bed would wake Will Jean. If so, she chose not to appear.

I took my place on the deck chair with little hope of falling asleep. My head exploded with thoughts about Uncle Bob and all had elements of a drama that was sure to end badly. That was the way it usually went with books and movies.

I must have fallen asleep after deciding to approach Mr. Baker for advice about Uncle Bob's problem. At some point, I jerked awake to a motor cranking. It was Uncle Bob's car going down the hill. I jumped off the porch and gave chase, screaming for him to come back. I watched until it disappeared. "Oh, God, please," I said. I was scared.

I waited in the deck chair for hours and watched daylight usher in a clear blue sky. A plate heaped high with breakfast sat untouched on a stool beside me. I had no appetite for food. I only wanted Uncle Bob back home safe.

7

The sun had cleared the top of Bear Mountain more than two hours earlier when Sheriff John's car turned up the lane. It moved toward me as if reluctant to reveal its purpose. I wanted to call Will Jean but couldn't move. My heart beat faster. She stepped out onto the porch as I stood. Two men were in the car. Only the sheriff got out and came toward us. I was afraid his bowed head told me more than I wanted to know.

"Will Jean, I'm sorry to bring back news," the sheriff said. "Your son was in an accident."

"But he's going to be okay," I said, trying to hold on to that sliver of hope that I knew wasn't there.

"No, I'm sorry. The car went off the road up on Bear Mountain. We're trying to determine what caused the accident."

An audible cry came out of the stunned silence. Will Jean backed toward the door, shaking her head, moaning, "no, no." She threshed the air with both hands until she turned and rushed inside.

Moments later windows closed and curtains were drawn. I felt pressure pushing against my eyelids. No tears would come.

The other guy, much younger than the sheriff, climbed out of the car and spoke as he approached, "My dad thought you needed company about now and sent me along. He said if you need anything to let him know. Is your grandmother going to be okay?"

"I think so. She shuts herself up in the house when she wants to pretend something never happened. By this afternoon, she'll open the windows and start cooking."

The sheriff spoke. "You're Rudy, aren't you? I remember from the bear attack. This is Cliff Kellerman. His father, Homer, owns the local newspaper."

"I know Mr. Kellerman. He's a standup guy, bought my gear for track a few years back. You're his son?"

He nodded. "Sorry about the accident. I'd like to hang around and keep you company."

"Thanks, but I don't need company. I'm fine."

"I'm sure you are, but I'd like to hang around anyway. Mr. Baker said he wanted us to meet."

"You know Mr. Baker?"

"I do. He's a great teacher. Without him keeping me on track, I wouldn't have gotten into college. I'm now doing an internship to become a doctor, thanks to him."

"I guess we can hang out," I said.

"One other thing, Rudy," the sheriff said. "Robert had identification, but we need a family member to officially identify the body. He had an insurance card in his wallet. We want to be extra careful and follow the book. I hate to ask Will Jean. Is there another relative that could identify him?"

I took a breath. "I can do it."

"Are you sure?"

"Yeah, I'm sure."

I crawled into the back seat of Sheriff John's car. My feelings were locked in a struggle between anger and hurt. Loneliness slowly consumed me just as it did the day the police first confirmed that Mama wasn't coming back. I wanted to blame Will Jean for Uncle Bob's suicide or chalk it up to bad breaks, but I knew it was a selfish act that no one could justify.

"We're here," I heard the sheriff say.

I looked up and saw the word mortuary over the entry way. A chill crawled up my back and spread throughout my body. I pushed away the urge to run and told myself there was no one else to do this. I had no choice.

"Are you okay?" Cliff asked as I climbed out of the car.

"Yeah," I muttered, knowing I wasn't okay.

It felt like we moved into the building in slow motion. A short balding man offered condolences and then led us down a narrow hall into a cold room that caused the chill to return. Uncle Bob's body lay on a steel table draped in a white sheet. The reality of the moment caused me to tremble. I pressed my jaw tight, but it helped little.

The balding man turned to me. "He's really beat up. It'll take only a quick glance to confirm that it's him."

I felt Cliff's hand on my shoulder and braced myself. Uncle Bob's bruised and mangled face was suddenly before me. "It's him," I muttered.

I began to shiver, like being cold and wet in a thunderstorm. I pushed Cliff aside and didn't stop until outside. I leaned against the car gasping for air. Cliff had followed and stood a few feet away.

"You okay, Rudy?"

I kicked the side of the car and didn't answer.

Cliff caught my shoulder. "Take it easy. I understand you're angry. No one is ever prepared for something like this."

"He killed himself. The asshole killed himself and I hate him for it."

"Sheriff John considers it an accident."

"The fucker killed himself. I knew his state of mind and could do nothing. I tried, I really tried."

Cliff looked uncertain for a moment. "Why don't we get away from here? I'm parked over there." He took my arm and pointed toward a yellow Camaro.

I assumed he was taking me home until he failed to turn left up the mountain road. "Hey, you missed my turn."

"If it's okay, I'll take you home later. I thought we could drop by my house and get a bite to eat. Mom's gone shopping. I can make a wild ass beef and cheese sandwich with hot sauce."

I didn't bother to object. I didn't care where I went at the moment. I only wished I could stop trembling. Images of Uncle Bob's happy smile and his death mask changed places in my head like a slide show.

The Kellerman house was perched on the side of the mountain surrounded with various shades of lush green foliage. We entered the house by the back door, passing by a large oval pool with a waterfall spilling out of the hillside. Once inside the spacious kitchen, Cliff pointed to a small breakfast table in front of a large window with a view of mountains beyond. After placing a soda in front of me, he went to work building the sandwiches. They soon appeared on the table, along with chips, and then he settled into a chair across from me. "Mr. Baker said you'll be a senior this year and you're considering a couple of scholarships for college. I hear you're Barbourville's track star, perhaps good enough to earn a scholarship or two."

"I might pass on college."

"Why? Mr. Baker said your scores were off the chart, not to mention your track record."

"Yeah, well, my life's been off the chart since the day I was born."

He stopped chewing and stared. "You okay? You're shaking."

"Yeah, I can't seem to stop."

"My dad has some bourbon in his office. He says it takes the edge off of a rough day. It'll smooth you out. You want a little in your coke?"

"Why not, if it'll help knock the shakes."

He took my glass away and returned shortly. The strong taste of bourbon hung in my throat, but the stinging was a small price for what followed. The tension was soon gone, replaced by a warm, relaxed glow much like the little white pills had done after the bear attack years before. "I've never drunk before." I chuckled, feeling strangely happy with the results.

"Take the booze with you. The next few days will be rough since all the arrangements will fall on your shoulders. It's half empty. Take it. You might need it to get some rest."

"I don't think so."

"Take it anyway. There are a lot of details like burial site, casket, flowers, and choosing someone to conduct the service. It could be overwhelming."

"Oh, I hadn't thought about that."

"My dad said to let you know he would help out if you needed him."

"Help out? What do you mean?"

"Pay expenses."

"We can take care of ourselves. We don't need handouts."

"It's not like that. He's been successful with the newspaper and it's his way of giving back to the community."

"Thanks, but we don't need his help."

"The offer is open, okay? Sheriff John suggested we locate the burial site today in case a road has to be cleared with a dozer. He remembered a family cemetery up the mountain behind the house. He assumes Will Jean will want him buried there."

"Who knows? I guess. I can ask her."

The doors and windows were open when we arrived back at the house. Cliff waited on the porch while I went inside. All burners on the two stoves were in use with pots stacked on top of pots. Will Jean hummed what I thought was a church song as she kneaded bread in a large wooden bowl.

"Uncle Bob's going to be buried in the cemetery up the hill," I stated.

"What are you talkin' about? Now get out of here so I can finish my meal. Bob's gonna be hungry."

I stared for a moment, and then walked out, knowing she could not accept the reality of the moment.

Cliff followed as I led the way up the mountain, pushing through weeds and past scrub bushes. We reached a small clearing a quarter mile up and saw markers mostly obscured by weeds and vines. About ten feet off of what was once a trail, I stared at eight small markers made of stacked stones. The tiny graves were cleared of weeds, each with a mason jar filled with wild flowers. I moved closer and saw the words *Willa Jean's baby* painted on each stone. I dropped to my knees as tears gathered.

"What's wrong?" Cliff squatted beside me.

I pointed. "The graves. They're Will Jean's babies. Her old man beat them out of her belly before it was time for them to be born."

"The son-of-a-bitch," Cliff muttered. He placed an arm around my shoulders.

Cliff left with plans to accompany me tomorrow as I made preparations for the funeral. Using his wheels made me realize how much I needed a car. That could only happen by dropping track and taking a part-time job after school.

Knowing Will Jean would have a mouthful to say about the bottle of bourbon, I took it to the barn before going to the house. She would think a few innocent swallows would turn me into an Uncle Bob.

I found her seated by the stove staring into space. Moments passed before she saw me watching from the doorway.

"Everythin's cold." She jumped up and began to empty pots into bowls until the table could hold no more. I slipped into my chair and then saw a plate set for Uncle Bob.

She saw me focused on the plate and growled, "We ain't waitin' on him. Go on and eat."

After a moment, I muttered, "He's not coming back."

"What?"

"Uncle Bob is not coming back."

She snarled. "Just like him to leave again. He could have said goodbye."

A rush of adrenaline brought me out of the chair. I shouted, "Don't you understand? He's dead."

She flinched. The hurt in her eyes made me ashamed. "I'm sorry, Will Jean." I settled back into my chair with no appetite left.

She pushed her hair back and rubbed her cheeks with the palms of her hands. "I made him a blackberry cobbler and he ain't here. Guess I can warm it up, maybe add a little sweet cream." She moved to the window and whimpered. "He ain't never comin' back to see me again?"

"No, Will Jean."

She walked past me and down the hall to her room. I listened at the door and heard her crying. I wanted to tell her everything was going to be all right, but I wasn't sure anything would ever be right again. The room felt small and the air thin. I couldn't stay. Anger and hurt took me out the door . . . running at full speed. Wind brushed tears from my cheeks and grasshoppers took flight as I raced across the meadow and into the woods. A trail took me to the crest of the mountain where exhaustion brought me to my knees. I lay curled on the ground and cried. A ton of memories about Uncle Bob flashed through my head. I wanted to remember none of them. Not the good. Not the bad. I wished I'd never met the man.

Fireflies were out of hiding and shadows had dissolved into blackness before I left for home. The house was dark. Bowls of food remained on the table and stacks of unwashed pots and pans were on the stove. I tiptoed down the hall and cracked the door. Will Jean had not left her room. She sat in a rocker by the window, gently rocking back and forth as she hugged a baby picture against her breast. It must have been a picture of Uncle Bob.

"Are you all right?"

"Why wouldn't I be?"

She pointed toward the foot of the bed. Bills in all denominations were lined up next to a cigar box. "There's fourteen hundred I've been savin' to put me away. Robert was good-lookin' like his daddy, but not as mean. He was handsome. Make sure he looks fittin' for people to see."

"I don't know how much it will cost."

"You've got to make do with that. It's all I got." She continued rocking.

I gathered up the money and turned back at the door. "I love you, Will Jean."

The rocker halted. I waited. She said nothing and then continued to rock. I slipped out the door and made a second trip to the barn before curling up in the deck chair to wait for sleep that was slow in coming.

8

After a night of fitful dreams with Uncle Bob's dead face talking, I welcomed the familiar sound of rattling pots and pans from the kitchen. Order had returned when I stepped inside. Will Jean was quick to set a plate of hotcakes, eggs, sausage, and grits in front of me. "I'm gonna pick some green beans for cannin' before they get too tough. You want to help?"

I looked at her in disbelief. "Have you forgotten about Uncle Bob's funeral?"

She shook her head. "I ain't forgot. To put bad stuff out of my head keeps me from goin' plum crazy."

I wouldn't be available to pick beans. I had plans but none to share with her. I was going to visit Irene.

"I'm going down the mountain this morning to pay for the funeral. Okay to take the truck and pick up a sack of feed while I'm there?" She acknowledged with a nod. I felt guilty by lying, but I had to know if Bob had visited Irene last night. Was it his visit that sent him over the edge?

I took a couple of swallows and slipped the nearly empty bourbon bottle under the truck seat before heading down the mountain. Corbin was a small mountain town fifteen miles away. I could deal with Uncle Bob's insurance and see Irene while there. After the funeral tomorrow, I'd put death behind me and forget I ever had an Uncle Bob. Just days ago, I wanted to be like him. Stupid! Even the thought made me angry.

The booze relaxed me, and the sun warmed like a blanket as it danced across the windshield on the climb up Bear Mountain. The feeling that I had left the gloom of death behind was short-lived. Near the top a path of uprooted bushes and sheared tree tops stretched down the mountain from the edge of the road. I climbed out of the truck and stared at the twisted ball of metal that lay a hundred or so feet down with little resemblance to a car. "You're a coward, a loser!" I screamed. The echo came back. I dropped to my knees and cried, but it helped little. There was no way to unwind the coil of confusion in my head.

The insurance agency was located at the edge of town. An elderly lady sat behind a desk stacked high with folders. I stated my business and she rattled off condolences like a recorder. I felt sure she'd repeated them hundreds of times until no feelings were left in the words. With robotic efficiency, she concluded that all papers were in order and a ten-thousand-dollar check would be in the mail after legal proof of his demise reached her desk. I inquired about directions to Irene's shop and learned that it was only two blocks away.

The shop was attached to the front of a house in a residential area. After parking, I took the last swallow from the bottle before stepping down from the truck. As I entered, a young girl smiled from behind a white wicker desk. Five or six ladies appeared to be at various stages of having their hair styled on the other side of a lattice wall.

"I'd like to see Irene," I said, feeling the calming effect of the bourbon.

"Mama doesn't do men cuts, only Charlene does those. Her baby is sick and she's not due in until this afternoon." She smiled again and it was then that I saw a little of Uncle Bob and realized she was my cousin. She also had his complexion and brown eyes.

"I'm not here for that. I need to speak with your mother about another matter."

She turned toward a side door and called her mother. A slender, light brown-haired woman with each curl in place came out of an office door. She was beautiful with an easy smile that ignited sparkling blue eyes. With her hand extended she approached. Suddenly her smile disappeared and she withdrew her hand. "What can I do for you?" she asked in a tone that didn't match her earlier smile. She must have smelled the booze.

I glanced at my cousin, then back at her. "Please, could we talk outside?"

After a moment of uncertainty, she indicated with a gesture that I should lead the way. "What's this about?" she asked, while keeping her hand on the door knob.

I started to speak, and then realized her daughter could see us through the window. I moved a few feet away thinking she would follow, but she remained at the door.

"What is going on with you other than being half drunk?"

"No, please, I'm not. I don't know if you've heard about Robert Kelly. My Uncle Bob?"

67

For a moment, she looked confused. "Who are you? Did he send you?"

"No, no. He's dead."

She gasped.

"He ran his car off Bear Mountain last night."

"You said ran. An accident?"

I hesitated. "I don't think so."

"Oh, my God, no, no," she cried. I grabbed her as her legs buckled and she dropped to her knees. I knelt beside her. Black mascara flowed onto her cheeks. "I caused it, I caused it," she muttered.

I knelt beside her. "Nobody caused it. He did it."

"I should have known it was bound to happen sometime." She used a finger to wipe tears from her cheeks. "I've expected it for years."

"He still loved you."

"I know and I loved him. Our relationship . . . it never would have worked. He felt guilty about being born. Couldn't feel any other way. You would know had you known him. What's your name?" she asked again.

"I'm Rudy, Margaret's son."

"I didn't know she was back here."

"She's not. I haven't seen her in nine years."

She touched my cheek. "I'm sorry. Bob and Margaret were born under the wrong stars."

"It would seem that way. I take it you saw Uncle Bob last night."

She nodded. "Like I've done so many times over the years. But this time I told him I never wanted to see him again. Oh, God, why did I say that? That's why he did it."

"No, stop thinking that way. The authorities ruled that it was an accident. He left some insurance. Half goes to you."

She rose. "God, no, I don't want it. I can't take it. You keep it."

I followed her up. "Half goes to me. He wanted the other half for your daughter."

"Keep it, keep it all. I do well. Gloria wants for nothing. I won't take it."

Silence fell between us for a moment. "He told me he could never love another woman after you."

"I know. I did what had to be done to take care of Gloria. I would do it again."

"I don't know why, but I want to give you a hug for some reason."

She opened her arms and we hugged. I immediately felt embarrassed. It was out of character for me to ask for a hug. I had no good answer as to why. Perhaps it was because I realized how strong she was and wanted to absorb some of her strength.

I invited her to the funeral, but she didn't commit. She had been tied to the past as much as Uncle Bob, but there was a difference. She was strong enough to make the right choices even when it hurt. Maybe now she would leave the past behind, but somehow I doubted that she could.

Will Jean was in the kitchen half humming and half singing some religious song when I entered. She faced me with a raised brow, which meant questions would follow. "It took you a long time to get a sack of chicken feed. Where have you been?"

"There was the funeral home and then the corn had to be ground. You know Mr. Shubert never gets in a hurry. Besides, there were people ahead of me with grain to grind."

"Don't lie. You're gonna be like Robert with your whorin' around?"

"I'll never be like him," I shouted. "Not like him, not like Mama, and not like you." I turned and shot out of the door.

I crossed the meadow and was well up the mountain trail before stopping. Two young eagles were making trial runs out over the valley. I longed to be like them. They were free.

Darkness had closed in when I returned to the house. I expected the usual activity, but there were no pans sizzling or pots bubbling on the stove. The room remained in shadows. From somewhere in the house a radio played religious songs. I found Will Jean on the front porch rocking gently.

"Are you okay, Will Jean?"

"Why wouldn't I be? I worked my ass off gettin' them beans canned. I could of used some help."

Her continued denial about Uncle Bob's death made me angry. I had no desire to shadow dance with her while trying to bring reality into a conversation. I slipped onto the deck chair and watched the last sun rays crawl up the mountain. Soon lightning bugs moved out of hiding in the meadow below the house. They added an array of sparkle to the night, though it did nothing to lift my spirit.

At some point exhaustion put me into a deep sleep. When I awoke Will Jean's rocker was empty. My watch showed the time approached midnight. I rolled over in the deck chair and hoped that sleep would soon return.

I was nearly asleep when the screen door opened and closed ever so gently. Will Jean tiptoed across the porch and down the steps. The moon was bright and I watched until she turned the curve in the lane before following at a safe distance behind.

I was right in thinking she was going to say goodbye to Uncle Bob. When she entered the mortuary, I hurried to the side of the building and clawed my way past tall shrubs until reaching the window. She stood in the doorway for what seemed an eternity, just staring at the open coffin. She began to cry and moved slowly to the casket with a handkerchief pressed against her mouth, though it failed to smother her sobs.

She took a red rose from her pocket and stuck it in Uncle Bob's lapel, and then kissed him on the forehead several times. She turned away and staggered before sinking into a nearby chair. I was ready to go to her when she pulled herself up and continued toward the exit.

I followed her back up the mountain. Her pace had slowed and she often paused to get a breath. If she noticed me gone from the deck chair, she made no mention of it.

I slept little that night and was awakened by noise in the kitchen and the aroma from breakfast cooking. Will Jean had resumed her normal routine.

I stepped inside and without looking my way, she said, "I hope you're hungry. Robert didn't come home last night."

I stared for a moment. How could she not remember seeing him last night? "He's dead, Will Jean. You kissed him goodbye last night, remember?"

She froze for a moment. Her shoulders slumped. "I guess I forgot. That was not a dream?"

"No. Uncle Robert is gone for good."

She turned slowly and shook her head. "He was my baby," she whispered. "I loved him once." She fell to her knees, sobbing.

After a moment of indecision, I dropped down beside her and gathered her in my arms. She clung to me and continued to cry.

Later that morning, I made a two-hour run along the base of the mountain with the funeral only hours away. Perhaps it was an attempt to leave behind the anger and confusion that had dogged me since the suicide. I arrived back at the house with just enough time to dress for the funeral. Will Jean made no effort to change into Sunday clothes. I finally asked if she was going.

She looked at me for a brief moment, then without a word turned away.

There was no way to explain what was in her head. I doubted that she remembered or would admit that she cried on my shoulder. That was proof she had human emotions, something I'd witnessed again through a mortuary window.

Cliff arrived to accompany me to the funeral. I was not in a talkative mood during the ride down the mountain. He asked if I was okay.

"Yeah," I muttered, which wasn't the truth.

"Are you sure we don't need to talk?"

"Wouldn't do any good."

He pushed a pack of gum toward me. "Maybe you should chew a couple of sticks. Your breath smells like a brewery."

"To hell with my breath, I just had a sip."

He shot a quick glance my way. "Okay, no big deal."

"Sorry," I muttered. I had no right to be pissed at him.

"Before I forget, Dad said you should come in and talk to him after all this is behind you. He needs some part-time help. He'll arrange a work schedule so you can remain on the track team."

The news gave me a lift, the first positive feeling I'd felt in days.

We entered the funeral home with soft organ music drifting down from overhead speakers in the dimly lit room. A scattering of people sat in fold-up chairs, mainly my teacher friend, his wife, and my track team buddies. Teammates gave me a subtle thumbs-up or a pat on the arm as we were shown seats on the front row.

A spray of yellow and blue mountain flowers draped the closed end of the coffin and multicolored baskets lined the floor in front. The extra large wreath that stood alone caught my attention. The words *I'll always love you* were printed in gold on a white ribbon that stretched across the wreath.

I whispered to Cliff. "The big wreath, who is it from?"

He retrieved the card and placed it in my hand. *Sleep in peace, my love* was scribbled on it. There was no signature, but I knew it was from Irene. They'd never stopped loving each other. The thought sent a wave of sadness sweeping over me. She could never forgive him for leaving her pregnant and he could never forgive himself. I wondered if it was useless to expect to find love in my life.

I remembered little about the service. It started with a couple of songs, followed by prayers and a short speech. Regardless of how hard I tried, my thoughts drifted away from the service to the time I'd spent with Uncle Bob and him talking about his unresolved relationship with Irene. They were involved in a duel within themselves over what they wanted and what they feared. Both lost, and that was the saddest part of all.

The service was soon over, and people paid their respects by passing by the coffin. Accompanied by Cliff, I went last and stared down at Uncle Bob. Where was his smile? Where was the charm that I'd planned to copy? What happened that was bad enough to send him over a cliff? The plugged up dam behind my eyes broke and tears gushed forth. My lips remained sealed. I wiped my eyes with a handkerchief Will Jean had put in my pants pocket, and then walked out of the funeral home feeling more confused than ever.

No more than a dozen people continued on to the burial site and half of those were my track teammates. Will Jean watched from the kitchen window. I couldn't imagine why she wasn't with me.

When the burial was complete, I requested time alone at the grave. I stared at the mound of dirt, hoping to find a way to forgive Uncle Bob for what he'd done. He'd been my hero, the man I wanted to be.

An eerie feeling of uncertainty hung heavily around me as I descended the hill. I couldn't make myself face Will Jean and shot out across the meadow as fast as I could run.

My shirt clung to me and perspiration dripped from my chin when I dropped to my knees beside the pool where I swam with Uncle Bob. I needed to cry, but couldn't. I thought about Mama and doubted that she ever thought about me.

I slipped out of my clothes and dove into the water, kicking and pawing to reach the bottom. Then I remembered that Uncle Bob had done the same the day he wanted to die. The thought sent me fighting to reach the surface.

9

I saw little of Will Jean during the weeks after the funeral. She fell back into the same pattern of living as if nothing had happened, though I sometimes saw her stop and stare into space while going about her daily chores. If Uncle Bob's suicide affected her in other ways, I never detected them, though it certainly did me. Dreams became nightmares that brought to life all the bad things that had happened in my life. Gone were the dreams of naked magazine girls. I often awoke crying and begging Mama to come back and get me, and at other times I relived the camping trip with Mr. Wells, right up to the moment the bear charged. But the most haunting dream was when I watched Uncle Bob's car shoot off the mountain and heard his voice begging for help as it sailed out over the valley, dropping in slow motion, down, down, until the explosion brought silence and left me gasping for air.

I would usually find myself on the floor beside the deck chair soaked in sweat. Increasing the booze did little to stop the nightmares. It left me feeling like crap to do my five-mile run each morning.

I'd started work at the paper two weeks after Uncle Bob's funeral. One afternoon Mr. Kellerman asked me to drop by his office at the end of the day. Cliff had told me that his dad was pleased with my work after my first week. I sat across the desk feeling relaxed as he placed elbows on the desktop and leaned forward. "Rudy, I'm pleased with the initiative you've taken in being a part of our team, but I'm concerned about something else. School will be starting soon. This will be your senior year. School should come before work, especially with scholarships to think about."

I explained that my grades were good and that I never neglected my school work.

"Being 'good' isn't enough to get you accepted by an outstanding school." He smiled. "Acceptance to the school of your choice requires better than good."

I dropped my head. What he said was true. "Please, Mr. Kellerman, I need to work. I wouldn't have a way to pay you back for the car if I don't work. I'll drop out of track."

"No, I don't want—"

A loud clap of thunder turned both our heads toward the window. The sky was dark. Leaves on the trees were belly up, a sign to expect wind and rain, according to Will Jean.

"We have a thunderstorm brewing." He turned to me and caught my eye. "I don't want you dropping out of anything, Rudy. I expect great things from you and will do all I can to help. Your mentor, Mr. Baker, and your track coach approached me. They're concerned that you may be stretching yourself too thin. Your coach suspects laxness in training."

"Please, Mr. Kellerman, I can do better."

"I know you can. It's Homer to you. I've told you a dozen times to call me Homer."

I nodded, though I wasn't ready to call him by his first name.

He added, "If you need to talk, come to me." He caught my eye until I glanced away. "You're special."

I nodded. *Expects great things . . . I'm special . . . Wants to help me. Why?*

He noticed my frown and added, "What I mean is . . . you're, uh, special because you're smart. Mr. Baker and I want to give support while you're pursuing a career."

He leaned back in his chair. I assumed he'd finished and thanked him for his advice and assured him I would improve, though I left puzzled. I was a nobody. This man considered me special and wanted to help me. He owned half the town and wanted to personally help. It made no sense.

I returned to the pressroom, thinking it wasn't natural for Mr. Kellerman to help to the extent he'd indicated. I'd noticed him staring at me in an odd way before and marked it up to my imagination. Now I wasn't sure.

Joe, the pressroom manager, who'd called me "kid" since we first met, had finished the Friday run. I began to bundle papers for deliveries to businesses around the county when he broke the silence. "Kid, you're as quiet as a cat waiting to catch a mouse after meeting with Homer. Something on your mind?"

I hesitated and then asked what he thought of Mr. Kellerman as a boss.

Joe frowned. "He's a class act as a man, and a boss. That's what I know. Kid, you had a reason for asking."

"Not really."

"No one asks a question without a reason behind it. If not, you'd have no question to ask."

"He seems like a perfect boss. I wondered if there was another side to him."

"See what I mean? There was a reason behind your question. What you see is what you get with Homer. He likes to help people. Nobody has done more for this community than Homer."

It was time to move away from the subject, but nothing had quieted the little voice that told me things didn't feel right.

The storm unleashed its fury and we moved to the window to watch. Lightning flashed. Thunder rolled. Sheets of rain pounded the roof and trees bowed to the breaking point.

Vickie, Homer's secretary, slipped into the pressroom unseen until a waft of perfume announced her presence. She put a hand on my shoulder and leaned against the glass to look up and down the street. A cascade of reddish-brown curls fell over her shoulder. "Aw, geez, I chose to walk to work today and the street is like a river." She turned sparkling blue eyes toward me. "Sweetie, it's gonna ruin my new shoes and the flood gate will close and delay you gettin' back up the mountain. It sucks for both of us, don't it?"

"Yeah, I guess."

"It'll probably slack soon," Joe said. "That old river rises and falls fast with water coming down from the mountains."

"Look how hard it's rainin'," she said. "The darn flood gate will be closed in an hour or so for sure."

"Yep, it could be," Joe answered.

She moved further into my space and spoke in a pouty voice, "The rain is gonna ruin my shoes." She stuck a leg out and lifted her skirt a bit to reveal red three-inch heels on long shapely legs. "Rudy, would you be a sweetheart and give me a lift to my house? I live just past the flood gate." She caught my eye and smiled. "I'll make it worth your while."

"I guess so," I said. Was it just wishful thinking that her smile and the inflection in her voice meant something other than money? "I won't charge." I said.

"I didn't think you would." She gave me a quick hug and pressed her boobs against my shoulder. "Let me know when you're ready to leave."

I watched her walk out, curious about how she'd intended her remark to be taken. I couldn't be that lucky.

Joe chuckled. "Kid, put your eyes back in their sockets."

I blushed. He laughed again.

The storm had moved past and darkness began to close in when we left the office. Vickie climbed into the car and kicked off her shoes. "It's rough to break in new pumps," she whined. "My feet hurt like hell. I need a foot rub." She placed her foot on the dash and began to massage with long even strokes from her ankles to her knees. Each stroke moved her skirt down her leg, closer to her thighs.

She changed feet, moving her skirt even more, enough for me to see a flash of pink lace.

"Do you like massages?" she asked.

"I've never had one."

"You should try it. Just to lay back and feel hands movin' over your body. It feels great."

I didn't need her to describe hands rubbing body parts any longer. My imagination did that without any help.

The flood gate remained closed as we drove past. I had an hour to wait or take the catwalk across, but I didn't want to leave the car. Besides, something happening with Vickie was possible. Though eager for the experience, I had misgivings about performance. It would be embarrassing if it was all over before it started.

How should a thirty-year-old woman be approached? A slap in the face could be the result of a misread signal. But Vickie seemed to be doing everything but asking me. Should I just ask her? Should I tell her it would be my first time? No, I couldn't say that. She'd think me a wimp or worse. Another problem came to mind. What if Will Jean threw away the rubber I had in my wallet? She did every time my wallet was left unguarded.

Vickie pointed and squealed, "That's my house. Oh, my God, look at the yard. It's turned into a river."

A modest-sized stone house stood about fifty feet from the street. Water covered the yard and looked an inch to several inches deep in places. She followed me out of the car. "How am I gonna get to the door?" she cried.

I slipped out of my shoes and socks. The water looked shallow enough to wade along the high ground next to the yard fence. "I can hold your hand and lead you to the end of the porch. Along the fence looks like the best route."

"Oh, my God, no. What about snakes? I've seen copperheads when the river floods. Could you carry me, please, Rudy?"

"I'm not sure. It could be slippery."

"Oh, you're not strong enough?"

"That's not it. I'm *strong* enough."

"Then you have to carry me." She hooked her arm around my neck and I had her cradled in my arms before I knew what had happened.

"You're strong." She snuggled against my chest. I got the full effect of both her perfume and her gaping blouse.

I started toward the porch, zigzagging to find shallow water and moving slowly to find sound footing. With each step, her butt rotated against me and her breasts rubbed against my chest. The age difference never entered my mind. I was in the moment. Her hand settled on my crotch. She cut her eyes up at me and smiled. I knew this was the day.

She slid out of my arms onto the porch and led me inside. "Do you need something to drink, because I know you drink?"

"No," I said. A large photograph with Vickie wearing a wedding dress and a man in a tux caught my eye. She must have seen me looking. "That's my old man. You want him to face the wall?"

"Maybe I should go. I don't want to be in the middle of something."

"Baby, you're not. The marriage is over. He does his thing. I do mine. Now, don't go anywhere. I'll be right back, 'cause I promise we're gonna have fun with what you brought to the party."

It would have taken forty men to pull me out the door after that promise. I didn't move except to drop my hands in front of my bulging pants, and it was then I remembered about the rubber, again. I was pulling apart my wallet, hoping the old imprint meant I had a condom with me when she returned.

She held up a condom. "Looking for one like this?"

I blushed and nodded.

Her blouse hung loose and she wore no bra. I placed my hand on her breast. She smiled and felt me up again. I was close to going over the edge until Will Jean's fiery eyes flashed across my brain. I feared going flat until Vickie unzipped my pants, while staring into my eyes.

More than two hours later, she patted my butt as I stepped out the door. "You were good," she said. "Would you like to do this again?"

"Yeah, like tomorrow after work."

"We'll see." She giggled. "Tell your grandma you've been playing with a friend."

I chuckled, thinking that wasn't likely to happen. The explosion would demolish this side of the mountain.

10

Vickie and I continued our relationship for the next few weeks. In the back of my mind guilt kept poking at me. She had a husband, and I couldn't forget that a college scholarship might be at stake should we be caught. As time passed I became more concerned and decided more than once to break it off. I even voiced my concern to her. She smiled and said all I had to do was to be careful that no one at work learned that I was a drinker. From then on, though subtle, she brought up the subject about my drinking. She passed by my worktable several times a day and often asked if I'd had a drink and could anyone smell my breath. Then she would whisper what she was going to do to me after work. By the end of the day I would decide to see her just one more time.

A couple of weeks after school began Cliff came home for a quick weekend visit. He suggested we let off steam at a honky-tonk joint not far out of town. I was ready. The aftermath of Uncle Bob's funeral, my affair with Vickie, training for track, working at the newspaper, and attending school had left me uptight.

We'd finished off nearly a pitcher of beer when Cliff changed the subject. "Listen, Bro, depression often follows the sudden death of a family member or close friend. It can affect you months, even years after a tragedy. I'm aware your Uncle's death hit hard. How are you doing?"

"Fine."

He paused briefly. "Really? You're not yourself, Rudy. You're late to work half the time, keep to yourself. You're not the quiet type. What's going on?"

"Who's been talking to you?"

"Dad. He's concerned."

I looked away. "It's taking a little time getting past all the crap with Uncle Bob."

"I understand that. My concern is booze. Someone told Dad you had liquor on your breath at work."

"That's a lie. Did Vickie say that? She just wants me to screw her."

"Vickie? Is she after your ass? How do you know?"

"Well, she, uh, asked if I dated, if I had a girlfriend. And when I'm setting type, she rubs against my ass when there's room behind me to pass without touching."

He chuckled. "Give her a roll in the hay. It might make you feel like a new man. Good therapy."

"She's your dad's secretary. Too old for me." I sucked in a breath. I hated lying to Cliff and wanted to change the subject. "I know you're here as a friend and I appreciate that. But I'll be okay. There's this girl at school. We're both seniors. She's the prettiest girl in school, too pretty for a guy like me, but I'm going to ask her for a date if I can get up the nerve."

"Why are you waiting? School started . . . how many weeks ago? Some other guy will make a move if you wait too long."

"I don't know . . . I just . . ."

"Just what? Why wait?"

"She could turn me down."

He chuckled. "Come on, Rudy. Not likely. You're a good-looking guy, not to mention being the school track star. You've got wheels now. Promise me you'll make a play for that girl. Romance in your life will bring you out of the dumps."

"I'm not in the dumps."

"Of course, you're not. You're living it up . . . getting all the sex you want."

"Maybe I am, smart ass."

"If you were satisfied with what you're getting, you wouldn't be goggle-eyed over the girl at school. Talking about her made your face light up like you were a different person. Don't wait around. Go for that girl."

All I could think about was to get a date with her. September temperatures remained the same as that of July and August. Large fans placed in classrooms moved hot air around but offered no real relief. During study periods students were permitted to study outside under the trees.

The prettiest girl in school sat alone on a bench under a shade tree. I decided to take Cliff's advice and make a move. I'd watched from the classroom window for ten minutes or more before gathering the nerve to approach her. I was granted permission to study outside and chose a nearby bench. I stared at her while pretending to focus on my book. After a while I finally spoke. "You've found a cool place to study. Classrooms are like furnaces about this time in the afternoon."

"That's for sure," she said. "I'm working on an English assignment. Girls usually excel in English. But grammar is confusing for me."

I crossed to her. "Guys are supposed to be super in math. It's not for me."

"Oh, I love math. My favorite subject."

"I love English. Maybe we can help each other." I sat beside her. "I'm Rudy Kelly."

"I know you. I've watched you run. I'm Lou Ann Warren."

Up close her eyes were blue-green. I could just about melt looking into those eyes. "You're new this year. And you're hot. I would have remembered a body like yours if you'd been here before."

She glanced away. "We moved here two months ago."

"I'm real, real, real glad you did."

She sighed. "Will you stop it? Lines full of bullshit don't impress me."

Heat flushed my face and I felt as stupid as a goat. She would tell me to take a walk unless I was honest. "That was silly and stupid for me to go on like that. That's not really me. I was nervous about asking you for a date. I hope we can still be friends."

"Just friends, okay. I have a steady boyfriend in Lexington."

How unlucky could a guy get. "That shouldn't keep us from being friends. I have a girlfriend."

"Really? I haven't seen you with anyone."

"Uh, she lives in another town."

She focused her gorgeous eyes on me and her mouth spread into a smile. "You're lying like a hound dog. You don't have a girlfriend."

"No, I don't. The truth, I've wanted to ask you out for the last two weeks. You're the prettiest girl in school and that's no line."

"How nice of you to say that."

"How did you know I didn't have a girlfriend?"

"I asked around, checked you out."

"You asked around, about me? Wait a minute. You'd do that with a steady boyfriend?"

She giggled. "I don't have a boyfriend."

"You don't?

"Nope."

I laughed. "Okay. Would the prettiest girl in school go with me to a movie Saturday night?

"I'll ask Mama."

"Is she going?"

"No, you silly. I tell her everything."

I left with excitement coming out my ears. Her checking me out meant something. This date had to be planned in detail. It had to go right. What to do? A movie for a first date?

The newspaper listed two possibilities: *Thoroughly Modern Millie* and *Bonnie and Clyde*. The first one was too girlie, but the *Bonnie and Clyde* movie sounded promising. The name itself suggested a dreamy love story between two people. Just what I wanted . . . perfect.

On Saturday afternoon, I bathed with Ivory soap and dabbed on a few drops of cologne, careful not to overdo as I'd done before. I wore a new designer pair of jeans and a blue tee shirt that worked well with my eyes. After dressing, I walked out and asked Will Jean if I looked sharp? "Like a pimp," she answered.

I arrived at Lou Ann's house timed to the minute. She opened the door. I couldn't say a word and stared for a moment. She could have walked off the silver screen with matching white pants and top, a perfect choice to show her summer tan.

She ushered me in to meet her parents, a requirement from her dad before we could leave. Her mother served coconut pie and iced tea. While her father was nice enough, he had less to say.

What fascinated me the most was the interaction as a family. No doubt love was in the room. I watched how they spoke, how they smiled at each other, and how they seemed at ease with each other. I wanted that someday. Being part of a loving family must make for a perfect life.

When we rose to leave, Mr. Warren followed us to the door. "Young fellow, what time do you have?"

I checked my watch. "Thirteen minutes after six, sir. "

"My watch shows the same. We'll meet again when both our watches say eleven. Do we understand each other?"

"Yes, sir," I said.

Meeting her parents had interfered with the time schedule I'd prepared. It made us arrive late at the theater and center seats were the only ones left. Previews were under way, which made it difficult to see as we struggled past knees and feet to reach our seats. A stout lady rose to let us pass. Her elbow sent our popcorn box airborne. It landed a few rows away. With no popcorn, we pushed forward and reached our seats. As we sat a coke spilled on Lou Ann's white pants.

She giggled and told me not to worry, it was only pants. I settled back and slipped an arm across the back of her seat, thinking nothing else could happen now. Wrong! It proved not to be a dreamy love story after about sixty seconds. The blood and guts, shoot 'em up, movie was not working. She said nothing, but seeing her with both eyes closed confirmed that I'd made a mistake. She seemed pleased when I suggested we leave.

We drove away with my mind going like a buzz saw. What could I do to make this date a success? I wanted to see her again.

A large billboard announced that the annual Daniel Boone Festival was under way. Hoping the carnival atmosphere would appeal to Lou Ann, I suggested we go. She was excited and I was again hopeful that the date would be turned into a success.

The festival was swarming with people, along with all the sounds and smells of a carnival midway. Barkers stood in front of every attraction, trying to pull people in to see everything from a bearded lady to a three-headed snake. Screams and laughter came from the various rides, with long lines waiting.

We walked the midway, sometimes stopping to test our skills at game booths. We usually lost, but at one I was lucky enough to win a teddy bear. The man presented it to Lou Ann, winked at me, and whispered, "I made you look good in front of your lady." I gave two thumbs up. He smiled and I knew the win was rigged in my favor.

Being with this girl was fun. She was fearless and eager to try all the rides. My life would be perfect to have her as my steady girl. Surely the early mishaps had been forgotten since she was enjoying herself so much.

On a lark, we had our fortunes told and giggled during the whole ordeal. With strange and mysterious music in the background, someone chanted in a language other than English as we entered. The lights dimmed and the crystal ball began to glow. A curtain opened and the fortune teller stepped into the tent wearing a heavy veil and dressed in a black robe covered with glitter.

"Give me your names, please," the fortune teller stated.

"You go first," Lou Ann whispered.

"Rudy is my name."

"Rudy, you and Lou Ann will always be connected by your spirits. You are both guided by the same star. It has been your good fortune to find each other at a young age. There will be many children."

Lou Ann blurted, "How did you know my name?"

"The spirits know everything. You must remember that everyone has a soul mate. Happiness can never be completely achieved until the two come together. You're fortunate that you've found each other."

"Can you tell us the names and sex of our children?" I asked.

"Of course, for only ten dollars more."

"Too much," Lou Ann whispered. "Let's just wait."

"Whatever you say, dear." We rose.

"It's time to close. For you, I give special price. Five dollars."

"When the little lady makes up her mind, she doesn't change it." I ushered Lou Ann toward the exit.

Once outside we howled with laughter.

"I know he was a fake, but how did he know my name?" Lou Ann asked.

"I think he heard me call you Lou Ann when I asked if you wanted your fortune told. Do you believe in soul mates?"

"I'm not sure. I read a study where one spouse died and the other died the next day for no medical reason. As if they were meant to be together. Their love was so strong, one couldn't go on living without the other."

On the way to Lou Ann's house, we talked more about the possibility of soul mates and kidded about names for our twelve children. She also thanked me for the teddy bear and told me how much fun the fair had been. I was upbeat, feeling certain that a second date was in my future, perhaps even a goodnight kiss.

We reached the front door and she looked up at me. I started for a kiss and realized I was thirty seconds late when the porch light clicked on. She gave me a quick hug and told me she'd never had more fun.

"How about next Saturday?" I asked.

"No, I'm sorry," she said as the door behind her opened.

Her father smiled and pointed at his watch. "I like guys who do what they say they will do."

I cranked the car and headed home. How could I feel so low to have felt so high just minutes before? I would have taken bets on a second date. She turned me down flat. For her to say she'd never had as much fun was a nice thing to say, but I didn't want nice. I wanted her to be my girl.

That night sleep came in fitful dreams that had me awake to see the sunrise. Perhaps it would be a nice day for everyone but me. When I felt disappointed, angry or hurt, I always ran for the mountains. This morning was no different. Lou Ann's turndown took me lower than low. I gathered my gear and headed up the mountain to spend time alone. Fall was a closing down time, a changing time for all of nature. Flowers would soon bow to the first frost and leaves would begin to take flight. Flocks of geese were already making rest stops at valley lakes on their way south, and wildlife was putting the final touches to a place for the winter.

Not the best place to be this time of year for most people, but it suited my nature. I sought solitude when disappointed. But the mountains were rejuvenating for me regardless of the season.

11

I awoke Monday morning ready to acknowledge that Lou Ann would never be my girl. I needed to look to the future and started with a five-mile run along the base of the mountain. My grades and track record this year could be a turning point in my life. A ticket to a new life, I told myself each time after a run-in with Will Jean, which happened on a daily basis since I now made my own decisions.

I was nervous about seeing Lou Ann at school. I wasn't sure how to approach her now that she had no interest in dating me. I'd expected to see her in the hallway each time a class changed, but at the end of the day, no Lou Ann.

That afternoon I went to work at the paper feeling as upbeat as possible. I rushed into the pressroom with only minutes to spare.

"Hey, there, kid," Joe called.

I waved, pitched my book bag into the corner, and continued to the back room to change out of my school clothes into a pair of ink-stained jeans designated as work pants. Will Jean complained enough about my laundry without providing additional reasons by having ink on school clothes.

Joe was doing a last-minute check before the press started spewing out the final run when I returned to the pressroom.

"How's it going?" he called as I approached. "Are you getting any these days?"

My surprise at the question must have shown on my face. Had Vickie told him about us? Before I could respond, he laughed and added, "Just kidding. I hope you had a nice time with that girl you had the date with Saturday."

"We had a great time." I added with a touch of sarcasm, "She had so much fun with me that she doesn't want to date me again."

"What happened? Is she a nice girl?"

"Yeah, she's a nice girl."

"You sound like the turndown got to you. It doesn't mean a thing. It took me three months to get a first date with my wife."

"Really?"

"Yeah. If you really want something, go after it. You're a nice kid and good-looking. A lot of girls would be thrilled to be with you."

"Not this one."

"Is she worth fighting for? That's what you have to decide. You're a good kid and I wouldn't want to see you get into trouble with an older woman, especially if they're married."

What he said made the hairs rise up on my neck. Did he know something? I could no longer take chances. I had to break it off with Vickie today. "Thanks, Joe. I'm going to try again with Lou Ann."

He smiled. "Glad to hear that. That also solves a problem for me. Gladys is a fine reporter but has an overgrown imagination."

The mention of Gladys brought a feeling of uneasiness. "What does she have to do with me?"

94

"She thinks you're a nice kid, but she's concerned that you and Vickie are a little too chummy around here. You drive her home most days. There've been whispers about your car being parked down that way."

"Gladys is a gossip. You know her column is mostly that, yet she reports it as local news."

"Now, now, kid, she was a crackerjack reporter in her day. Give her a little slack. She's close to eighty and deserves respect."

"I'm sorry, but I don't like rumors. As for my car being seen, it's a good place to fish. I sometimes throw a line in there and have trout for supper."

"I'll handle things with Gladys. Just didn't want talk to get out of hand."

I hoped that was the last lie I'd ever tell about that subject. I also knew that breaking it off with Vickie couldn't wait.

I left work at seven with plenty of time to see Vickie before her husband arrived at ten. Rather than park in the usual place, I parked around the corner from her house. Cutting through an alley behind a wooded area took me straight to Vickie's back door. A tap brought the sound of footsteps.

Her eyes widened when seeing me. "Why in the hell are you here?"

"We've got to talk."

"About what?"

"Us. People at work may know."

"Have you been running your mouth?"

"No, I wouldn't do that."

"Are you sure you haven't told your friends what a stud you are when not drinking?"

"I haven't told a friggin' soul. You're pissed because you learned at work that I had a date with Lou Ann. It's over with us." I turned away. She grabbed my arm and pulled me back.

"Wait, baby. I'm sorry. I was teasing. I'd never say a word about your drinking. You surprised me being at the back door . . . Jake is due soon."

"You said never before ten. It's just past seven."

"I thought it was later. I'm sorry, baby. You've found a girl you like. Maybe we should call it quits. No reason we can't part as friends." She moved against me. "Baby, I want you now one last time. You're so damn good. I promise never to let anyone at work know you drink or about us after this last time." She took my hand and led me inside.

12

I had one leg in my briefs when a male voice shouted, "Hey, Vickie, I'm home."

I froze for an instant. Vickie popped out of the bathroom, looking wild-eyed. "It's Jake," she whispered.

"Where are you, baby? I need a beer."

"Get me one too," she answered. "I'm in the bathroom, be there in a minute."

Footsteps moved toward the kitchen.

"Go out the window," she whispered. "He can see the back door from the kitchen." I started for my jeans beside the bed and she stepped in front of me. "No, you've got to go, now."

Footsteps grew louder coming down the hall. Vickie kicked my jeans under the bed as I went out the window. I hit the ground running and took the same route back to the car. I rounded a corner and collided in the alley with a woman carrying a sack of garbage. She screamed and let go of the bag, sending garbage flying in all directions.

A shot rang out as I jumped in the car. "Oh, my God," I gasped. What to do? My head was empty except for the fear that told me to run. Thankful that I'd left my keys in the ignition, I pushed the car into gear and shot down the street without lights for two blocks before slowing. I wanted to believe the shot came from another house, but I knew better. I remembered hearing a scream just before the shot. Going to the police was put aside. I had to get back up the mountain, but first I needed jeans to wear.

I circled back to the newspaper office, grateful I had a key to the back door. It took only seconds to climb into jeans and head home. A whirlwind of questions! What to do? Oh, my God, I was losing it.

Will Jean was waiting on the front porch. "Why are you barefooted?" she called as I climbed out of the car.

"I don't know," I answered and walked past her and out the back door. I continued on to the barn where I turned up the bottle and chugalugged a few times. It soon worked it magic.

Will Jean was busy at the stove when I returned to the house. With hands on hips, she focused on me. "Why was you late today? Somethin's happened."

"I had a lot to do at work."

"Don't they have a telephone? Everythin's cold. Probably nothin' fittin' to eat."

"I'm not hungry." I continued out to the porch and fell into the lounge chair. She followed.

"Have you got yourself in some kind of trouble?"

"No trouble. It's just a headache."

"You need an aspirin?"

"No, I need to be left alone and have some quiet time."

She stared for a moment and then went inside. I wanted to sleep
. . . not to remember anything, but that didn't happen. Every kind of
scenario rambled around in my head most of the night. One minute
I'd convince myself it wasn't a shot at all, more like a car backfiring.
Then the next thought had Vickie shot and me the reason. It crossed
my mind that never to wake up would be better. Tomorrow was
Saturday, judgment day for me. I was scheduled to work at eight.

Little sleep and too much booze left me feeling washed out the
next morning. I sat up in the lounge chair as the first glimmer of light
spread a warm glow across the top of Bear Mountain. I mumbled a
prayer that all would be well, something I hadn't done since Uncle
Bob's suicide. The thought that I'd caused Vickie's death was too
much to handle alone, yet I was afraid to seek advice. Should I
confess my affair or take a coward's way out by lying? I'd already
done that with Joe and it left me feeling like crap.

Stomach nerves fluttered like dying butterflies as I headed
down the mountain. Paralyzed with anxiety, I parked behind the
newspaper office, thankful the police I'd expected weren't there. I
wanted to think the shot had missed, but it was possible that her
body hadn't been discovered. My heart skipped when I realized she
might have been wounded and suffered an agonizing death alone.

"You doin' okay kid?"

I dropped the bag of garbage and whirled around. Joe stood five
feet away. He chuckled. "I didn't mean to scare you. I called when I
came in the door."

"I didn't hear you."

"I guess your mind was on what happened. A terrible thing."

"What do you mean?"

He frowned. "Vickie. Didn't Homer call you?"

I managed to shake my head.

"Somebody shot her."

I was afraid of the answer but had to ask. "Is she . . . going to be okay?"

"No, kid. He pointed. The bullet got her right here in the head."

I shut my eyes against the image that flashed before me. Nausea rose up in my throat as I grabbed a work table to steady myself.

"Kid, are you okay?"

I managed to nod. I couldn't say a word but knew I had to pull myself together or Joe might become suspicious. The choice to lie had been made. I pulled in a deep breath of air. "A robbery?"

"Oh, no, it was murder. This is not for public consumption, but Captain Johnson told Homer that Vickie's husband got home last night a little after ten and found her. She'd been dead awhile. An autopsy will determine just when she died."

Her husband was the killer, but I had caused it by being there.

"Kid, you're as white as a ghost. You sure, you're all right?"

"It's my stomach . . . must have eaten something bad."

"The bedroom window was left open. Cap Johnson thought it was a robbery or burglary, just like you said. Then he discovered she'd had a lover."

"Why do they think she had . . . somebody?"

"She'd just had sex. A condom was left in a Kleenex on the nightstand. There was nothing out of order to suggest she'd been raped. A naked man running from her place nearly knocked a lady down in the alley as she was putting her garbage in the can."

Perspiration crawled from under my armpits and around my back. The urge to run, to get lost in the mountains came to mind.

100

The back door opened. Homer entered, followed by a tall, middle-aged police officer. "This is Cap Johnson," Homer said. "He wants to interview everyone on the staff. Others should be arriving within the next fifteen to twenty minutes." He turned to me. "You okay, Rudy?"

"Yes, sir."

"You'd left when I called your house. Your Grandmother was not happy when I told her about the shooting. She thought I was blaming you." He chuckled. "I'm not sure I convinced her otherwise. You may be in for some tough questions when you get home."

I tried to laugh. "That's Will Jean."

"Rudy, have you met Captain Johnson, the head of the police department?"

I shook my head.

The captain stepped forward and shook my hand. "Glad to meet you, son."

"Thank you, sir."

The captain turned to Homer. "I don't want to keep everyone here all morning. Since these two are here, why don't we get statements from them first?"

Homer suggested I go first. My legs would barely support me as I followed the two into the conference room. My heart beat so loud against my chest, I was sure the captain could hear.

A long table surrounded by stuffed chairs stood in the center of the room. The captain took the end chair and motioned toward a chair to his right, with Homer across from me. With his arms folded, Captain Johnson leaned back and stared at me for a moment. I looked away to avoid his dark, piercing eyes and then remembered that I should have met his gaze to avoid appearing guilty.

101

"Rudy, how well did you know Vickie?"

I swallowed to clear the cotton from my throat. "Not well, just around the office."

"You never knew her outside the office?"

"No, sir."

Though subtle, his brow went up and I quickly added, "I gave her a lift home a few times when the weather was bad."

"Did you go inside when you took her home?"

"No." I answered.

"We lifted a lot of fingerprints last night. None could be yours?"

"No, sir, I've never been in her place."

"Can you think of any reason a person would shoot her?"

"No, sir, unless it was a robbery."

"What size jeans do you wear?"

Oxygen became thin and my body flashed hot. "I'm, uh, not sure."

The Captain just stared. Homer frowned.

I quickly added, "Will Jean buys them."

"Will Jean has good taste. You have on the trendy cut, I believe. Isn't that the latest style?"

"Yes, sir. I bought these. Didn't look at size. Just tried some on until a pair fit."

"Then we should talk to Will Jean about your size, right?"

"I guess so," I muttered.

"Could we check your jean size?"

Too scared to speak, I looked at Homer.

"Cap, is this necessary?" Homer asked. "Rudy couldn't be a suspect. He's a nice kid."

"I'm sure he is, Homer. At this point, no one is a suspect. Questions are to eliminate those close to the victim."

I stood up, unbuckled, pushed my jeans down, and turned my back so he could check the tag for size.

"Thanks, Rudy. You can go now."

"Thank you, sir." I pulled my pants up quickly. Anxious to leave, I hurried toward the door.

The captain called. "Rudy, do you know your shoe size?"

I stopped, but every nerve in my body said run. I swallowed, turned back, and shook my head.

The captain stared long enough that concern washed across Homer's face.

"You can go for now, Rudy." The captain had spoken in a voice absent of the warmth that was felt when he shook my hand earlier.

I closed the door and leaned against the doorframe, gasping for air. I'd screwed up, really screwed up.

"Was it that rough on you, kid?" Joe asked from the hallway.

I brushed past him without answering. "I'm sick to my stomach. I've got to get away from here. I'm going hiking and watch the eagles fly."

The question about shoe size echoed in my head as steady as a drum beat all the way up the mountain. Any creditability I might have had was blown when I lied about the shoes and pants. They were proof that I was involved with Vickie, and the lady in the alley could place me there when the shot was fired.

Knowing that I had been responsible for Vickie's death put me in a dark place with no way out. Lies I'd told or even the truth couldn't change the fact that I'd caused her to die. The guilt was too much.

Just to feel nothing would be welcome. A thought that kept going through my head scared me, but it was the only solution.

Will Jean was waiting on the porch. Anger wrinkled her brow as I climbed out of the car. "You've got yourself mixed up in a murder. Don't expect nothin' from me. You're no good just like your mama."

Her words stopped me cold. How could she declare me guilty without giving me a chance to explain? I swallowed the hurt and continued on to my room. After grabbing my backpack from under the bed, I turned to find that Will Jean blocked the door. "I want the truth. Did you kill that woman?" she shouted.

I pushed past her into the kitchen without a word. She followed. "You ain't nothin' but trouble," she shouted. "Only God knows why you was ever born."

I cringed. She was right. The urge to cry was strong. I faced her. "You're a mean old woman. You shot me down when all I needed was a hug."

Her hand caught the side of my face and sent me reeling. I recovered in time to dodge the next blow and grab both her wrists. "Goodbye, Will Jean. I'll have no more of you."

She broke down and dropped to her knees. I went out the door with her begging me to come back. I felt strange, disconnected from everything, as I cut a length of cord from the clothesline and stuffed it into the backpack. I thought about the eagles. How free they were. How much I longed to feel what they felt.

I grabbed a bottle of booze from the barn and headed across the meadow. Hours later I reached the campsite. I was a loser like Uncle Bob, just a mishap of nature with no place in the world.

I dropped down on a boulder beneath a tall tree and took a few swallows from the bottle. I hoped dying was being free, the way eagles appeared to be as they floated and glided above the valley. There were no eagles to be seen today. Their absence made me anxious. I pulled binoculars from the backpack and scanned the sky. Where were they? I searched near the nest on the rocky ledge. There were none to be seen.

I finished off the bottle. Everything around me became blurred. I thought about Mama and felt that I would never see her again. The bad things that had happened in my life floated past. Tears spilled onto my cheeks and rolled down my face.

I wasn't sure how long I sat feeling dead inside. As if watching myself in a dream, I removed the length of cord from the backpack and made a hangman's noose. After a few drunken attempts, I managed to toss the cord over a tree limb and secure the rope to a nearby sapling. After several attempts, I kept my balance on the boulder and slipped the noose around my neck. While praying for courage to jump, I fell. My head snapped back and the rope jerked tight seconds before I crashed to the ground.

Voices grew louder. "Check him out," someone shouted.

"What was he trying to do? Oh, no, the rope. God help him."

Something was being pulled from around my neck.

"He's got a bad rope burn," a man said. "It'll hurt like the devil when he gets sober. It looks like he failed to tie the rope tight and the knot came loose."

"Thank God it failed," said a familiar voice.

I opened my eyes, unsure of where I was and what had happened. I blinked and Homer's face came into focus. I struggled to sit up.

He pulled me to a sitting position. "Rudy, what were you trying to do?"

I looked away.

"Rudy, talk to me. What were you trying to do, man?"

My neck was on fire. I ran my hand lightly across it, thinking the stranger with Homer was here to arrest me. I looked around. It wasn't morning any longer. The sun hung low in the sky and would soon drop behind the mountain. "I wanted to see the eagles," I said.

"You came to watch eagles?" Homer asked. "They're here in the spring, not now. What were you trying to do, son?"

No one had called me son in my whole life. It triggered an avalanche of emotion. I began to cry. "I didn't shoot Vickie, I didn't shoot her," I sobbed.

The stranger stuck a handkerchief in my face. He waited while I wiped my eyes.

"Feel better now?" he asked.

I nodded. "Are you here to arrest me?"

"I can't arrest anyone. We need to talk. Let's get you up on your feet." He slipped his hands under my arms from behind and lifted me up as if I was light as a feather. I felt a little woozy and stumbled. He guided me to a boulder to sit. A giant of a man looked down at me. His eyes were a piercing blue that seemed to soften as he smiled.

"Rudy, this is a friend," Homer said.

The curly red-headed Irishman must have weighed three hundred pounds and looked to be all muscle. "My friends call me Preach," he said. I hope you'll call me that."

"You're not here to arrest me?"

"No. But we need to talk. Why were you trying to hang yourself?"

"I wasn't."

"Yes, you were," he snapped. All the softness had left his eyes. I looked away again.

"Tell us what you know about Vickie and then we'll tell you what we know. Is that fair?"

"I guess."

"Bullshit on the guessing. It's not a time for playing games. It's time to man up. You either killed the lady or you didn't. Which is it?"

"I didn't."

He stared into my eyes for a moment. "Okay. I'll believe you until someone proves to me that I'm wrong. What was your relationship with her?"

"She was a friend at work."

"You were banging her. That makes her more than just a friend, right?"

I looked down. "Yes, sir."

"For how long?"

"A few weeks."

"Think before you answer. I need the truth. When did you see her last?"

I pushed aside the urge to lie and said, "The night she was killed."

"Rudy, for God's sake, please tell me you didn't do it," Homer begged.

"I didn't kill her, Homer. I promise I didn't. I'm not lying."

"Your pants and shoes were found at her place," Preach said. "You lied to the law and that goes against you. You can't deny the clothes are yours with printer ink on them. A lady saw a young man running from the house. Was that you?"

I nodded.

"She described you to a tee. But there's one bit of news that could be good. She said the shot came just seconds after you ran by. The distance between Vickie's place and hers would require more than seconds regardless of how fast you were running."

"I had passed her and was getting in the car when the shot came."

"The lady is elderly. The defense will argue she's confused about the time or else she heard a shot from someone's TV. Most all neighbors admitted they were watching Gunsmoke at eight o'clock. Many had their doors open to let in the cool night air."

"But the lady saw me and I was without pants or shoes."

"That could be a thin argument at best. Some teenage boys in the neighborhood have been pulling pranks by streaking."

"I didn't kill her, believe me."

"I told you Rudy was innocent," Homer added.

"It was her husband," I said. "He killed her."

"How do you know that?" Preach asked.

"He found me there. I jumped out the window and ran as he came into the room. That was shortly after eight o'clock."

"You're saying her husband killed her at eight. He reported her dead at ten."

Preach and Homer exchanged looks.

"You've got to believe me. I didn't do it."

"We'll talk more when we get off the mountain. We need to leave now."

I still felt the effect of the booze as we prepared to start down the trail. Preach reached an arm around my waist and lifted me to my feet. In spite of feeling wobbly, we moved fast and I had no choice but to keep in step. "I'm going to be straight with you, Rudy. The sheriff agreed to give us until six o'clock to get you back home before bringing in the dogs. We don't have much time."

"Then you're taking me to be arrested?"

"Probably. It's just a part of the process at this point," Preach said.

"Maybe not," Homer added quickly.

Preach frowned. "Homer, you know they'll take him in for questioning and will probably press charges after having his pants and shoes."

"If they do, I'll put up bail and have him out in no time."

"It might not be that easy," Preach said, "He'll be considered a flight risk after taking off."

"So, that means jail," I said.

"No," Homer snapped.

Preach looked even more puzzled, but said nothing. We continued down the mountain with thoughts bouncing around in my head. Trying to hang myself seemed more like a dream than real. It seemed logical at the time. Now it was stupid. I was embarrassed.

Fear rose up like a fast-moving dust cloud when I saw the sheriff's truck with two cages of barking bloodhounds in the back. The sheriff rose as we drew near. "I'm glad you come in, boy. You've got to go with me. We need to talk."

"May I say goodbye to Will Jean?"

He nodded.

I looked around for her. She stood watching from inside the screen door as unnoticed as a shadow. In spite of our poison words and ongoing storms of anger, she was my only family and I needed to feel like I belonged to someone right now, even Will Jean.

I pulled the door wide. She stood with hands clasped and arms resting across her breast. She appeared calmer than I'd ever seen her, though her eyes held a sadness that offered no description. "I haven't killed anyone, Will Jean."

The corner of her mouth quivered and her eyes continued to study me for a moment, and then she reached up and smoothed down my collar three or four times as if trying to keep everything in place. I'd thought of her as being tall. For the first time, she looked tiny. I kissed her on the cheek. She seemed startled, but never moved.

The ride down the mountain was done in silence, except for the sheriff telling me he'd called ahead and arranged for the rope burn medication to be waiting at the office.

"Is it hurting bad?" Preach asked.

"I'm okay," I muttered.

My attempted suicide must have been mentioned when the three men were huddled together while I said goodbye to Will Jean. I wondered why Preach had accompanied me instead of riding with Homer. I assumed he was my watchdog to make sure I didn't try to run again.

I snuggled in the corner of the backseat and closed my eyes, but it did nothing to eliminate the nightmare of uncertainty that was my future. Time spent with Vickie floated through my head, and with it came sadness. I'd only thought about saving myself to this point. She deserved to be remembered. I wasn't in love with her, if I knew how

110

being in love should feel. Yet, we shared moments of tenderness, of laughter, along with deep felt passion. She had taken me across a threshold into manhood. From her I'd learned the feel of a woman and it would be imprinted in my senses until I took my last breath.

I felt the car slow down and opened my eyes as the sheriff pulled into a reserved space at the back door of his office. He turned toward me. "You'll be questioned by Captain Johnson. Until he gets here and bail is posted, you'll wait in a holding cell."

"I didn't kill her, sir."

"I hope not, kid. I'm glad I'm not the one to decide."

The sheriff led us into a room with a couple of chairs and a faded, blue sofa. Across the room a lady dispatcher, surrounded by blinking communication equipment, glanced up.

Homer had followed in his car. He came in the door and demanded that I was not to be locked up. The room fell silent. Preach stepped forward. "Homer, could I see you in private for a moment?"

Homer hesitated, and then followed Preach into a side office.

"Homer's got faith in you, boy," the sheriff said. "I hope you deserve it." He motioned me forward.

A cold chill crept across my back as we approached a small cell at the end of the hallway. The walls were made of cinderblock with bars across the front. A chin high peephole window offered a view of more cinderblocks across the alley. No sky. No mountains. I cringed at the thought of being convicted and never enjoying a sunrise again or hearing all the sounds of the mountains.

The cell door shut with a bang. For a split second I felt an urge to cry.

"Captain Johnson will be here soon," the sheriff said as he left.

The cell smelled of pee and cigarettes. The furnishings were sparse: a cot, a stool, a sink, and commode. Biblical graffiti covered the walls. It struck me that people who believed in God rarely talked to him until they had their lives threatened by something. I wished I knew how to pray, but I had no right to be heard.

The stale air made breathing difficult. I jerked my belt from its loops and flopped down on the cot and closed my eyes. The feeling of helplessness hit me. I tried to pray again and then the sound of someone coming brought me upright. It was Preach.

"You okay?" he asked.

I nodded.

"The sheriff sent some ointment for your neck." He unlocked the cell and stepped inside.

His expression changed. "Where's your belt?"

"My belt?" I glanced toward the cot.

His forearm went under my chin and slammed me against the wall. "I'm not going to let you do it."

My attempt to break free failed. A scream for help brought Homer and the sheriff. They pulled him away from me. "It's okay, Preach," the sheriff kept repeating as he slowly guided the big man outside the cell. Preach looked spacey for a moment, then blinked and looked around. "Sorry," he muttered. "I thought I was somewhere else."

"I know, Preach," the sheriff said. "It's okay."

Preach hurried down the hall.

The sheriff saw my concern. "It's okay, kid. Preach used to be a Marine and was reminded of something he doesn't want to remember."

"My attorney is out of town until tomorrow," Homer said. "Will you be okay here for a while? I'm going to talk to the judge about getting you out tonight."

"Thanks for doing so much to help me."

"I wish I could do more."

I watched the two men disappear down the hallway. After applying ointment to my neck, I flopped down on the cot again. Silence soon filled the void, except for an occasional delivery truck or someone taking a shortcut through the alley.

Feeling dead tired, I tried to clear my mind for sleep, an undertaking that proved impossible. How did I explain all that had happened? Lou Ann would never be allowed to see me again. Any hope for a college scholarship was gone. "Oh, dear God, help me. You know I never killed Vickie."

I wasn't sure how long I'd been asleep. I sensed someone was watching and jerked awake. Preach stared down at me through the bars.

"Rudy, I'm sorry about what happened earlier. Forgive me, please."

The only thing I could think to say was to tell him it was okay. He shot back that it wasn't okay, that he'd promised to shoot straight with me and wanted me to listen. He explained that the war left him with a problem, that he sometimes thought he was still living the nightmare. He'd noticed my belt gone and thought I had planned to hurt myself again.

"You don't have to do this."

"Yes, I do. Please listen. The streets of Philly were home to me. I never knew my old man. He left when I was a baby and my mother

113

used booze to medicate her heartbreak. I became a petty thief and finally found my footing as a man after joining the Marines. Seeing buddies die was too much for my head. I kept seeing their girlfriends, their wives, and children in my head."

At this point tears rolled onto his cheeks. "The hospital was my safe haven for a while. I left with an ache in my heart to do something to help people. I worked with kids on the streets for about three years while studying to be a counselor. My old way of thinking returned. Too much partying and running with old friends that were being arrested finally triggered my thinking. I needed a change and took a job with the orphanage here. During my first month, I met William, a fifteen-year-old kid who was bright but had lived a life of highs and lows, much like mine and probably yours. One Saturday afternoon this kid, William, was in a bad way. I thought I'd talked him down and left for a hot date."

Preach dropped his head and said nothing for a long count. He finally muttered, "William hung himself. In hindsight, I knew I shouldn't have left him. I also knew that I chose to get laid instead of saving William's life. Now the guilt gets mixed in with what happened in the war and my head gets off track. I pray my work serves as some kind of penance. When I saw your belt, I knew that to lose you would be losing another part of me. I refuse to lose you. You hear me?"

I started to speak but could say nothing when I saw his sleeping bag spread in the hall outside the cell door.

13

A night of bad dreams left me damp with perspiration. The sky was still dark and the building was quiet except for an occasional toilet flushing from a row of cells down the hall. The interrogation last night had lasted for hours. I was accused of being a killer and hounded about what I did with the gun until my head felt as if it would burst. Homer's attempts to intercede failed. He was finally shown the door and told to go home.

The prodding and accusations made me angry with more determination to defend myself. The session ended after midnight. Captain Johnson closed by saying, "Here's something to think about before we talk tomorrow. We have your pants, your shoes, and a witness. She can place you at the murder scene when it happened. We questioned the lady in the alley again and her memory has changed somewhat. She made two trips carrying garbage from her kitchen to the trash can the night of the murder. She now thinks it could have been the first time when she heard a shot and you ran past on the second trip."

Footsteps grew louder coming down the hallway. I rose with one shoe on and the other one in my hand as a lady approached the cell door. She wore heels and a soft, rose-colored suit. She could have stepped off a magazine cover.

"Are you Rudy?" she asked.

I nodded and matched the woman to a Cadillac I'd seen her driving around town.

"I'm Virginia Kellerman."

She was Homer's wife. The newspaper often covered events at the country club and she was always smiling in the pictures. Her tightly drawn mouth suggested she was not in the mood to smile this morning.

"Homer is quite upset about this murder thing you've gotten yourself mixed up in."

"I didn't do it."

"The court will decide that. If you escape the situation you're in, I suggest you resign from the paper and get a job bagging groceries at the local store. Many of the orphan children work there.

"I'm not an orphan," I snapped. "Is that what Homer wants?"

"People like you will not be allowed to blacken the reputation of the paper. It's been in my family for over a hundred years."

She never answered my question. I was curious about Homer's opinion. No one had ever had my back like him. He'd earned my trust. Before I could speak, she added, "What little scheme did you use to make Homer think you're his son? The idea is more than ridiculous, it's disgusting."

I was too stunned to sort out what she'd said for a moment. Then it hit me. That's why Homer had shown such concern about my welfare. I'd daydreamed about my dad coming to rescue me from all the slaps, knocks, and abuse. It pissed me off to learn his kindness was an older man's guilt. "The son-of-a bitch," I screamed and threw the shoe. It struck her jaw and took her to her knees. Her screams brought running footsteps from the far end of the hall.

I spewed out obscenities while turning the cot upside down, poking the glass out of the window with the stool's legs, and then beating it against the sink until I was grabbed from behind and slammed to the floor. A knee pressed against my neck until I heard the click of cuffs.

A deputy leaned close. "What were you trying to do, boy?"

I turned my face away and began to cry. I wasn't sure why. Perhaps it was because this felt like the death of hope for me.

The deputy flipped the cot back in place, picked me up by my arms, and dropped me on the cot, face down. Mrs. Kellerman was still crying somewhere down the hall.

"Son, you only make more trouble for yourself by acting this way," the deputy said.

"Fuck trouble," I muttered. I could only think about Homer knowing about me all those years and doing nothing. He should have been there for me when Mama's boyfriends came in drunk and knocked me around.

I shut my eyes and tried to go to the mountains in my mind. I wanted to stop feeling, to stop remembering. Being in the mountains always calmed me, but the emotion of what had just happened kept pulling me back. I couldn't keep the images of eagles flying, of flowering meadows, or bubbling streams in my head long enough to escape from the present.

I heard the cuffs on my wrist click open. I jerked awake. My arms were free. I started to sit up until I felt a hand on my shoulder. "Take it easy, Rudy, it's me, Preach."

The deputy locked the door and left. Preach grabbed my legs and swung them around onto the floor. I leaned forward and cupped my face with my elbows resting on my knees. Preach dropped down beside me. "What happened, Rudy?"

"Nothing," I muttered. He placed a hand on my shoulder. I shook it off.

"Come on, Rudy. Talk to me."

"I just got fucked for the last time."

"Everybody gets fucked a few times in life, some people more than they deserve. I've been there. I know the feeling. I also remember how I hurt, how alone I felt. Someday you're going to meet a girl and have babies and give them all that you've missed."

"I wish I could believe that."

"There's someone down the hall who wants to see you."

"I knew Will Jean would come."

"It's not her. It's Homer."

I came to my feet. "No! No way will I see him."

"Just talk to the man."

"Have you become his errand boy?"

He shook his head. "No." He held my gaze until I looked away. "Rudy, we all make mistakes. This is one Homer would like to do over. You should know that he's not one hundred percent sure you're his son."

"And that should make me feel better?"

"Probably not, but for him to extend a helping hand should mean something. Your mother said he was not your father, but Homer thinks she might have lied."

I circled the cell and turned back. "What reason would she have to lie?"

"I wish you'd please let Homer tell you."

"No!"

Preach started to walk away. "You could do me a favor," I said.

He turned back. "What?"

"Go talk to this girl. Her name is Lou Ann Warren. I don't want her to think I'm a bad person. Tell her I didn't kill anyone. She's special and I don't know why."

"Are you serious with this girl?"

"I don't know. It doesn't make sense after one date, but for some reason we connected. I can't get her out of my head."

"Some might challenge your seriousness by being involved with this other woman."

"I know. I went to break up with Vickie that night. I never intended to see her again after meeting Lou Ann."

"What do you want me to tell this girl?"

"That I never killed Vickie. Tell her she's special and I'd dreamed about her being my girl."

A recognizable voice shouted, "You can kiss my ass. I'm takin' food to the boy no matter what you say."

There was no mistaking Will Jean's voice. I looked down the hall as she came forward with a straw basket resting against her hip. It was large enough to hold food for a dozen hungry men.

"Please, Miss Will Jean," the deputy pleaded. "It's regulations. I need to see what's in the basket."

"Nothin' but stuff to eat. My gun is under the truck seat on the driver's side if you're lookin' for weapons. If you don't believe me, go check and leave me the hell alone."

"Please, let me help you with the basket."

"So you can sneak a sausage and biscuit?"

"It's policy to check."

"Not mine. I know what's in it."

"Please, don't force me to take the basket."

She whirled around and faced him. "What did you just say?"

The deputy backed away. He looked like he wanted to laugh but didn't dare.

"Will Jean, he's a good Joe," I shouted, "Let him look."

She rolled her eyes and pulled the dishtowel up, then flipped it back into place. "Everythin' is gettin' cold. Now, leave me be."

The deputy smiled as he turned to leave.

Will Jean's expression was sad as she looked at me and then at the cell. "This ain't the first time I've been here. Used to come to this very cell when Robert was in trouble. You ain't gonna be like him, are you?"

"No, I'm just me."

"A man from some college come lookin' for you. I told him he could find you here."

My heart sank. Hope for a scholarship was gone. "Did he say anything?"

"Not much. Just that he was disappointed to find you in jail."

"Did he mention the scholarship at all?"

"Nope. Would you bein' in here make a difference in gettin' it?"

"Yeah, it could."

"Was you tellin' me the truth about not killin' that girl?"

"God in heaven knows I was."

She stared for a moment then sighed. "I'll sell off some of that meadow land and get a lawyer. Old man Johnson's been wantin' to buy it."

"No, don't sell anything. I've got insurance money that Uncle Bob left me."

"What do you want from me?"

"Tell me about my dad." The request startled her. She grabbed the basket and began passing food through the bars while mumbling about everything being cold because that fool deputy kept trying to keep her out. I repeated my question.

"You ain't never had a daddy," she snapped.

"I used to believe that, but I'm old enough to know better."

She sighed. "There was two or three boys talked about, which ain't sayin' much for your mama."

"I know all about what Mama was. I want to know about my father. Was Homer one of those men talked about?"

"He might have been."

"Come on, Will Jean, stop stalling. Tell me."

"It ain't gonna do a damn bit of good to remember all that old stuff."

"Please, Will Jean, I need to know."

She slowly nodded. "Yeah, he was. Margaret wouldn't say much. She was protectin' somebody. Don't know if it was Homer, but she hung around with him some. He dropped her off at the bottom of the hill a few times. Me and Margaret had a fight out by the stables not long before she run away. I asked if it was Homer. She wouldn't answer. I slapped her hard. I don't know who your daddy was. There was a couple of other boys she was runnin' with."

"So, you don't know?'

"No. Homer was married and had a kid four or five years old. Heard he had to get married before that kid was born. That's why I kind of thought it might be him. Ask Homer if you want to know."

"He's not sure either."

She picked up the basket to go and turned back. "Forget about who your daddy was. You ain't him."

I watched her walk away and wondered if she'd told me all she knew.

I had all morning and half the afternoon to ponder our conversation. Other than a deputy bringing a bowl of cold soup and a bologna sandwich at noon, I saw no one after she left. Where was the lawyer I'd expected? Homer promised I'd be out before now. I felt more antsy as time dragged on. I circled the cell a thousand times growing more pissed by the minute. Homer must have changed his mind about getting me out.

Footsteps turned me around. Preach came down the hall. Seeing him smile pissed me for some reason.

"Homer promised I'd be out of this dump before now. This fucking place is driving me crazy."

"Hello to you too, Rudy."

Without a word, I kicked the stool across the cell and moved to the window. The broken glass allowed fresh air to brush past my face.

"I could leave and come back later if you want, or I could leave and never come back."

"Why are you helping me?"

"Someone has to.

"This cell is bugging me."

"I gathered as much. I've got more bad news. You can kick stools and break the place into pieces or sit on your ass and make plans on how to clear yourself. You're not being bonded out. You can probably guess why."

I muttered, "Shit," and circled the cell again. "Homer changed his mind after the shoe throwing, right?"

"Wrong. It was Virginia who furnished the judge reason not to give you bail. Homer moved out, left his wife. He's still trying to help in spite of you being so ungrateful."

"Ungrateful? Homer owes me."

"For what? He may or may not be the man who gave you life, but he's trying to help now. He owes you nothing either way."

"Why don't you just go?"

"Why don't you cool down and stop throwing the F word around. It doesn't make you tough and it's not cool. You don't talk like that and it sounds dumb coming from you. You're in trouble. You might as well hear it all. You've been scratched from the track team's fall schedule. Parents complained. Either in jail or released, you're off the team."

"Just as well."

"Rudy, anger blinds a person from making good decisions. You have reason to feel that everyone in your life will abandon you at some point. I'm never going to do that. I told you about the kid I left for one night to go out and get laid. He killed himself. I'm haunted by it every day because I can't undo what happened."

Guilt swept over me. I dropped down on the cot and cupped my face. I was being an ass. "Sorry, Preach. Why do I always mess up?"

"You're human," he said. "That's what humans are good at."

"I don't know what to do."

"Praying might help. It helps me."

"Never helped me before."

"Maybe you never knew how before."

After a brief silence, I asked him if he would pray for me. He told me he did every day. I looked up at the guy. He was a special human being. Always relaxed, peaceful with an aura that seemed to counter any negative. He looked tired today. No doubt it would be hours before he saw a bed. He cared for the orphan kids and was available to strays like me twenty-four hours a day. "Preach, I'm sorry for being such an ass."

"Apology accepted. Do you know why you felt pissed at me when I arrived?"

"No, but I feel like crap now."

"You're trying to run me away before I walk out on you. Others in your life walked out. I'm not walking out."

"No, I don't think that."

"Just think about it. Do me a favor, will you? Just think about it."

"If it's to meet with Homer, I can't."

"Why?"

"I don't know. I might punch him in the nose and I can't tell you why."

"How about Cliff?"

"He's an okay guy. What happened between Homer and my mom has nothing to do with him."

"He's back in town. Came home after hearing about his mom and dad's separation. She had every stitch of Homer's clothes on the sidewalk when he arrived. Cliff wants to see you."

"Sorry Cliff was pulled into this mess. Yeah, I'll see him."

Preach started to leave and turned back. "Rudy, praying is letting your heart talk when you know you don't deserve the break you're asking for."

The next morning, I heard Cliff talking to a deputy at the end of the hall. He and I had some of the same facial features: a wide mouth, strong cheekbones, olive complexion, and brown hair that turned lighter during the summer. I felt nervous about our meeting. It would be awkward.

Cliff came forward smiling and called out, "Hey there, butt face. It's a raw deal to have a brother so fucking ugly that girls have to be paid to go out with him."

I smiled. He chuckled. Then we both were laughing. He'd broken the ice and my concern about awkwardness was gone.

"I'm cool about having you as my brother," he said. "How do you feel?"

I shrugged.

"I'm not talking about how you feel by being locked up. That probably makes you feel like crap. I mean being lucky enough to have me as a big brother."

"It might be okay," I teased.

"I rate myself higher than an okay." He stuck his hand through the bars to shake. "I consider us friends already. It could work, don't you think?"

"Maybe."

"Dad is a great father. My mother is a great mother. I love them both, but they don't love each other right now. I think they did once. I learned not to lay blame years ago. When your uncle passed, Dad told me about him and your mother. He sent me to be with you and give you any help needed, and to suggest a part-time job at the paper."

"Why aren't you pissed about having a bastard in your family?"

"Dad doesn't consider you a bastard and neither do I. You're my friend . . . perhaps my brother too. I've wondered if your mother would have given my dad the happiness he deserved. When he talked about your mother there was sadness in his eyes and in his voice. I don't know if you're his son or not, but I believe he had feelings for your mother. Now, here's my question to you. Are you okay being my brother?"

I nodded and smiled.

"Could you leave biology out and consider Homer a special friend?"

"Not yet."

"That's fair. So, we're off to a good start as brothers."

"Cliff, I never killed anyone."

"You didn't have to tell me that. I never thought you did. You played on another guy's playground and that's always dangerous."

"Yeah. I need to apologize to you. I went a little crazy and threw a shoe at your mother. I'm sorry."

"She told me and we talked about it. I asked her how she could blame you, the victim, for her trouble with Dad? She couldn't. I suggested she might want to reconsider what she'd done. If I know my mom, she'll talk to the judge about another bail hearing."

"You mean she's going to help me?"

He nodded. "I think so. Preach told me you were more lonesome for the mountains than anything. I'm here just for the weekend, but how about the two of us go camping for a few days this fall when the leaves are at their best?"

"I'd like that."

He extended his hand. "Good. Let's shake on it, brother."

14

A fly kept buzzing my head, making sleep a lost cause. My days and nights had merged. I couldn't remember which day Cliff had visited. Was it three days or four when he was here? I tried to stay hopeful that Cliff's mother would support my release, but it seemed less likely as each day passed.

Loud voices erupted from the sheriff's office. I raised up and listened. Will Jean was bullying the sheriff again, but louder than usual. He kept repeating that he was only following the law.

Seconds later Preach appeared in the hall and came forward. Will Jean trailed behind looking unhappy and mumbling about the sorry ass sheriff not being cooperative.

"You're going home, Rudy," Preach called. "We got the okay for bail."

I jumped to my feet ready to leave. "How much was bail?"

"It's been put up."

"Did Homer pay?"

Preach stopped and shook his head. "Rudy, don't you have an ounce of forgiveness in your whole body?"

"Did he? Was it Homer?"

"It wasn't Homer. The person requested not to be identified."

"You wouldn't lie to me would you, Preach?" I wanted the question back when I saw his hurt expression. "Sorry, Preach, I know you'd never lie to me."

"If you must know, it was Virginia."

"I don't understand. Why would she put up bail after what I did?"

"Virginia has a forgiving heart. Some people don't."

I looked away, knowing I deserved that comment. "I'm sorry, Preach. Will you thank her for me?"

"Why should I? You can thank her with a note if you can do so without being hypocritical."

I felt too ashamed to look at him. "Again, I'm sorry."

"So am I, Rudy. Let's get you out of here."

We returned to the sheriff's office and Will Jean continued to mumble and complain about the sheriff requiring papers from the judge before releasing me. I whispered for Will Jean to let it go. I wanted to go home.

"Course you do, boy," she said, with a look toward the sheriff that would kill a lesser man. "We would already be home if it hadn't been for—"

Preach interrupted. "Will Jean, may I speak with you?"

The two disappeared in the hall and the papers were completed by the time they returned. Preach stuck a newspaper under my arm and gave me a hug. "Keep the faith, Rudy. I'm praying for you."

On the ride home, my eyes were drawn to the majesty and wonder of the mountains. How I'd missed them. They had always given me comfort like a hug from an old friend. Will Jean continued to berate the sheriff until I finally focused her thoughts in another direction by asking her why she'd cried when I was released.

"I never done it," she snapped. "You ain't seen no tears in my eyes. With you in jail I didn't have to cook and clean up after you. It was a restful time with you gone."

I leaned my head back and chuckled. I'd seen her eyes tear up when the sheriff shook my hand and told me I could go home. I shouted, "I love you, Will Jean."

She coughed and cleared her throat. "Stop that silly talk. Look yonder, a summer storm is comin'. Clouds is boilin' up black as a coalminer's bathwater."

I chuckled again. I knew she wanted to distract me from any more talk about love, but not even Will Jean's odd and cantankerous ways could dent the excitement I felt about being free to roam the mountains again.

She glanced at me. "You're thin as a rail. I'm gonna put some meat back on your bones. The sorry ass sheriff would have starved you had it not been for me."

"I'm a runner, Will Jean. That keeps me thin."

"Runnin' up and down a mountain is the silliest thing I've ever heard of. It don't make sense and you don't earn a penny doin' it. Is Homer's boy a runner too?"

"I think so."

"I thought he was studyin' to be a doctor."

"He is."

"Is he? Well, he ain't never doctorin' on me. It's plum silly with you two chasin' around a mountain after nothin'."

I laughed. "It does sound silly the way you describe it, but it's good for me."

I told her I was going for a run first thing when we arrived at the house. Will Jean replied, "The hell you are. Not until I get some food in your stomach."

I started to protest but caught myself. She wanted to show some love the only way she knew. Nothing to do but wait.

I took the newspaper Preach gave me and sat on the end of the porch. Instead of reading I gazed at the mountains. They had changed in the few days I was away. The meadow was now blanketed with knee-high yellow and brown oxeye daisies. Wind from the coming storm rippled the top of the flowers and sent a rolling wave of color the length of the field.

Squawks from an unhappy bird drew my eyes to the end of the meadow where a trio of deer grazed the young tender grass with joe-pye weeds as a backdrop. The plants thrived in the damp, swampy area and stood six to seven feet tall with serrated leaves and masses of rose pink blossoms. From God's eyes to mine was what Preach would say. There was surely a God when I looked out at this serene place much as it was when it was created, yet outside this place the world had gone mad.

Preach had furnished me magazines and newspapers while I was jailed. Some were six months old, but even those helped me handle boredom. I read them from front to back sometimes more than once. They were sobering. We were losing the war in Vietnam and perhaps the battle for civil rights here at home. A few years before I had taken the names of casualties from the local paper and climbed to the top of the mountain and honored them and their families with a ceremony. Why had I stopped?

I unrolled the newspaper and stared in disbelief. The bold headline read, "Robert Kennedy Is Killed in California." Suddenly, I was frightened. The Tet offensive in January, Dr. King assassinated in April, and now Kennedy in June. He was the hope of many. And with his death, I could see myself fighting alongside guys my age a few months from now if not convicted of Vickie's murder.

The next morning, I parked on the hill above the school and waited for Lou Ann to arrive. I climbed out of the car and stood where she would see me. She arrived and looked my way. After pausing briefly, she came toward me.

She looked sad, but she was still beautiful. I wanted so much for her to be my girl. Something told me that with her I could be happy the rest of my life. I waited for her to speak. "Daddy doesn't want me to see you."

"I understand. I don't blame him."

"The man from the orphanage, Preach, said you were a good guy. He said you wouldn't kill anyone."

"I didn't kill Vickie. But I don't feel like a good guy anymore. I'd been seeing her for a few weeks and I knew she was married. That doesn't make me a nice person. I didn't want to see her ever again after meeting you. I went there that night to tell her I'd never see her again. Why did you decide to talk to me?"

"I don't know. Guess it was to wish you luck."

"Tell me why you turned down a second date."

"I wanted to date you. We connected. I really liked you. We had fun."

"You really wanted to date me?"

"Of course, I did. I was out of town the next weekend. I couldn't date you." A tear rolled onto her cheek.

"Why are you crying?"

"I don't know that either. It feels like I've lost something that I'll never get back. It makes me sad not to see you again." She gave me a quick hug. Without looking back, she ran toward the school, not stopping until she was inside.

Mr. Baker left word that I should go by and see him. He suggested there was no reason to put my life on hold because of a possible indictment for murder. He told me to petition the school to reinstate me based upon my disciplinary record and class standing. That, along with an exceptional SAT score, was my only chance for college in the fall.

I petitioned the school and waited. With my life on hold, it felt like I was balanced on the edge of a cliff and could fall either way at any time.

I spent each morning at the library and walked the mountain trails in the afternoon. Both were distractions during the day, but my doubts and fears gathered around me each night and made sleep difficult, enough to make me use booze nightly.

One afternoon when I was at a low point, I heard a car coming up the lane. It was Preach. I rose and Will Jean slipped outside the screen door and waited. Preach jumped out and hurried toward me. His smile was bigger than usual. "I've got good news."

"I'm being reinstated in school, right?"

"Better than that, Vickie's husband has been arrested for her murder."

I froze for a second. Tears rolled onto my cheeks as I dropped down on the steps and cupped my face. "Thank, God." I muttered. The thought of being convicted had kept me in knots. "How did they find out that he was the killer?"

"Homer had a private detective on the case from the beginning. A fellow truck driver testified that he dropped Vickie's husband off at home around eight and not ten. That finally got a confession."

Preach patted my shoulder. "You owe Homer. He didn't have to do that."

Will Jean blurted, "Now we've got grounds to sue that sorry ass sheriff."

I looked up at Preach who had red eyes and a broad grin. He couldn't have been happier if he'd been the one released. "You never stopped believing in me. Thanks, Preach."

"You're worth believing in." He added, "Homer also thought so."

"I guess I'm indebted to him."

"I don't guess. I know you are."

Graduating with my class at the end of June left me feeling charged with excitement about the future. Those in the know assured me my scholastic record would get me into college, and I knew that Uncle Bob's insurance money would see me through the first year.

I took a job at the drugstore for the remainder of the summer and waited as Mr. Baker continued the impossible task of trying to secure an athletic scholarship, though most were already awarded. My best hope was for someone to drop out.

I was determined to stay positive and train as if I'd been chosen to join a track team. I increased my training schedule and my time improved on the 1500. I'd decided to specialize in middle distance running, specifically the 800 and 1500. Those events demand an athlete have good aerobic and anaerobic energy producing systems, as well as strong speed endurance. Years of running the mountain terrain had served me well for those two disciplines.

My track coach, Mr. Helms, urged me to drop by the school and work out with the guys who would make up the team next year. He was big on qualities such as pace, race tactics, and endurance, explaining that speed was becoming less important and endurance more so. Human physiology dictates that a runner's near-top speed cannot be maintained for more than thirty seconds before lactic acid builds and causes oxygen deprivation. It was at such a workout one afternoon when I saw a man sitting alone on the top bleacher with a broad-brimmed hat pulled low. It looked like Homer, but the hat and rays from the afternoon sun made it impossible to know for sure.

I nodded toward the man. "Coach, who is that?"

"That's Homer. He's watched all of your workouts."

"Why? How did he know I'd be here?"

"Why don't you ask him?"

Anger sent me climbing up and across bleachers until I came within ten feet of him. "Why are you here?"

Homer only shook his head, looked down, and said nothing for a moment. "I'm not sure, Rudy. I think it has to do with memories and regrets. Don't you have regrets?"

I thought of Vickie and the question pissed me even more. "Everyone has regrets, but you and I have no connection. No reason for you to be here. I'm not your son."

He stared hard at me as if my face was a mirror. "If I knew that for certain I could sleep at night."

"Did you lose sleep after sending a pregnant sixteen-year-old girl out into the world alone?"

He dropped his head and spoke barely above a whisper. "I didn't know she was going. If I'm guilty of anything, it was not being able to go after her. But I was married with a baby."

"You had a choice I never had." Seconds passed and he never responded. I started back down the bleachers and turned back. "Preach thinks I owe you for hiring a detective to solve the case. What's your price?"

"It's free for you, Rudy, even if you're not my son."

I stared at him for a moment, then without a word continued down the steps. I never saw him watching me again. I heard he took a trip to Europe a week later.

PART TWO

15

Mr. Helms delivered good news near the end of August. Kent State made a last-minute decision and granted a full scholastic scholarship, along with an invitation to compete for a slot on the track team. On the day to leave, excitement brought me out of bed earlier than usual for a run before leaving for Ohio. I would miss the mountains and took my time running the trail, sometimes stopping to listen to the sounds that were as familiar as my face in a mirror.

I knew Will Jean hated to see me leave, though she denied it each time leaving was mentioned. When I returned from the run, she came puffing up from the basement, her flip-flops whacking against the stairs. "Thank the Lord you're leavin' and won't be in my hair no more." She thrust an old dust-covered suitcase toward me and then used her apron to wipe beads of perspiration from her forehead. "You'll have to make do with this, 'cause I ain't made of money." She grabbed a wet dishtowel and smeared months of dust around on the case. It belonged to Uncle Bob and had been stored in the cellar after his death.

I laughed and told her it would be fine. Her red eyes told me how she really felt about me leaving.

Preach waited at the bus station to see me off. He wished me luck and asked me to write, and then, without a word, unzipped my suitcase and pushed a Bible inside.

As I prepared to board, Will Jean hit me on the shoulder and advised in a loud voice that I should keep my thing in my pants so as to stay out of trouble. Her suggestion left a surprised woman in line behind me with her mouth open.

"You're gonna get skinny," she said. "They ain't gonna feed you half good." I saw tears threatening before she turned away.

I had mixed feelings as I watched her standing on the boarding platform. A part of me tugged in her direction and the other part looked forward to being away from her.

The Greyhound driver turned the key in the ignition and the bus vibrated as the gears caught. We moved slowly away from the terminal as Preach and Will Jean stood waving. I watched until we passed out of sight behind the building. Words that would describe Will Jean were hard to find. I decided she was a paradox. Women were complicated enough to write a book about and I might do that someday.

I'd never left the mountains since arriving ten years before and a little sadness crept in as they slowly disappeared behind us.

We crossed into southern Ohio where flat rolling cornfields stretched from the highway to the distant skyline. A touch of uncertainty floated up from inside as the bus traveled alongside the Cuyahoga River, passing near the Kent State campus where brick structures in various shapes and sizes stood like giant puzzle pieces. The perfectly clipped blanket of grass that stretched between buildings had turned yellow from the cool September nights. Flowers that lined the walkways had tasted the sting of frost.

An old man carrying a broom and dustpan walked over to me at the bus station. "Young feller, you look lost." He smiled, showing a perfect set of teeth in a lean face with skin like brown crepe paper. He must have detected my concern. "You'll make it fine," he said. "Go one block over, turn right, and go until you reach the administration building. They'll tell you from there."

The ivy-covered brick and marble administration building stood at the end of the street and looked to be the oldest and grandest of other nearby structures. A sign out front read "Room Assignments." Marble steps led to double doors that opened into a lobby where chatter and laughter came from a line of students that filled the long hall. Many had luggage on the floor beside them and pushed it forward with their feet as the line moved. Three bearded guys with long hair stood at the end of the line. They looked me up and down when I approached. One whispered something and the other two laughed.

Were they laughing at me? My expression must have shown my disapproval. The tall one wore Jesus sandals, wrinkled pants, and a tee shirt with "Stop the War" printed across the front. He came forward and extended his hand. "Welcome to Kent State."

I took his hand, thinking he could be setting me up to look like a fool in front of his two friends. He smiled. "I noticed your army issue case. I was telling my friends that my dad had one just like it."

"This one belonged to my uncle. You have to make do at times."

141

"That's for sure," he said.

This was my first opportunity to see a protester up close, though I'd seen pictures and read about them in the newspaper. We chatted a bit and all three seemed amiable enough. We exchanged information about where we were from, what we planned to study, and the protest that became violent at the Chicago Democratic convention. They supported protests against the war, but I wasn't ready to take a position and added little to the conversation. The quiet guy must have noticed and changed the subject by making comments about a group of girls in miniskirts who walked past. And from then on, we turned to sports and shared opinions about girls who giggled and wiggled their butts past us in the hall.

We reached a large room where each of us was directed to the appropriate alphabetized station to receive room assignments. We promised to hook up sometime and grab a beer. The campus swarmed with students who strolled about. Some with maps in hand rushed past on a mission to find their dorm. I flagged down a guy who came hurrying toward me and asked where to find Ordway Hall.

"I don't know, man," he said as he flew by. "I'm as lost as you look."

I didn't count myself lost until I realized I stood in front of my assigned dorm, the one he'd just left and the one I was trying to find. I pegged him a smart ass and me half blind.

Ordway Hall was constructed of dark red brick with stone trim. Double doors opened into a rectangular lobby. Clusters of sofas and chairs were spaced around the room. Portraits of unsmiling old men in gold baroque frames hung on the walls.

A muscular young man with horn-rimmed glasses sat behind a folding table inside the entry door. He asked my name and began searching through an index file. Seconds later he looked up and smiled. "I'm Frank, your RA for the dorm." He pointed over his shoulder toward a door in the corner. "My digs are back there." He extended his hand to shake. "Welcome to Ordway Hall."

He explained that Ordway Hall was the oldest and smallest dorm on the campus. It was divided into suites. Each suite elected a spokesperson for their group who reported any problem to the RA. There were four units attached to the lobby, six suites in each unit, two levels high, with two students to a room. He handed me a pamphlet and two keys and said, "The pamphlet is about being a gentleman at all times. No girls in your room after eleven, which means no overnight female guests." He pointed to my right. "You're in Unit A, suite 100. There's a packet of material in the room assigned to you. I suggest you read it first thing. The suite door should be unlocked."

I thanked him and climbed the five steps to a small landing. Door 100A opened into a study lounge with a long table in the center surrounded by chairs. A large bulletin board hung on the wall announcing campus events for coming weeks.

Two guys in a room off to the left were playing cards. The gaunt-faced one glanced at me. "Man, don't you know how to knock?"

The other fellow, a bruiser type who would top two fifty on any scale, pushed back from the table. "What do you want, dude?"

I set my case on the floor. "I'm assigned to this suite."

They glanced at each other. "What's your name?"

"Rudy Kelly."

"Oh, yeah. You're in the corner room straight past the bathroom. The only room with two windows. I'm Russo Moretti. This is Tony Ricci. We're from Chicago."

"Good to meet you, guys," I said, not sure I was being honest. They gave off vibes that were reminiscent of Mama's Chicago boyfriends.

Russo reached behind him and took a coke from a small waist-high refrigerator. He set it on the card table and pointed toward an empty chair. "This coke is on me. No drinks are to be brought in from outside. I have the only refrigerator. You buy from me for a dollar each. Coffee is fifty cents a cup."

I stared briefly. "You're price gouging."

He pretended not to hear and continued on. "We have this room next to the lounge for a reason. The RA has appointed me as spokesperson for this suite." He opened the coke, set the bottle back on the table, and looked up at me and smiled. "I consider myself a benevolent dictator with the authority to keep harmony in our little group." He nodded toward the chair again. "Sit."

I remained standing in the doorway without answering. If I was right, he used his size and bluster to intimidate. It was a test that spelled trouble if I failed now.

Russo turned toward Tony. "Tell Mr. Kelly how I manage."

Tony spoke with a crooked-toothed grin. "He hangs guys by their balls if they get out of line."

I chuckled, knowing my butt was mud if I'd misjudged him. "I'm fond of both my balls." I caught his eye. "I don't like trouble. Don't make trouble. But I've never run from it either. I'm from Chicago too." I picked up the coke. "No need to let this get hot." With the coke in one hand and my suitcase in the other, I disappeared down the hall and took a good, deep breath once out of sight. Mama's boyfriend used to say, "If they don't come in five minutes, you've won." I checked my watch.

The room had two beds, two desks, and double closets. More room than I could imagine, even with a roommate. I knew I could be happy here unless Russo gave me grief. All tenants had to pass by his room to reach theirs and that could be trouble.

My roommate had already settled in. His bed was made and his clothes hung neatly in one of the closets. I noticed we had something in common. In the bottom of his closet sat an old leather pouch-like case that looked worse than Uncle Bob's.

I flung myself on the mattress and stretched, feeling pleased with my new home. A picture sat on the windowsill between the two beds, facing away from me. It was probably his girlfriend. If it was his mama's picture, I'd move to another room. I picked it up and a pretty black girl stared up at me. My roommate had a black girlfriend or he was black. I reminded myself that I was up North now. I could make it work either way.

After waiting five minutes I assumed that Russo wasn't too pissed and closed my eyes. At some point, I heard movement in the room and sprang to my feet with fists drawn. A muscular black guy went into a crouched position ready to take me on.

I dropped my hands and backed away. "Sorry. I must have been dreaming. I'm Rudy Kelly." I extended my hand.

After a slight hesitation, he shook as if the white might rub off. "Charles Sanders."

We stared. Awkwardness became more pronounced. I spoke up. "I see you've unpacked. When did you get here?"

He nodded. "Earlier."

Was he playing games? We both knew he arrived earlier. Our eyes met and he glanced away.

"Where are you from?" I asked.

145

"Chicago."

Was everyone from Chicago? I considered throwing up my hands and calling it a lost cause, but decided to try one more time. "I'm from the Appalachian mountains. Some people call us hillbillies."

Not even a hint of a smile. I got it, the guy didn't like white people. Will Jean always said black people never liked us. I thought they had reason based on history, but I'd done nothing to this guy. He didn't want me as a friend.

I grabbed my case and began unpacking. He dropped down at his desk and pulled a Bible from the drawer. I rolled my eyes and turned away. God forbid if he started quoting scripture. Preach would like this guy, but he'd shown me nothing other than not caring for white boys.

I unpacked in silence and then pitched Uncle Bob's case into the closet. It appeared that the two of us would live like two monks who had taken a vow of silence. I had envisioned hitting it off with a roommate, maybe hanging out together. That wasn't likely to happen with this one, but at least he was the neat type if his appearance and the way he'd organized his side of the room was an indication. I was a people person and pissed that he'd refused my friendship. Then I remembered Peach lecturing me about the need for tolerance in one's life. It wouldn't hurt to try one more time, but not now. I needed a break and it wouldn't be sitting in the room and watching him read the Bible all afternoon. There were things to do and see. Perhaps check out the track field, maybe drop by the library and scan today's paper. No doubt the latest political talk would dominate the news and I didn't want to be the only dummy should a conversation occur.

I sent Preach a postcard and wrote Will Jean a note to let her know I'd made the trip fine and was pleased with my room and the school. I thought about telling her my roommate was black but shelved the idea. Our only discussion about desegregation happened once and was short-lived. She made the comment that she didn't like "them" people. I asked her how many blacks she'd known. She said, "None." What else could I possibly add to a discussion after such an answer?

It dawned on me how free and relaxed I felt being away from Will Jean. For all the years I'd lived with her, a subtle, underlying anxiety existed from not knowing what kind of reaction to expect. Approval was met with silence and disapproval came with an unbridled barrage of hurtful words. She gave me food and cared for me well, but that never substituted for the assurance that I was wanted and loved.

Russo chuckled and ask how I liked my roommate when I passed his door. I patted my ass, which was to say "kiss it," and sailed out the door without a word.

16

The late afternoon sun sent rays of light through a row of maples in front of the dorm. I paused a moment. The sun would be feathering the tree tops on Bear Mountain about now. Night creatures would soon come to life with the sounds of a mountain night.

Homesickness swept over me but disappeared quickly. I continued across campus, passing through The Commons, a grassy knoll traditionally used as a gathering place for rallies or protest marches. A few flowers were still beautiful, but most beds around the Commons had bowed to cool September nights.

I entered the track field through an unlocked gate and stared wide-eyed at the stadium. It surpassed any I'd seen before. The equipment and spaciousness made any kind of field and track event possible. I fell into a slow jogging pace that ended halfway around the track when I saw a girl in pink sitting alone on the top row of bleachers. The wind lifted then released her long, light brown hair. She never moved, only her hair. Something was wrong. Why would she be alone up there? She was on the top tier. The height behind her had to be over thirty feet. What if she had thoughts of jumping?

I climbed the bleachers and came within a few feet before she looked my way. Her eyes were red. Was it the wind or had she been crying?

"Are you okay?"

Using an arm, she held a mop of windblown hair away from her face and looked up at me with light blue eyes. "Who are you?"

"I'm Rudy Kelly, a student."

"Me too. I'm Annie Edmond."

"Why are you crying?"

She glanced away. "My cousin was a star runner here a few years back. He could maintain near top speed for forty seconds. Thirty seconds is considered good."

"Yeah, I know. I'm a runner."

She smiled. A sweet smile that seemed so pure and sincere. She was pretty in a soft, glowing way. Nice build, great eyes that held a hint of sadness. "What events did your cousin run?"

"His favorite was the 100 meters."

"I'm a distance man. You haven't told me why you've been crying."

She pulled the light pink sweater that draped her shoulder snug around her neck. "Jim was my cousin. He was killed by a land mine in a rice field three days before he was scheduled to come home."

To say I was sorry seemed so hollow, but I said it anyway.

"I'm not a crier, but I remember so many things about Jim. He'd planned his life. The baby he'll never have was going to be a track star, according to him."

The mention of a baby reminded me of Benny. He wasn't a baby any longer and would soon be old enough for the new lottery draft. With Mama's screwed up life, she may have left him with strangers.

Him being mulatto, with racial hatred and unrest across the country, made me more concerned than ever. How could anyone hate Benny with those big brown eyes and near perfect milk chocolate complexion.

"Do you have someone in the war?" she asked.

I dropped down beside her. "Not in the war. A brother somewhere that I haven't seen in years."

"You have no reason not to think he's still alive. I'm sure you'll find him again."

She'd tried to comfort me. There was nothing I could say or do for her. She was pretty. I'd lie my butt off just to make her feel less sad. "Let me walk back with you. Maybe we can get a sandwich, coffee, or even grab a beer . . . something?"

She looked out across the stadium. "It feels like Jim is still here."

"I'll stay here as long as you want, all night if you say so."

She faced me and smiled. "What a wonderful thing to offer. That's sweet of you, Rudy. I came here to say goodbye to Jim and offer a tribute. I might as well get on with it." She stood and handed me her sweater and then dug into a large handbag and came out with a handful of flowers. I rose and held the bag as she stripped blooms from their stalks and tossed them into the wind. I thought about the mountain ceremony I conducted for dead soldiers. Why had I stopped?

She whispered, "Goodbye." After a moment of silence, she turned to me. "You want to know something funny? I stole the flowers from beds in the Commons where all the signs say not to cut the flowers. It's something Jim would have done." Her expression changed as she took my hand. "We have kindred spirits, Rudy. I'm happy you

151

found me here. I'd love to walk back with you, even let you buy me a beer. How about you and I . . . what is it you guys say . . . get shit-faced drunk tonight?"

I laughed. Was she serious? No way could I see this girl doing that.

"I want to get drunk to celebrate something . . . like meeting you. That's reason enough. Would you take care of me like Jim did?"

"I will," I answered, anxious to know her better.

"Don't get the wrong impression. I'm a touchy, hands-on kind of person. Every guy's sister, it seems. You want to be my buddy?"

"Do I have other options?"

She gave me that smile again. "Let's go."

I let her lead the way down the bleacher steps. We found that the entry gate had been locked. The fence was constructed of woven chain links and much too high to climb over. For some bizarre reason our situation struck us as funny. We laughed our way around the perimeter while searching for a way out. We found a narrow opening between a leaning fence post and a corner bleacher that offered an escape. She squeezed through first. I followed, sucking it in and pushing hard. A loud ripping sound stopped me.

She giggled. "Was that your pants? It sounded like the whole seat went."

"No, I think just the pocket." To have my rear end stuck between the fence post and the corner of the stadium was a bit embarrass-ing. Willing to sacrifice a pocket, I lunged forward and ended up on my hands and knees with my butt in the air. Annie erupted with laughter. A rush of air across my bottom told me the reason. I came to my feet and heat moved across my face, but I managed to laugh along with her, though I didn't think my exposed rear would increase my chance for a date.

"Here, let me see what happened." She turned me around to have a look. She giggled. "I knew you'd have a nice butt."

"Have you been checking me out?"

"Of, course. Haven't you me?"

"No, I'd never do that."

"Liar. I guessed you wore briefs." She raised her brow. "But the pink surprised me."

I chuckled and turned red. I'd forgotten. That explained my new roommate's peculiar expression when I changed pants earlier. "I can explain the pink."

"You don't have to." She turned and began walking away. "Your preference for pink undies is your business. Are you gay?"

"No, I'm not. I can explain the pink." She kept walking and I hurried to catch up. "My grandmother washed them with a red shirt just before I left to come here. There was no time to bleach them before leaving."

"There's nothing wrong with pink. My sweater's pink. Butts look better in briefs regardless of color. You've proved that, don't you think?"

"Well, I, I've never thought about . . ."

"Don't you notice guys in the locker room?"

"Nooo. I mean . . . I don't know what they wear. Guys don't peek at each other or do things like that. At least I don't."

"I do when I think I have better boobs. Girls are competitive. They compare bodies all the time. Jim said guys compare sizes."

I turned red again. "Stop teasing me. Come on, we've got to get out of here." I turned to leave.

"Wait. Do you want to spend the night with me?"

I turned back. I could tell she was teasing. "Will you stop it? The answer is, yes. I would in a flash, but you're just toying with me."

"Are you a virgin?"

"Will you stop? I don't discuss my sex life with strangers." I turned to leave. "I'm going. Are you coming?"

"We've got to cover your butt first." Holding the sweater by each arm, she reached around my waist and pulled the sweater sleeves in front and tied them while staring into my eyes. Suddenly, I touched my lips to hers. She didn't resist. Our kissing became intense, so much so that I pulled away.

"What's wrong? You didn't like my kiss?"

"The kiss was great. Fantastic."

She laughed. "You're such a tease."

"You're the tease, Annie, but you just wait and see. We're going to be more than friends."

She laughed. "Don't I have a say?"

"Of course, you do. It'll be your decision when we sleep together."

She laughed again. "Look, I'm acting a little crazy carrying on like a bad girl. You're fun to be with. I couldn't keep from teasing you. I love the way you blush and smile at the same time, but you should know that I'm engaged to a guy studying international law in England."

"You're joking . . . you're teasing me again."

"No, it's true."

Our gaze connected. I knew it was true. Her eyes said so. "Then he's the wrong guy for you."

"How do you know?"

154

"An old fortune teller told me that I'd meet you. We could be soul mates."

She caught my eye for just a moment and looked away. I had a feeling her relationship with this guy was not without problems. Maybe she didn't know it now, but she was my girl. Not tonight, maybe not tomorrow, but it was going to happen. Joe's advice was to go for what you want. I wanted this girl.

We left the stadium and headed to my dorm across campus to get pants for me. Annie became quiet. Was it because of the kiss? As we entered the dorm, she turned to me. "Could we talk serious a moment before you go up to change?"

I pointed to a sofa and sat beside her. "Is this about what happened between us?"

"I shouldn't have kissed you. I don't know why I acted the way I did. I've never done anything like that before in my life. I teased and carried on like a bad girl. I own you an apology. That's not who I am."

"Why did you do it?"

"I'm not sure and that's what bothers me. I'm embarrassed now."

"Don't be. I don't regret kissing you."

"Of course not, you're a guy. You've got to understand it'll never happen again if we're going to be friends. David is a good guy."

"I'm sure he is, but even as a good guy he's not right for you."

"Why do you say that? It irritates me when you say it."

"Annie, I'm sorry, but I'm just being honest. There's something special between us."

"My God, listen to yourself, Rudy. You don't know me. I don't know you. We just met."

"I know you're special."

She laughed and shook her head. "Do you approach every girl you're attracted too like this?"

"How many guys have you kissed since becoming engaged?"

"None, of course."

"Doesn't that make you question why you kissed me? Why are you engaged to this guy?"

"He has a name, Rudy. It's David. I'm in love with him."

"How do you know that?"

"Well, I've known him all my life. Our parents are friends. His dad and mine are law partners."

Her reasons made no sense, but they pleased me. "You kiss me and then toss me aside. You're forcing me to accept buddy status forever. I hope I'm still your buddy?"

"Of course, you are. You're my best buddy."

I rose. "Be back in ten." I turned and started toward the suite, feeling more convinced than ever that I was right about us. Russo and Tony stood inside the entry door watching. They rushed to catch up.

Russo laughed. "Kelly, you lucky prick. Have you already found you some stuff?"

My first impulse was to punch him out. I faced him. "If I ever hear you refer to her as 'stuff' I'll break your fucking neck, even if I have to do so in your sleep."

Before he could react, I turned and shot up the steps, surprised at the extent of my anger. I wanted to smash his face. My reaction toward him had been spontaneous, yet I considered myself more methodical and not just acting on impulse. It felt right to defend and protect this girl. I could feel the connection that existed. Annie was my soul mate.

The last two suite mates had arrived and looked my way as I passed their door. I had no time to introduce myself with Annie waiting. I would look in on them when I returned.

I popped in the door and staggered backward with my hands raised. "It's me, it's me," I shouted.

Charles lowered the bat and expelled a rush of air. "I'm sorry, I thought . . ."

"Man, you were ready to brain me. What's going on?"

"Nothin '." He dropped down at his desk and cut his eyes toward the sweater hanging from my waist.

"The sweater belongs to my girlfriend. I ripped my pants. What's going on with the bat?"

He shrugged.

"Look, man. We've got to live together. I'd hoped we could be friends."

His eyes widened. "Me too."

"That means we talk. If you have something on your mind, you spill it. What happened while I was gone?"

"The big guy in the front room put the squeeze on me. He wants money each week because I go past his room. Is it just me or is it you too?"

"Oh, crap. It's me too. He's a dick. I'll talk to him."

"Are you sure?"

"Yeah, I thought we had an understanding."

I gave thumbs up to the two new suite mates and continued on. Tony stood in the doorway talking to Russo. "Pardon," I said and nudged past him. Russo leaned back in a chair drinking a beer.

I pointed. "I don't believe that's legal in the dorm."

Russo chuckled. "I don't believe so either."

"You tried to shake down my roommate. It's not going to happen. You're out of business, period. No cokes, no coffee, no nothing for sale. If you attempt to continue I'll go to the administration and let them settle the matter."

Russo laughed. "Listen, country boy, nobody tells Russo what to do. You cross me and your ass will be in trouble."

"It's been in trouble before. The last time was for murder." I waited for that to sink in then left. Before I'd taken three steps, I heard him say, "That hillbilly don't stop Russo." I halted to listen. "That little bitch in the lobby won't recognize him when I'm finished."

I whirled around and started for Russo. Tony caught me from behind and pinned my arms to my sides. I kicked, struggled, and danced around, trying to get free. Russo came to his feet and gave me a solid left in the jaw. I kicked him in the crotch, hard. He howled and doubled forward. I broke away from Tony, and in the process elbowed him under the chin. He went staggering backward into the study lounge. When I turned back, Russo came with his head down, sending me against the wall. His body pressed against mine with a hand on my throat. I pounded his fatty sides with both fists. It never moved him. I gasped for air. Out of the corner of my eye I saw the coffee urn on the table an arm's length away. I grabbed the handle and dumped its contents down his back. He staggered backward into the lounge area, clawing, ripping, and pulling at the steaming tee shirt, with screams that could be heard throughout the dorm.

I stood with fists ready when five or six guys from the suite next door poured into the room. They moved in between us, all talking at once, telling us to "cool it" before security arrived.

"Come on, man. It's over," a tall guy said, taking my balled fists and urging me toward the other side of the room.

Russo lay on a sofa moaning with three guys gathered around, all trying to remove his shirt. "Damn, look at his back. This guy needs to see a doctor," one of them said.

"Somebody call an ambulance."

The RA rushed into the room and looked around. "Who's involved, other than him?" He pointed to Russo. I raised my hand.

"Those of you who didn't witness what happened move it outside. Where you involved in this, Charles?"

"No, sir."

"Then put the bat down."

I turned and looked behind me. Tony was glued against the wall with Charles holding the bat ready for a home run. I smiled. He smiled back.

Any hope to booze it up that evening was put on hold. Russo was taken to the emergency room, and those with knowledge about the incident were herded into a room and questioned by the RA. I waited in the lobby with Annie for the Assistant Dean of Men to arrive.

Time dragged on forever before Frank told us the dean was on his way. We were advised that he might not be in the best of moods after being called from a social gathering. His prediction seemed right on point when a short, chubby, grim-faced man finally arrived. He settled into a chair across from us. No smile. No handshake. Not even an introduction. Dark piercing eyes framed by curly, gray hair focused on me as if he was a mind reader, the kind that could spot a lie in a guy's head before a word was spoken.

He flipped through a folder for a good minute and then looked up at Annie. "I assume you're not involved in this matter. What are you to him?"

"Just a friend."

"Mr. Kelly, you want her to hear this?"

"Yes, sir, I have no problem with her being here."

He narrowed his gaze on me. "You're on campus less than a day and in trouble. What is it with you, Kelly?"

"Sir, I accept part of the responsibility for the fight. I'd intended to punch the daylights out of Russo. But the fact is, his friend grabbed me from behind. Russo hit first while I was being held." I touched my swollen lip. "He gave me this, and he was choking off my air. I couldn't breathe and had no choice but to dump the coffee down his back. I believe any reasonable person would have done the same."

"And what would an unreasonable person have done, Mr. Kelly?"

"Run, I suppose, but I don't run when my girlfriend is disrespected or my friends are threatened by extortion."

"Extortion?" He glanced at Frank who rushed forward with a paper extended. "Here's what his suitemates had to say."

The dean glanced at the paper for a few seconds and slipped it into the folder. "We must interview Russo before we can determine blame. You've presented your side of the story in a very simple and precise way, for which I commend you." He held the folder up. "I'm aware of your troubled past and see that you were accepted to the university under probationary conditions. Should your explanation of the incident prove untrue, further disciplinary action could follow." He rose and walked out the door without another word.

Frank stepped forward. "All of your suite mates supported the extortion charge. I don't think you're in trouble, but be careful. The dean is not a generous man when handing out punishment."

I thanked him and he left. Once he was out of earshot Annie turned to me. "I've got a question. How did I get involved? I'm not aware I was disrespected."

"You were. Russo referred to you by an unflattering word. I'd warned him before, so I was going to let him know it shouldn't happen a third time."

"You were fighting for me?"

I shrugged.

Her eyes widened. "You were. And you lied."

"About what?"

"You said I was your girlfriend. Just minutes before I'd told him we were just friends."

"I didn't say girlfriend, did I? I said friend."

"Rudy, you said girlfriend."

"Well, you . . . you are my friend, right? My buddy? And you're certainly a girl. Wow!"

She laughed. "You silly thing, I've got your troubled history figured. You were dropped on your head as a baby. That would explain your pickup lines. They make you weird."

"I'm not weird. I'm just different."

"And that can be weird."

"Point well taken." I checked the time. "It's getting late. Are you sure you want to party tonight?"

"Not really, not after all of this."

"I don't either. Let's go find a sandwich, wash it down with a beer, and go for a walk. There's going to be a full moon."

"Oh, my God, Rudy."

"Wait, wait. I've walked in the moonlight with my guy buddies and we've never held hands."

"Sorry, point well taken."

"Thank you, lady. I bet walking down by the river is nearly as pretty as being in my mountains."

"Your mountains. Why would you call them *your* mountains?"

"I went to live with my grandmother when I was eight and fell in love with them. They've always boosted my spirit."

"Rudy, what happened just now? When you mentioned going to live with your grandmother, your expression changed. You looked angry."

"Did I? It's a long story. I'll tell you when there's more time." I rose and pulled her to her feet. "Right now, I'm starving. What about you? I know nothing about your past. You're the only buddy I've ever had that I can't talk with about which girl is putting out."

Her mouth fell open. "You would tell?"

I ran my hand across my mouth as if to zip my lips. "No, never." Annie laughed. "We're off subject. Do you have siblings?"

"Yes, I'm the youngest, the renegade according to my family. My sister is the oldest and married with a baby. My brother is at West Point, my dad's an attorney, and my mother's a doctor. I'm going to become an attorney."

"I've heard little girls are close to their dads. How long have you wanted to become an attorney like him?"

"Actually, I haven't. I've dreamed about being a journalist."

"Then why don't you study journalism?"

"My family doesn't support the idea, so I'm going to become an attorney."

The sound of her voice told me she was not happy with their choice. I thought it odd that she had no say in choosing her own career, but then I knew nothing about how a real family functioned. "Why don't you sign up for a course in journalism just for the fun of it?"

"Why would I do that?"

"We'd be in the same class."

She stopped and stared up at me. Her mouth widened into a smile. "I just might do that. It'd be dangerous for you to run free all the time."

We both laughed.

There were a hundred reasons why I wanted this girl. Was it her smile? Was it the way she touched my swollen lip after the fight? Or was it because I felt better with her than being on top of the highest mountain in the world?

The park stretched along the river with a walking trail near the water's edge. A full moon danced across the bubbling water and spread its magic over flower beds, climbing vines, and other vegetation that hugged the river, giving a fairytale quality to the night.

Couples strolled arm in arm along the winding trail. She walked so close I didn't speak for fear it would break the illusion of intimacy felt. We hadn't touched hands or spoken a word since entering the park.

A night bird somewhere in the midst of darkness sang a song that sounded right for lovers. I reached for Annie's hand to assist in crossing a marshy area where irregular placed stepping stones were nearly emerged in water. She smiled and thanked me when we reached the other side. This moment, this girl . . . there was no other place to be. A fantasy of us being a couple was complete when she hooked her arm in mine. "I feel like we've met a hundred years ago."

"Do you believe in reincarnation?" she asked.

Had she been thinking about me? I wasn't sure she was conscious of hanging on to my arm. "I never have before," I said. "If you had a buddy back then, it had to have been me. My life must have been a hundred percent better back then."

Concern spread across her face. "Has your life been bad?"

"No, no, uneven might be a better way to describe it." I chuckled. "My family is insane."

She laughed. "There's a little mental illness in all of us. It's the degree of madness that separates us. Mad men started this war. Now the world is in step with insanity leading the way."

"No talk of war, not tonight. Let's make it off limits. This night gives promise to good things. I refuse to dwell on the war."

"What good things?"

"Well, I met you. I have a new friend, a new buddy."

She laughed.

"What is the one thing you want most in your life right now?"

"To study journalism," she blurted.

I saw the excitement in her eyes and encouraged her to go for it regardless of what her parents wanted. I felt no such passion about a career and spoke in general terms about my love for books and became brave enough to reveal a secret about becoming a famous writer. For years, I'd been privately writing poetry, convinced it was the best genre to describe something as mysterious and beautiful as the mountains.

"You've got to let me read your poems," she said.

"I'm not that brave."

"I think I'd love them."

I chuckled, surprised at the response. "Why would you think that?"

"I believe in you."

We'd better get back. I reached for her hand. She never pulled away and we held hands all the way. It must have felt as natural and right to her as it did to me. Maybe the magic of the night got to her too, and perhaps she wasn't even conscious of us holding hands. It could be another sign that we were meant to be together.

Annie lived two blocks off campus in a garage apartment. She preceded me up the stairs and turned back when I hesitated at the bottom. "Do you want to come up?"

"I'd better get back to the dorm." The impulse to go up tugged at me, but the night had gone well and I couldn't take the chance of messing up. "Tomorrow we register for classes. You want to have breakfast with me and stand in line together?"

"Sure."

"I had a great time with you Annie."

"It was fun for me too, Rudy."

I threw her a kiss.

She laughed. "Do you always throw kisses to your buddies?"

"Only to those who wear skirts."

Laughing, she came running back down the steps, hesitated a moment, then threw her arms around my neck. "I have to hug you for making me come to my senses. I'm taking journalism and my parents are going to flip out."

I held her close and only released her when she pulled away. Our eyes met. She looked confused, befuddled, and walked backward a few steps, then without a word shot up the steps.

I watched her go and whispered, "You're my girl, Annie. You don't know it now, but you will."

I headed back to the dorm too wound up for sleep. Knowing I would need a couple of shots to turn off my head, I stopped by the liquor store and picked up a pint.

The two suite mates I'd never met were in the study room. With handshakes and introductions behind us, I dropped down on a sofa across from them. They were also first year students and total opposites in appearance. Gene was a tall, thin, red-haired guy, who'd played high school basketball, confirmed by his lettered jacket. His roommate, Randal, called Randy, was muscular and short. Both gave thumbs up to the way Russo went down. I chatted with the guys for a while and learned they were from a little town in southern Indiana. The two seemed like standup guys that anyone would welcome as roommates. I was surprised when Randy lowered his voice and whispered, "You pulled the short straw when getting a roommate. What are you going to do about the black guy?"

"What do you mean?" I asked, though I had an idea what he meant. The two exchanged quick glances. Gene spoke. "If he leaves me alone, I'll leave him alone. Live and let live, I say."

"That's fair," I said. "I hope you two will have the same attitude toward me."

Both guys chuckled. "Yeah, yeah, you're a good guy," Gene said.

Randal added, "You've proved that already."

"His name's Charles. Did you give him a chance to hang out with you here?"

Another look passed between them. "We talked about it," Gene said, "but weren't sure what to do."

"Give him a chance, will you? He had my back during the fight with Russo, so I'm going to have his."

"Sure we will," Gene said. Both nodded.

I found Charles at his desk with a mouth full of cookie. I gave thumbs up as a hello and stepped behind my closet door to remove the pint from my waistband. I needed a good hiding place, but for now I slipped it into the pocket of an old winter coat that Will Jean insisted I bring.

"My mother sent some cookies. Would you like one?" Charles asked.

"Sure," I nodded. A sweet cookie sounded good.

He opened the pouch-like bag that lay on his desk. In lifting the cookie tin from the case an old gray and white photo fluttered to the floor.

It was the picture of an elderly Negro man. I picked it up. "Who is this?"

"My great grandfather." He held the tin toward me. "Take a couple. He made the bag from a cowhide. When I was a kid, my mother told me about his journey."

I pushed a bite of cookie to the side of my mouth and asked, "What kind of journey? Was it like when he came to America?"

He smiled. "No. It was . . . my great grandfather was a slave. He carried his belongings in this bag and walked from a plantation outside of Charleston to New York City."

Hearing the history of the crude leather-stitched bag left me stunned. I ran my hand across the case, somehow needing to connect. I had read about slavery but had never thought about it in such human terms until now. "When did this happen?" I asked.

"In the eighteen fifties. I'm told he hid in fields, swam rivers, and lived off wild berries and tender grass." Charles stroked the dried leather case, running his fingers across scrapes and smudges on the raw leather. I imagined each scar had its own story.

He reached for the picture on the nightstand. "You had a girl with you today." He held the framed picture toward me. "This is my girl. We're getting married when we both finish school."

"That's terrific, but that's four years out," I replied with a mouth full of the second cookie.

"She's worth waiting for. Time will pass fast."

I stared at the picture and thought about Annie. "When did you decide that this girl was your soul mate?"

He took the photo, stared at it and smiled. "When her face got in front of every other girl's face I'd had thoughts about."

A chill crawled up my back. That's the way it was with Annie.

While Charles showered, I took a couple of swallows from the pint and chewed two sticks of gum. The booze soon took me down a couple of notches, enough so that I went to sleep shortly after crawling into bed.

The night was filled with fitful dreams, all about looking for Annie. At some point, I must have fallen into a deep sleep. I awoke with light coming through the window. Frightened that I'd be late for breakfast, panic brought me out of bed on the double. Filled with excitement, I took a quick shower and rushed out the door to meet Annie.

17

I was first in line at the cafeteria at six o'clock. Half an hour later the line had grown long and disappointment simmered, enough so, to make me pace up and down. I thought Annie would be the punctual type. Then seven came, followed by seven-thirty. I was growing more concerned by the minute. The clock neared eight and still no Annie. To hell with breakfast, I bolted across campus at full speed, breaking stride only when meeting a couple on the narrow sidewalk near her apartment. I reached the stairs that led up to her place with beads of sweat running down my forehead. Circles of perspiration colored my new shirt. I'd chosen to wear blue, hoping Annie would like it with my eyes.

I banged on the door even though no one was there. Frustration mounted. Where the hell was she? I gave the door a solid punch and dropped down on the steps with scraped knuckles. Annie could have a reasonable explanation, and I was acting like a nutcase. Perhaps she overslept. It nearly happened to me. I'd find her in line registering for a class somewhere.

I spent the morning looking for Annie and trying to fit classes into suitable time slots, succeeding with only two, both required for all beginning freshmen. I decided to take a break and resume after lunch. That was the time scheduled to register for journalism. I was sure to cross paths with Annie there. We both would be in the same class. With an hour and a half of free time, I decided to go back to the dorm and freshen up after the morning run to her apartment.

Charles sat in the study room with papers and a class schedule spread across the table. "Did you get the classes you wanted?" I asked.

"All except one," he replied. "Oh, the girl you were with yesterday came by this morning and left a letter. I put it on your desk."

I hurried down the hall, thinking how thoughtful Annie had been to leave a note. I should have known she would have a reasonable explanation. The letter was sealed and I hurriedly tore into it.

> *To my Favorite Buddy*
>
> *Thanks for such a great time yesterday. It will have a special place in my memories, forever. David called last night and I told him about my decision to take a journalism class and what a wonderful time we had, but to my surprise he objected to both, especially our friendship. I disagreed vehemently, but after giving it some thought, I've concluded he was right now that he and I are engaged. I hope you understand. It's best that we make other friends.*
>
> *Annie*

I threw a book against the wall and yelled, "Nooo, damn it."

Charles appeared in the doorway, looking concerned. "Are you okay?"

"Sorry. Annie is trying to drop me. I think I'm in love with her."

"I thought you two had just met."

"Yeah, yesterday."

"Isn't it a little quick to be . . . in love? Find another girl."

"No. She's the one." He frowned. "I'm okay. The note pissed me off. I'm embarrassed that you heard. I'd appreciate if you'd let it slide."

"Sure, I'll do that."

"Thanks."

"Are you sure you don't want to talk to someone? The student handbook said counseling is available around the clock."

I chuckled. "I'm not nuts, Charles. I just got pissed off and wasn't thinking clearly. Besides, I can't picture myself spilling my guts to a stranger."

He smiled. "I hope not everyone has that attitude. I'm planning to become a therapist."

"Are you lining up business already?" I teased.

We both laughed.

"I'm going to shower and then find Annie."

"Are you sure you should do that . . . maybe give it more time?"

"Charles, I'm fine." He looked like he didn't believe me. "Come on, Charlie, it's over . . . all behind me. I need to explain some things to her and everything will be fine with us."

He nodded and left, though he didn't look convinced. I hollered after him, "Charlie, it's okay."

After a couple of minutes with cold water gushing over me, I was in control and developed a game plan to make Annie realize I was the guy for her. Dozens of ideas had sailed through my head. I settled on emphasizing the friendship angle until she recognized the depth of her feelings for me, even if it took all year.

The cattle call, a name given to registration by students, began in a large room where students waited. When their name was called, they were taken to various locations in the building to register for their chosen classes. Annie sat in a far corner reading a pamphlet and never noticed as I approached.

"Hey, buddy," I said.

A smile appeared for only an instant, but long enough to know she was glad to see me. "Hi," she said. She blushed and seemed embarrassed.

I sat beside her. "Are you getting the classes you want?"

"Yeah, just one to go and I'm waiting for that one now."

"I know you wanted journalism bad. I'm sorry you're not taking it."

She glanced down. "Actually, I'm taking it."

I waited.

She continued. "I changed my mind an hour ago. Dad's going to be furious, but I'm taking it anyway."

What could have changed her mind? Maybe she'd had second thoughts about both journalism and our friendship. "I'm glad about journalism," I said. "Have you changed your mind about anything else, such as us being friends?"

She looked down. "Rudy, I'm sorry. I was too much of a coward to tell you face-to-face."

"I can see it would be difficult to tell a friend you no longer want to be friends for no reason at all."

"I don't want you to feel that way. We're still friends. I like you the same as before."

"David must be a special guy to choose and pick your friends."

"He doesn't do that. This is really unlike him. I must have talked about the fun we had yesterday with so much enthusiasm, he was afraid our relationship went, well, you know . . . beyond friendship."

"But you know we're just friends. I'm confused. It's not like we were having a hot affair. Surely, he's not the type to control you by limiting your friends?"

"Stop it, Rudy. He doesn't control me."

"If you say so, but I would suggest that the word 'control depends on the degree to which he controls you. Does David view our friendship as if we were two married people?"

She shook her head. "Of course, not, that's ridiculous."

"Of course, it is. I'm sure you've never fantasized about being with me, uh, in a sexual way. It's pure friendship, right?"

"Yes, of course."

"We did kiss, remember?

"That meant nothing."

"And you said I had a cute butt."

"Lower your voice," she whispered. "People can hear you. I never said cute. I might have said nice."

"Come to think about it, I believe you did say nice. You know, Annie, we're destined to be friends. Can you believe it, we've both agreed on most everything just now, and you've solved a problem for me. You see, I didn't know how to tell you that I met this cool little number at registration this morning. I'm to meet her and need to cancel our walk in the park we'd planned for later. She asked me out, can you believe it?" I chuckled. "First time ever to be asked by a girl! I've heard that when a gal asks a guy out, it promises to be a hot date. What do you think?"

"I wouldn't know," she snapped. "I don't ask guys out."

"You should have seen the short shorts and the halter she wore . . . unbelievable. She was a knockout."

An announcement came over the intercom. Annie rose. "Was that my name they called?"

"No, it was for a John somebody."

"I'm not sure, I'd better check." She hurried to the front of the room and engaged in animated conversation with the lady at the desk.

A part of me hated all the pretending, but another part of me relished the fact that she was glad to see me and irritated at the notion of me dating.

I watched her check her watch every two seconds, and she looked unhappy. I hated that.

I registered for the journalism class, careful to choose the same time and session Annie had chosen. I wanted to see her often and enable her to see me interacting in a playful way with girls in class.

I'd made Annie unhappy and left the building feeling down. The only defense against such moods was a couple of drinks or a long run.

I returned to the dorm, slipped into sweats, and headed across campus to the stadium for a run. I hit the track at a fast pace and kept moving until exhaustion took me to the ground. I sprawled on my back and looked up at the sky, a pure September blue now that the summer heat had moved on. A few stray clouds floated in a vast sea and looked as lost as I'd felt much of my life.

Just recently an unthinkable feat was accomplished. Neil Armstrong announced that "The eagle has landed." It'd traveled 238,000 miles to reach the moon. It was an example of America's exceptionalism and a tribute to its people. It inspired me to write, to put my feelings down in black and white. It also convinced me that Annie would ultimately choose me regardless of her engagement.

Playing mind games with Annie left me flat, yet she'd confirmed that her feelings went beyond friendship by an unintended display of jealousy. While I was happy that she cared, I returned to the dorm feeling contradicted, upbeat and hopeful one minute, then guilty and down the next.

Letters from home offered a slight mood change, even though they were only short notes, most likely mailed the day I left. The one from Preach was filled with encouragement, along with a blunt reminder that eighteen-year-old guys attracted trouble like a dog does fleas, especially if they were inclined to be hotheads. He underlined, "I believe you know someone of that nature." His advice was to think twice and then do nothing in most cases.

His closing line left a lump in my throat. "I love you like a son, kid, and I pray for you every day." He'd never said that before. What reason did he have to love me? I took a moment to think, but arrived at no answer.

Will Jean's letter set a tone that only she could write. "I'm still here," she wrote. "If you don't get this let me know. But if you don't it won't matter much anyway. Pearlie had her calf. I do worry they ain't feedin' you good. It's real peaceful not havin' you here. I don't have to cook my ass off feedin' you three times a day. I hope you ain't homesick." It was signed, Will Jean. She'd written in pencil something that had been erased. I squinted and saw the words, "I love you" barely visible beneath the smudge.

I muttered, "I care for you too, Will Jean." How could I not? She took care of me when no one else would. I wrote Will Jean a short letter and ended it with "I love you" in big capital letters. I also wrote to Preach, careful to keep it upbeat. I wished I could talk to him about the way I felt about Annie, but I didn't dare. He'd cut to the chase and tell me it was just an overdose of testosterone at work and to take a cold shower and get over it. A quote he often threw at me came to mind. "Doing the right thing sometimes means being unselfish and doing what is best for the other person."

I threw a book across the room and sank back in my chair. "I'll be damned," I muttered. Mama did to her boyfriends what I was doing to Annie. She'd tried to manipulate them to make them jealous.

On my way to the closet I threw the letter to Preach in the waste-basket and grabbed the bottle from the coat pocket. I was taking a second swallow when the door opened and Charles stepped inside. He looked away, but I knew he'd seen me.

"You want a shot?" I held the bottle toward him.

"No, thanks." He slipped into the chair behind his desk.

I felt pissed and wasn't sure why. After an awkward moment, I stammered, "Uh, the day was kind of rough with my girl trying to drop me. I needed to take the edge off."

"Some days are just that way," he said in a monotone without looking in my direction. I watched as he focused on repositioning items on his desk, making sure each was perfectly lined up

I blurted, "You're OCD, aren't you?"

He looked up at me and held my gaze. "Do you think so, Rudy?"

I looked away. What was happening to me? Why was I angry with him? He'd refused to drink with me. Maybe it was because he was black. He had no right to disapprove of what I did. It was obvious that he disapproved. I'd heard it in his voice.

Mixed in with my confusion was a feeling of guilt for what I'd said and what I was thinking. "I'm sorry, Charles. My comment was out of line."

"It's okay," he said. "I've been called worse."

I knew enough to understand that what was not said spoke the loudest. His response had made me feel even worse. "I'm truly sorry," I added.

He looked up at me. "The line between being neat and a neat freak is very thin and always fluctuating, based upon each individual's perception."

I assumed Charles was smart, but I'd just learned how clever he could be. His point hit home. "You mean drinking alcohol to take me down a notch could lead to something more serious than just social drinking. You're saying I wouldn't know when I crossed the line."

He looked at me and smiled. "I'm driving home on Friday afternoon to pick up some things. I'm coming back on Sunday. Would you like to come along, see what Chicago looks like? My parents said they would love to have you visit. We could hang out . . . shoot some hoops . . . swim at the Y?"

I was surprised and couldn't respond immediately. I'd never thought of having Charles as a friend. Was it because he was black? I didn't know what to say. "What about your girl? I wouldn't want to be an extra spoke in the wheel."

"You wouldn't be. She's out of town. You don't think I would invite you along if she was there," he teased.

I laughed. "May I give you an answer tomorrow?"

"Sure."

"I'm going for a run in the park. You want to come along?"

"Thanks for the invite, but I have things to do. I thought you did a few laps at the stadium earlier."

"Yeah, but I need to run again." I turned to leave.

"If I ran as often as you, I'd be running away from something."

I chuckled and turned back. "You're a smart ass, Charlie, but I'm going to like having you as a friend."

"Why? I am black."

"I hadn't noticed."

We both laughed.

"I accept your invitation for the weekend."

I'd hoped to reclaim the moon's romantic vibes that I'd felt with Annie last night, but an overcast sky blotted out the moon. The park felt strange, filled with dark shadows that changed shape as the wind nudged trees. I'd never felt more alone in my life and picked up my pace, running at full speed until nearly colliding with a man at a bend in the trail.

I finally stopped to take a breather, but my imagination was working overtime. I felt as if I was being watched.

At one point, I glanced behind me and saw what looked like a man dart into the shadows. Then, farther down the trail where visibility was at least two hundred feet, I saw him again. I continued on, picked up speed and slowed down. The figure did the same, keeping the distance between us the same.

Instead of returning to the campus exit, I took the next one available, which connected to what students referred to as Hangout Row. It was the main connection between town and the campus. Neon lights were ablaze from one end to the other. Small bands, hoping to make it big, appeared regularly at the small joints that lined both sides of the two-block area. I slowed to a walk, glancing behind me often. No one was there.

My eyes were drawn to crude, handwritten signs tacked on buildings and light posts, announcing an antiwar meeting at The Place tonight.

Farther down the block I came upon The Place. It was a one-story, rock building that stood on a corner with a banner above the door that announced the meeting. A guy on the sidewalk was selling antiwar tee shirts. I shook my head "no" and slipped inside to a packed, standing-room-only crowd. It appeared to be a mixture of students and older hippie types. Messages on new to faded tee shirts were walking billboards against the war. The speaker on the bandstand was the only person in suit and tie, but he had hair and a beard like most of the others. He'd connected to the crowd that gave hoots and shouts of approval.

I made my way through the crowd and found a spot in the corner next to the bar. I ordered a beer, chugalugged it down, and waved for a second one. I soon realized that within the crowd a debate between a peaceful protest and anarchy might also be determined by perception. I wondered if Charles would agree.

18

I avoided Annie the three days prior to leaving for Chicago to the extent of being a no-show in the journalism class. No doubt she would notice my absence.

We were at the point of departing for Chicago when I developed second thoughts about going. A scary feeling from out of nowhere had me on edge. A shot of booze was what I needed, but I didn't dare drink in front of Charles. I was constantly concerned that he'd learn about my drinking. The drama of Mama leaving me tugged at my nerves with such intensity, I realized something had to give. Being back there would make memories too real.

I'd stopped packing and was mumbling to myself when I realized that Charles was staring at me with a strange expression. Had he understood or even heard what I'd said?

"Sorry, I might have been talking to myself about something that happened years ago."

"Yes, you were."

Our gazes connected for a quick second, and then we resumed packing. Why was I afraid of Chicago? I couldn't kid myself, the trauma of that morning when Mama left was still alive within me. Charles knew something wasn't right with me, and I couldn't afford to fall apart in front of him. "Charles, maybe it would be better if I don't go."

"Why?" he snapped.

"For personal reasons," I answered, unable to think of an excuse that would fly.

"Maybe you've decided it wouldn't work to have a black friend?"

"Oh, hell, no, it's not that at all."

He continued to stare.

I had to shoot straight . . . to tell him something. "Okay, Charles, I once lived in a motel on the south side near the Projects until I was eight. Something bad happened and it's affected my life ever since. To be honest, the thought of going back scares the hell out of me."

He grimaced and looked down. "Sorry, Rudy."

"I have a younger brother. We've had no contact since I left Chicago, but I've dreamed of finding him all those years. Now I'm afraid to look. What if I never find him?"

"Aw, man, you've got to keep thinking you will. How old would he be now?"

"About seventeen."

"My mom works in records for Chicago's Department of Education. If he's in a Chicago school, she could trace him down."

"You really think so?

"I know so, man."

I hesitated.

Charles added, "Why not let her try? Otherwise you'll never have closure."

After our conversation, I was surprised at how relaxed I became during the drive.

We were expressing opinions and exchanging ideas as if we were old friends. I told him about Chicago and being sent to the mountains, along with the sane part of my life with Will Jean. He shared some difficulties of growing up as a black kid and how important Dr. King had been in his own life and that of his race.

It's funny how one's mind will sometimes go blank while in the middle of a story. I'd started telling him something but went blank when an image of a bear chasing a boy flashed in my head. I couldn't recall what I was talking about.

After a few moments of silence, Charles glanced my way.

I chuckled. "Damn, I forgot what I was going to say."

He laughed. "You were going to tell me about your first camping trip."

"First camping trip?"

"Yeah, remember?"

I couldn't recall. "I don't remember my first camping trip."

Charles gave a quick glance my way again and then jumped into a story about his experience while camping up in Michigan with an uncle. I knew it was to cover my awkwardness, but it helped little.

We lapsed into silence and after a few minutes I suddenly blurted, "It was with Mr. Wells." My eyes filled. "I saw him killed by a bear."

"What are you talking about?" Charles asked.

"I went camping with Mr. Wells. I saw him killed by a bear."

"Oh, Rudy, no wonder you had a lapse of memory."

Why would I forget that? "I can't believe I didn't remember."

"Our minds have a way of protecting us," Charles said.

185

After that conversation, we talked little and what said was mostly about the landscape, which was pretty impressive with a vast array of reds, yellows, and browns that were ushered in by an early frost.

The Chicago skyline was something to see. I didn't remember the buildings being so tall. Charles's family lived on the Southside in an upscale middleclass neighborhood called Groveland, a relatively short distance from the area where the motel stood near the Projects, but miles away in terms of living conditions.

His parents couldn't have been more gracious in welcoming me. We arrived near dinner time and his mother had prepared a special meal that included her son's favorite foods. Topping the list was a sweet potato cobbler made from a recipe passed on by his Alabama grandmother from generations before.

After dinner, his dad took us to the local Y for a swim, but the pool was so crowded we chose shooting hoops instead. I learned that Charles was a better athlete than I'd imagined. I considered myself fairly good, but I couldn't hold a candle to him. He beat both his father and me. I'd been good enough to make the basketball team while in high school, but had dropped it after running track became my passion. Charles teased and rubbed in his win so much, I vowed to challenge him to a race at some point in the future. It made me realize that guys are most competitive with their best friends. Would Charles someday become a best friend?

When we returned to the house, Charles told his dad that we were going to cruise around for a little. The man's brow went up. "A kid on the streets on Friday night after eleven is primed for trouble." Without another word, he walked into the house.

Charles chuckled. "Dad wanted to say, 'No, you're not going,' but he settled by reminding me that my butt would be in trouble if I wasn't back at a decent hour."

"I thought it was kind of nice that he cared," I said.

"You wouldn't if you'd heard it for years. I guess your dad never gave you a curfew."

"No, he never did. It's going to sound strange, but I kind of wish he had. I never knew him."

"Sorry, I'm always putting my foot in it with you."

"It's all right."

He shifted into gear and moved down the street. "You mentioned living near the Projects. They're not far away. You want to cruise past the motel and see if it looks the same?"

"I'm not sure about that."

"Why not?"

Perspiration popped out across my forehead. "No reason not to, I guess."

"Then let's do it."

The motel was gone and I felt an immediate sense of relief. A new building that went up ten to twelve stories high stood in its place. Gone was everything, but not the memory.

We failed to make curfew and slept in the next morning. Charles's parents were gone when we awoke. He made pancakes and eggs for breakfast. They were good, especially the pancakes with hot maple syrup. I was reminded that had I not been naturally thin and a runner, Will Jean's cooking would have turned me into a linebacker by now. Thinking about her made me a little nostalgic. I wondered if she missed me. I'd thought of her often, which surprised me.

Charles's mother returned shortly after ten. She greeted me with a smile, and then her gaze focused on Charles.

"Nothing?" he asked.

She shook her head.

"Rudy, we had hoped to surprise you. Mom went to the office and tried to locate your brother. No luck."

"I'm sorry," she said. "I only found one Benjamin Kelly."

"Maybe that's him," I said.

"No, baby," she replied. "He was black."

I stammered, "That's Benny, that's my brother."

"You have a black brother?" Charles asked.

"Yes, yes, his dad was black."

Charles laughed and grabbed me up in a bear hug and danced around. His mother clapped and shouted, "Praise the Lord. Thank you, Jesus."

Emotion silenced me for a moment. I had questions, but couldn't get them out. "Where is he? How do we find him?"

"Oh, my Lord, I didn't look. I saw he wasn't white and didn't go through his file." She grimaced. "This may not be good, but there was a page on top that said something about him being sent to the farm."

"What does that mean?" I asked.

Charles and his mother exchanged looks.

"Being sent to the farm could mean being sent to prison or jail," she said.

Charles added, "It's a southern term that relates to chain gangs in some southern states, but it's also slang sometimes used in the North, especially among the prison population."

On Saturday morning, the City School Records building was deserted except for a lone security officer at the front door. Without the usual shuffle and bustle of people the building gave off an eerie feeling like that of a mausoleum. Shadows filled the hall as the three of us moved silently toward the back of the building where a large rectangular room housed a maze of steel cabinets divided into alphabetized sections. Charles's mother wound her way around the room with us following until she reached the Ks. My heart beat faster as she pulled a folder from the drawer and spread it on top of the open file. I held my breath as she read.

After a moment, she smiled. "It was a baseball camp, sometimes called a farm since its purpose is to grow young hopefuls into major leaguers. According to these dates he spent a couple of months in Florida last summer." She looked at me and smiled again. "Do you want to see his picture?"

My hand shook as I held the photo. I could hardly believe it was Benny. In my mind's eye, I still saw him as a little boy, but he was all grown up and wore a Cub uniform. A hint of a smile left dimples in his cheeks as he sat with arms crossed. His hair was dark and his complexion was like tanned leather. He still had Mama's blue eyes and her round face. I looked nothing like Mama and couldn't help but wonder if that was why she took him and left me. "He's a good-looking kid . . . I mean young man." It hit me that we'd missed much in not growing up together. My eyes blurred as I flashed back to childhood games we'd played. Mrs. Sanders must have noticed me struggling to keep my emotions at bay and reached to hug me.

"It's all right," she said. "There is nothing wrong with tears at an overdue homecoming." After the hug, she returned to the folder.

"There's an address for a Richard and Martha Stanley. He must live with them."

"Can we go there?"

"Of course, we can. In fact, it's near where we live. Get this, Charles, he goes to your old high school."

"You're kidding."

"No, that's what it says right here. 'Seventeen-year-old Groveland Park High School baseball star, Benjamin Kelly, was invited by a Cubs scout to attend a training camp in Florida. He has the opportunity to prove himself good enough to join their stable of upcoming players.'"

Charles reached for the folder. "5384 Laurel Street. I know the street. Let's go."

We hurried from the building and suddenly the world felt rosy. I was going to see my brother.

There was no way to explain the growing excitement I felt during the drive over. When we knocked on the door I was nervous, excited, and scared all at the same time. How would we react to each other after years apart? My emotions had always played close to the surface and I didn't want to cry, but to keep a lid on when seeing Benny was going to be difficult.

The door opened on the second knock. A tall, thin, graying man in his mid-fifties glanced at each of us. "What can I do for you?" he asked in a less than friendly sounding voice.

"We're trying to find Benjamin Kelly. A family member is looking for him," Mrs. Sanders said. "I understand he lives here."

There was a slight widening of the man's eyes. He cleared his throat. "I don't know anyone named Kelly."

"His school records showed him attending a Cub's training camp in Florida last summer."

"I wouldn't know about that. Records must be screwed up somehow."

I felt nauseous and angry and wanted to scream . . . to break something. I turned and shot down the walk and climbed into the car. Charles followed.

"Rudy, I'm sorry. I shouldn't have pushed you to look for him."

"It's not your fault. It goes back to Mama. Why didn't the bitch just shoot me?"

"Come on, Rudy, you don't mean that."

"I fucking do mean it!"

The trip back to the Sanders' house was somber, much like following a funeral procession. I thought about Annie. Just to see her for a few minutes would make things a hundred times better. I was in no mood to talk and remained silent while Charles and his mother tried to make sense of what we'd heard. They theorized about a number of possibilities that didn't seem realistic and settled on flaws in record keeping by the school.

I sank into a dark mood. Calling Preach crossed my mind, but I decided against it. I wanted to be alone, not talk to anyone or see anyone. I needed a mountain trail to run off my anger.

I felt like a heel, but faked a headache anyway, explaining that I needed to be in a dark room to sleep it off. I even convinced Charles to spend time with his mother and was pleased when the two pulled out of the driveway to grocery shop. Once alone I reached for the bottle of rum that I'd seen on the top kitchen cabinet while Mrs. Sanders was making sandwiches for lunch.

It was old. After a few unpleasant swallows, I headed to the basement couch where it was pitch dark, but sleep wouldn't come. My mind refused to disengage. My thoughts kept returning to the meeting with Mr. Stanley. I went over every word, every expression. I suddenly sat straight up and shouted, "The son-of-a-bitch was lying."

I'd learned at a young age to read expressions when Mama or her boyfriend lied. I'd picked up clues. Why had I not noticed Stanley's eyes, his hesitant speech, his lack of eye contact, and clearing his throat. Things not found in a normal conversation. He was hiding something by trying to be so careful.

I left a note in the kitchen and headed out the door and down to the corner bus stop. A line of blacks soon gathered. I smiled and attempted conversation with a man behind me, only to have him turn away. An elderly black lady whispered, "It's best no white boy be down here alone at this time." I only smiled, but once on the bus, I wished I'd listened. I saw hate up close and dared not move until I stepped off onto Laurel Street. What was the number? Was it 56? No, no 58 something. I'd know the house.

I had no plan. What should I say or do? The only thing was to face the old man down and demand the truth.

My heart was pounding as loud as the knock I gave the door. A short, round faced lady with graying hair appeared this time. "If you're selling something, I'm not buying."

"I'm here to see Benjamin Kelly and I'm not leaving until I do."

She grabbed the door and pushed to close it, but I blocked it with my foot as she struggled to push it shut.

I saw Benny's photo on a hall table and shouted, "You're lying. That's his picture." I threw my shoulder against the door and sent the lady backward and stepped into the room. She screamed just as someone from behind the door grabbed me around the neck. I saw the flash of a knife and then felt the sharp edge against my throat. "Why are you here?" a voice asked.

"I'm looking for Benny." The pressure against my neck lessened.

"No one calls me Benny."

"I do, I'm Rudy."

He released the knife and my neck at the same time. I turned and faced him.

"You did come back," he whispered.

I nodded and opened my arms. He reached for me. We clung together for several minutes, then pulled apart and stared at each other. His voice crumbled. "Mom, this is my big brother, Rudy."

Preach would tell me that locating Benny was one of God's blessings. I wasn't much into praying, but finding my brother made me give it some thought. Perhaps it was an omen that good things were in my future. I felt compelled to do an act of penance. The amount of booze I was using to handle pressure and to sleep at night had become a little much. A daily regimen of exercise, such as running, could replace those nightly shots needed to shut out the world.

I'd never forget my weekend with the Sanders and felt certain that Charles and I would remain friends forever. It wasn't just finding my brother, but the extent to which the Sanders went to help me find Benny.

It had been Charles's opinion that Benny and I should have time alone to catch up on things. He took over and we were in a lakeside cabin that belonged to his future father-in-law before sundown on Saturday. My brother and I talked most of the night. The next morning, we took a dip in the lake and sat on a rock at the water's edge and watched the sunrise. It rose over the lake in a methodical way, moving like a cat stalking its prey. The glimmer of light grew until suddenly a ball of fire cleared the horizon.

I told Benny about my life, holding nothing back other than being selective in talking about Will Jean. Most people thought she was nuts. Perhaps she was, but I'd decided she was too complicated for me to explain or understand.

Benny related how he was found on the street, dirty and hungry. The Stanleys took him in and loved him in spite of his destructive impulses.

"Man, I was over the top," he said. "Busted a number of times as a teenager . . . was nearly sent away, but my parents had my back. Refused to give up on me."

"Did they know about me?"

"No, man. Not that you were my brother. I was seven when our mother dumped me. I would sit on the front steps for hours waiting for you to come for me. My parents assumed you were my old man. They were paranoid that someone could come for me all those years, or I would wind up in prison. I'm ashamed of it now, but I was such a bad-ass. Always out to have a gas . . . to stir up trouble. My dad finally got me into baseball and that turned my life around. You see, they were afraid because I'm not legally adopted."

"Why not?"

"They tried . . . got to the courtroom and the judge asked me if I wanted to be adopted. I said no."

"You said no why?"

He started to speak, and then turned away. A wave of emotion moved across his face. He dragged his hand through the gravel beside the rock a couple of times and spoke as he threw a stone skipping across the water. "I was trouble for my parents from day one . . . in fights, running away. I've tried to make it up, but now I live with a load of guilt. That's my incentive to do well in baseball."

"But why on earth would you say no to adoption?"

"I was afraid you'd never find me with a new name."

I pressed my lips tight. He'd been expecting me all those years. Tears pushed hard to get out. Benny looked to be having the same trouble. I chuckled and said, "What the fuck, I'm going to cry out loud." I let go, half crying and half laughing. Benny joined in. Tears rolled down our cheeks.

"I love you, Benny," I shouted.

I learned that he hadn't seen or heard from our mother since the day she gave him five dollars and sent him to the store for smokes. He never wanted to see her and I still wasn't sure. We said goodbye and left with the understanding that I would be back in three or four weeks. His parents told me I was family and welcome at any time. My heart was full for the first time since Mama left me.

The ride back across Ohio was silent for most of the trip. I relived the weekend minute by minute and said a prayer of thanks for finding Benny. Each time we passed a little white country church I was reminded of my blessing and the men fighting the war. I repeated a prayer for all the families who waited for their sons, husbands, and fathers to return. A senseless, stupid war, I decided. Would I be asked to go? What about Benny?

195

19

I was met with the news that a girl had inquired about me. After hearing the description, I knew it was Annie. She was concerned that I might be ill or had left school since I was not in class and hadn't been seen all weekend. Was it normal to feel about a girl the way I felt about Annie? What the hell was love about anyway? I'd dreamed about making love to her, but there was an undefined something beyond just wanting sex. Just to be near her made me feel like I was more alive.

The next morning Annie sat alone in the cafeteria reading in a corner. She glanced up as I approached. She smiled and rose as if ready to give me a hug, but then sat.

"Hello, Annie." I slipped into a seat across the table.

Her face glowed. "Hi, Rudy, are you okay? I've wondered where you were."

"I'm fine. I went away and had the best weekend ever."

Her expression changed slightly. I'd take odds that she thought I'd gone away with a girl. "Aren't you going to ask me where I went?"

She stabbed a grape with her fork. "It's none of my business. I'm glad you enjoyed yourself."

She didn't sound glad. "I wish you'd been along. I found my brother after ten years of waiting."

Her scowl melted into a smile and her eyes filled.

"You're crying. Why?"

"I don't know. I just feel like it, I guess. Rudy, I'm so happy for you."

"I'm happiest when I'm with you."

"Please, don't." She grabbed a napkin and wiped her eyes.

"Listen to me. We only see each other on campus by accident. I have to be honest. The girls you saw me with were to make you jealous. I'm sorry about that and it won't happen again. I wanted you to know that I've missed you." I rose and started walking away.

"Wait, Rudy. Please, we need to talk."

I slipped back into the chair and waited.

"I'm confused . . . I don't know what to do. My dad keeps pushing for me to become an attorney. Now he has Mom and my grandmother on his side. And David is impossible anymore. He wants me to go home and go to school locally."

"What do you want?"

"To do what I'm doing . . . stay here . . . study journalism."

"It wouldn't be fair to tell you what to do. You decide what you *want* and go for it. A nice old gentleman who works on the local paper at home gave me that advice."

After a moment, she nodded slowly and whispered, "Thanks, Rudy. That was good advice."

"You need to have some fun. Focus on something else. How about a movie on Friday night? It'll be Dutch, of course, since we're just buddies."

She hesitated and then smiled. "Dutch, it is."

On Friday evening, we took a swing through the park and followed the river into town. A harvest moon washed everything around us with a dreamy softness. Which movie to see became our problem. Two were getting good press with Oscar talk. One was *Easy Rider*, an adventure drama. The other one was *Cactus Flower*, a comedy with Goldie Hawn making her film debut.

Between giggles and laughter, we flipped a coin until *Cactus Flower* came up. We were determined to laugh and have fun, which meant it was necessary to see the comedy.

The movie gave us plenty of laughs and we left in high spirits. Again, we hooked arms and walked, stopping at The Place for sandwiches. War protesters had taken over and some even promoted anarchy.

I wanted to walk her home, but decided against it after recalling what happened on her stairs the day we met. I knew it could happen again. I left her at The Commons after a quick hug and headed across campus to my dorm. Questions about the war, about Annie, and about my feelings for her filled my head. I would need a shot of something to get to sleep tonight. I'd gone all week without one, but this was Friday night, a weekend. I'd studied hard and had good marks in all my classes. I deserved a shot of booze to get some rest.

I wanted to talk to Preach and thought about calling him, but I was going home for Thanksgiving in a few weeks and would tell him about Benny and bend his ear about Annie and me at that time.

199

A card game was underway in the suite when I arrived back. I was told that some guy was waiting for me in the lobby. I'd noticed a stranger there. He was older and distinguished looking. What could he want with me?

Charles had gone to play pool with a friend. I took a couple of shots to level me off before meeting the guy in the lobby.

The man stood as I approached and extended his hand. "I'm Annie's father."

I took his hand. "I'm Rudy, a friend." I knew Annie wasn't expecting her parents in town and sensed this encounter could be unpleasant. It was important that I stay cool and appear friendly. I smiled. "Would you prefer to talk standing or sitting?"

"We can sit," he said.

I motioned toward the sofa across from me that had broken springs, though it appeared soft and inviting. He sank to the bottom and dropped a file folder while trying to grab the sofa arm. "Oh, I'm sorry you've got the bad sofa. Do you want to change and sit over there?" I pointed to another grouping of sofas.

"I'm fine," he said. After gathering papers back into the folder, he struggled to pull himself more upright. "As Annie's dad, I'm a little concerned about her. She doesn't seem to be her old self."

"I wouldn't know about that since we just became friends recently. It would be unfair for me to comment."

The man's face reddened and his eyes narrowed. "My point is that I'm not happy with her crazy notion of becoming a journalist."

"Why speak to me? You should speak with Annie about her career choices."

"You know damn well that you've filled her head with dreams of becoming a reporter and maybe a lot of other stuff."

"I find Annie to be a bright girl who is capable of making her own choices without any advice from me. Shouldn't she decide on a career?"

Her dad's wrinkled brow held more frustration. He leaned toward me. "I don't play games. Let's get down to business. I've dealt with your kind before and they never win. Not with me."

"What is my kind?"

He ignored my question. "I'm holding a check for five thousand dollars. It's yours if you stop all contact with my daughter."

"You've got to be kidding."

His jaws tightened. "Five is my limit. Take it or be sorry. This is a certified check made to you." He pulled it from his folder and reached it toward me.

"I'm insulted that you would attempt to bribe me. I rose and headed toward the stairs."

"Rudy, have you told Annie about the murder?"

I turned back.

He smiled and held up the folder he'd been clutching. "The firm had you investigated. What will Annie think when she knows the truth about you . . . the murder, your wacky grandmother?

I moved toward him with fists clenched. He backed away. "I'm not going to fight you."

I stopped. A fight with him would ruin everything with Annie. "You'd better leave." I headed to my room with anger tapping every nerve. The son-of-a-bitch thought he could keep me away from Annie with a bribe. Nothing was going to do that. I reached for the bottle in the closet, but stopped . . . backed away. I'd gone running every night for a week just as planned and hadn't needed booze to sleep. A run in the park was better than depending on booze. I left a note telling Charles that I'd gone for a run and would be at the student union later if he'd like to get beat in a game of pool.

I headed across campus, passing through The Commons and into the park. After stretching to warm up, I hit the trail at full speed and reached the end in record time. In spite of the cool night, I'd broken a good sweat and decided to take it slower and cool down on the way back. My mind was buzzing with random thoughts, from wishing I'd told Annie about Vickie, about Will Jean, and all the other drama in my screwed-up life. Her old man was going to lie and make me look like a monster.

Scattered clouds were playing games with the moon, going from light to dark, sometimes making it difficult to see the trail. A sharp turn through a thick grove of trees marked the trail's halfway point. As I came out of the shadows a cloud moved past the moon. Twenty feet in front of me, Tony stepped from behind a bush holding a knife. I turned to run and saw Russo with the bat raised above my head.

20

Footsteps came near and then faded. My eyes were covered. Panic kicked in and I struggled to pull the bandages from my eyes until two hands pushed me back on the pillow. "Rudy, it's me, Charles. You're going to be okay."

"I can't see."

"You'll be fine. The bandages are to prevent strain on your eyes. You've had a bad concussion."

"I don't remember."

"It's all right. The doctor said your memory will come back in time."

"What happened? I dreamed I met Annie's dad."

"I'm told you met a man in the lobby. Was that her dad?"

"Oh, yeah, it was. He tried to bribe me to stay away from Annie. He offered five thousand dollars."

"Randy said after meeting the man you dressed in sweats and left."

"I think I went . . . maybe for my nightly run . . . I did, I went for a run. Yeah, I remember. Russo hit me."

"The police will be glad to know that. A man in the park saw the attack and intervened. Otherwise, you might have been killed. Doctors have had you sedated because of swelling."

"I need to see Annie. We need to talk."

"She's not in town. I went to tell her about you. Her parents took her back home over the weekend according to the landlady downstairs. I left her a note. She's due back later today."

"How long have I been here?"

"Three days. Your equilibrium will return to normal according to the doctor."

"I've got to talk to Annie. Her dad probably told her crap about me. He tried to bribe me to stay away from her. Can you believe that?"

"You can deal with that later. You need to take it easy. I'm sure she'll come to see you sometime today. Now I've got to skip out . . . get to class. I'll be back later." He turned to leave. I called for him to wait and ask if he'd been with me all the time.

"Yeah, except when I had a class."

"Damn, Charles. You did that for me?"

"Yeah, that's what friends do."

"That's what brothers do," I said.

"If you say so, brother."

When I awoke, I sensed that I'd slept most of the day. Nurses had checked on me every few hours, and as footsteps drew near, I assumed it was med time or a nurse with a needle.

"Rudy, it's me."

"Annie!" I reached toward her. "We need to talk." I heard a sniffle. Was she crying?

"Are you going to be okay?" she asked.

"I'm going to be fine. Just like new." She was crying. "Annie, what's wrong?"

"'I thought you were . . . dead."

"Dead?"

"At the nurse's station two nurses were talking about a young man who had died. I thought they were talking about you."

I tried to sit up, but dizziness sent me back on the pillow. "Annie, I need to tell you something. I'm not sure how to say it. I can't sleep. I can't concentrate. You should know that I love you, Annie. There's no doubt about it, I'm in love with you.

I waited for her to speak, but she said nothing. "Please say something. Tell me that you don't love me."

"That wouldn't be the truth. I do love you."

"Are you sure?"

"Yes. I knew it downstairs when I heard them talking and I thought you were dead. I couldn't see life without you."

She came into my arms. Our lips came together. Kissing her was like standing on the tallest mountain in the world. "I need to tell you something that happened with your dad."

"You don't have to tell me anything. I love you. I'm glad you two had a nice talk."

"We only met for a few minutes and . . ."

"I know. He said you two got on well."

"He probably told you stuff about me. I had no father and a lousy mother. I lived with my grandmother who is as weird as they come. I had a relationship with a woman and she was murdered. But I didn't do it."

"Were you in love with her?"

205

"No. She was nice to me and I cared for her, but I wasn't in love with her."

"Thanks for telling me, but I already knew. My dad told me he had a detective check you out. I was furious. Then he laughed and said he was joking. It was sweet of you to be so open and honest by telling him about your life."

I took a moment to catalog all the bad names that fit her father, but I was afraid to tell her about the attempted bribe. It would only hurt her and nothing would be gained. It seemed that her parents were trying another tactic by playing good guys. "Annie, you understand that I want to spend my life with you?"

"That's what I want too."

"You're sure?

"No doubts."

"You'll break your engagement to David?"

"Yes. I'd thought about it even before meeting you. It was something our parents wanted and we went along. But David left yesterday to go back to England. He won't return until April or May."

"Can't you write him?"

"No. I have to tell him face-to-face. I owe him that much."

"I love you Annie. I'm not a hotshot lawyer like David, but if given a chance I'll show your parents that I'm not a bad choice for their daughter."

"I'm not concerned about what my parents think. It's my happiness too."

The hospital dismissed me the next morning. I went to Annie's apartment and was back to normal in a few days. The months that followed were the happiest of my life. I'd never been so happy, nor had I ever felt so confident about the future.

Thanksgiving rolled around. We resisted being apart for only a few days, but there was no acceptable excuse for Annie to miss her family's gathering for Thanksgiving. Saying goodbye was like leaving a part of myself behind.

21

The bus left behind an early taste of winter. Snow had fallen during the night leaving mostly a world of gray and white, a scene that reflected my mood as desolate, snow-covered fields slid past the bus window.

I welcomed the amount of remaining fall colors as we moved further south, especially in the lower elevations near home.

Will Jean waited at the station. I waved to her through the window and she actually smiled. At least I thought she smiled until I stepped off the bus. Instead of a hug, she peppered my ears with complaints about the bus being late and her feet hurting.

Why did I keep expecting a hug from this woman who kept her feelings in a boiling pot? "It's good to see you, Will Jean. Just like old times," I said with a touch of sarcasm.

"Sure it is," she snapped. "Why wouldn't it be with me cookin' myself to death and waitin' on you hand and foot?"

No hint was needed to know it was not a good time for talking. With Will Jean driving we took a frightening ride up the mountain with few words spoken. Being back with her was like I had never left. She stated numerous times each day that I had become an even bigger pain in the ass since going to college. I ignored her complaints and complimented the special dishes she prepared while she continued to berate me as being nothing but trouble.

An embarrassing moment came when she found a condom in my wallet. I wanted to tell her she had no right poking around in my personal things, but I was much too wise to fuel the fire after an explosion had occurred. She sent me to hell and back a number of times and stated that I should say hello to Uncle Bob, because he would be at hell's gate to meet me. I soon realized that her constant criticism could best be handled by putting distance between us.

I took long walks along mountain trails just as I had done while growing up. It was during those times that I realized how much I'd really missed the mountains, but now I missed Annie even more.

The season's palette of brown, orange, and yellow was mostly gone. I spent hours watching and listening to rustling leaves flutter and crackle in the soft breeze. They seemed to whisper that it was closing down time and all was well. But not even the mountains could dampen my longing for Annie. Loving her convinced me to believe in soul mates. She was mine. I could never see myself without her, and knew without a doubt there could never be another woman to take her place.

It was good to see Preach. As usual, he was busy working to make sure that Thanksgiving was enjoyed by needy families in the valley as well as his orphan kids. I was drafted to help with food preparations, along with other volunteers. We scalded and plucked dozens of turkeys donated by a turkey farmer. The days were long and tiresome, but we shared the spirit of the season.

One day just before Thanksgiving, things suddenly changed when I reached inside a bird's cavity and pulled out the insides. I'd been doing that all morning, but for some reason I flashed to the camping trip with Mr. Wells and began to cry. I couldn't stop. Tears kept coming and I rushed outside hoping that no one saw.

Seconds later Preach popped out the door. I should have known the guy with eyes in the back of his head would have noticed.

"What's going on?" he asked coming forward. "Did you get something in your eye?"

"Yeah," I answered and turned away. He'd seen me use my shirt sleeve to wipe tears away.

He sat beside me on the truck's tailgate and leaned forward to look. "Did you get something in both eyes?"

"It's better now." I gave my eyes one more swipe.

"Let me have a look."

"It's okay, really."

"I know, but I'd like to look."

Irritated, I opened both eyes wide for a split second and then turned away.

Silence took its turn and then he asked, "What's going on, Rudy? You know you can shoot straight with me, don't you?"

Preach always knew the answer to a question before he asked. "Yeah, I do. I'm not sure what happened. Something weird."

He waited. I finally told him what had occurred. He put an arm around my shoulders. "I've had kids who have flashbacks after experiencing a severe trauma. When I got back from the war that was a real problem for me. If it continues, you need to talk it out with someone like I did."

"Why would that happen now?

"You've probably never dealt with it adequately."

"But I'm the happiest I've ever been in my life."

"Really? It's what I've prayed for. Want to tell me why?"

"Preach, I've met this girl. Her name's Annie. She's wonderful. I can hardly stand being away from her."

"Are you two intimate?"

"Damn, Preach. You don't ask a man something like that."

"Sorry. Do you think you're in love with her?"

"I know I am. I'm going to marry her."

"Not soon, I hope."

"No, it'll be awhile."

"That's good. Rudy, remember you're still young. Testosterone tends to have a mind of its own when making decisions that could affect your life forever."

"Come on, man, I know about the birds and bees."

"Do you know about love? Time and hardships are the real yardstick for measuring love."

"I don't need a yardstick or anything else to know how I feel. I'm not a fucking kid. Don't treat me like one."

"Using the F word doesn't impress me. I've told you that dozens of time before, boy. So, lighten up."

"Do you have to call me, boy?"

He chuckled. "Excuuuseme, I forgot. You're a college man now."

I couldn't stay pissed at Preach. I gave him the finger and a smile.

A couple of days later I was in the drugstore and came face to face with Homer. He appeared thin and bony with more wrinkles than his years should allow. Sadness left his face for a moment and his eyes brightened when he saw me. "Hello, Rudy, it's nice to see you."

"Thanks," I muttered.

"How is school? I hope you're enjoying yourself."

"Yes, sir."

"If you ever need . . ." He lowered his eyes. "Sorry. I was going to say . . . what I was going to say doesn't matter. I hope you find the kind of happiness that includes forgiveness someday." He turned away and then turned back. "Cliff's home. He wants to see you."

I watched him walk away and felt an urge to call him back. I wasn't sure why. Perhaps it was because the sadness that hovered around him had somehow affected me.

Cliff called that night and we arranged to have lunch the next day. I hung up the phone and found Will Jean standing beside me. She'd slipped in place without me noticing. Her disapproval about something was obvious by the way she stared down at me with hands on hips.

"Who was you talkin' to?" she demanded.

Irritated that she'd listened, I joked and said, "Just my brother."

"You ain't got no brother."

"Sure I do, Cliff Kellerman."

Her eyes widened. "Which son-of-a-bitch told you that? He lied."

213

I stood and faced her. "Will Jean, what are you saying to me?"

"I ain't sayin' nothin'." She hurried down the hall and into her room.

Had she confirmed something she'd always denied? Could Homer really be my father?

Sleep was slow to come that night. My thoughts switched back and forth between Annie and Homer. If Homer had loved my mother the way I loved Annie, he wouldn't have deserted her.

Cliff picked me up the next morning just before noon. We hadn't seen each other in months but connected as if I'd never been away. Being with him always left me with a good feeling.

We drove up Bear Mountain and stopped at a little roadside place with a sign that stated it had the best barbeque in the state. A warm fall breeze and a pitcher of beer made for a perfect day. We sat at a picnic table under a covered roof that extended out with a view of the town below. His intern duties had taken away some of Cliff's beach boy tan. I teased him about it being gone.

He chuckled. "I have no time for the beach. My schedule owns me day and night."

"Does that mean you really like being a doctor?"

"Yeah, I actually love it. The only negatives are lack of sleep and no chance for any kind of love life. I haven't had a real date in weeks."

"Sounds like your lifestyle has changed."

"It has. Mom and Dad's separation was a shocker. I'm not sure why since I've known for some time that they had issues with each other. They haven't acted like lovers in years. But their breakup hit me harder than expected. I used to think I wanted to make money, drive fast cars, and have a different chick every night. Now I hope to find the right girl and come back here and work with Doc O'Neil in his practice. I get a real high when I see how good medical care helps people." He chuckled. "Doc has dedicated his life to the mountain people in this area. I'd like to be just like him and help expand health care even more. What about you? Are you happy?"

"I've never been happier."

"Wow! Is it the intellectual challenge or the college lifestyle?"

"It's Annie."

Cliff frowned. "Are you saying it's because you two like to get it on, or more than that?"

"I'm in love with her."

"In love with her?" He chuckled. "You couldn't have known her long. Listen, bro, keep in mind that every chick has the same parts in the same place. Don't rush things. Our dad says a guy's mind is on sex and love and blurred until he's about twenty-five. You're special to me. I'd hate to see you get messed up."

I was being treated like a kid and felt a growing resentment. "Cliff, you don't know shit about how I feel. You and Preach treat me like I'm a kid. Well, I'm not. I love Annie and no one can change that."

"Hey, hey, man, cool it. Come on, I'm not trying to change anything. I just wanted you to be sure. I do care about you."

I took a moment. "Something has bothered me about you from day one. Just now you referred to Homer as 'our dad.' Do you know something I don't? I've trusted you as a straight shooter. I'd be disappointed to learn that you are not."

He dropped his head and then looked me in the eye. "Okay, Rudy, I don't want to see you hurt anymore. You are my brother. I tell you this because I care about you. We have the same father."

I opened my mouth to speak, but no words for a moment. "Are you kidding me?"

"No. I'm not kidding. I just broke a promise to Dad by telling you. He showed me the report yesterday."

"What report? Who was it from?"

"A detective searched for your mother. She was located living out West and agreed to talk for a certain amount of money. An agreement was reached not to reveal her location."

"My mother would lie for money."

"She didn't lie. Will Jean confirmed that your mother told the truth."

"Did Will Jean also demand money?"

"No, no. Come on, Rudy."

I rose and walked to the edge of the picnic area and stared out across the valley. Thoughts whirled around in my head like a top spinning. Mixed feelings . . . pleased that my birth father wasn't the lowlife Will Jean described. Cliff walked up and stood beside me.

"Rudy, we can't choose our parents or change what they may have done in the past. Dad harbors a tremendous amount of guilt about you. He'd like a father and son relationship. I'd also like that for you, because he's a great dad. But you've made it clear how you feel, and he doesn't want to do anything to add to your unhappiness. The report will remain closed until Dad's death, and then it goes to you." Cliff placed a hand on my shoulder. "Let it go, Rudy."

"I can't forget all the times Mama hooked up with a new guy, who beat my ass for a few months. Then he was gone. The next guy would do the same. I prayed for my dad to come and get me. He never came. At some point, I realized he never would . . . never cared. It makes you feel like shit to know that no one cares. How do I erase those memories and make everything okay?"

"Don't . . . no more, Rudy. Try to think about forgiveness."

"Don't ask for that, it's too soon to ask for that. I need to go home . . . I've got to run. Take me home."

The minute we arrived at the house I climbed out of the car and headed across the meadow. Cliff followed and grabbed my shoulder, turning me to face him. "Listen, Rudy. I shouldn't have told you. I know that now. Let's talk, let me walk with you."

"No," I jerked away and left Cliff looking helpless. Will Jean came out the door. She hollered and asked me where I was going.

I ignored her and broke into a run. I heard her say to Cliff, "You son-of-a-bitch, you told him, didn't you? I was promised he'd never know."

I increased my speed and was soon out of earshot. Running had always been the best way to clear my head and deal with a problem. But how could I reconcile this with all the built-up resentment I'd felt toward a man without a face or name?

I never stopped running until well up the trail. I dropped down on a flat rock that extended out from deep in the mountain and lay back with my eyes closed.

I wanted to be back with Annie and would have left immediately, but she was still with her parents in Chicago. She was my life now. Not Homer, not Will Jean, not even this town. Annie's smile, our lovemaking, and hearing the sweetness in her voice for the rest of my life was my future.

I must have dozed off thinking about her and awoke with someone standing over me. I jerked awake and came to my feet. "Who in the hell sent you?"

"Cliff sent me. Are you okay?" Preach asked.

I didn't answer.

"I'm here to find out what's going on in your head. I heard you got some . . . news today."

"News I don't give a shit about and could have done without."

"I always wanted to know about my old man. But my mother took his name to the grave with her."

"Maybe that was a good thing."

"Not for me it wasn't. I needed a dad back then. If your father was a lowlife, I'd be disappointed that you found out, but Homer is the opposite of a loser. He messed up big time as a young man and now he wants the best for you. I'm really disappointed, but at *you*, not him."

"At me? Fuck you. I've done nothing."

"I don't deserve that kind of talk from you. Yeah, Homer made a mistake, but you haven't been perfect yourself."

"I haven't sent a pregnant fifteen-year-old girl off to fend for herself. He did."

"And your mother deserted an eight-year-old boy. That kid grew up and left a lady to be shot by her husband."

"I didn't shoot her. That wasn't my fault."

"Nothing ever is, Rudy. Cliff is down there feeling guilty and all he did was welcome his brother into his family." He moved toward me. "I'm usually against violence, but I'm about ready to put that aside and kick your ass."

"Just try it, fat boy." I brought my fists up. With a quick move, he seized my wrists and whirled me into a bear hug, pinning both arms. I cussed, kicked, and struggled, but his weight and size locked me in like a vice.

"Stop resisting and listen to me, boy. You aren't going anywhere. Is nothing in your life ever your fault, Rudy? One would think God made you the perfect man. We're all human and subject to mistakes. Was it a mistake that you ran when Vickie was shot? I don't think so. The mistake was the choice made by her husband to shoot his wife. I can go further and say the first mistake started with you sleeping with a married woman. Was it a mistake that your mother deserted you? Yes, it was. She's made no effort to amend her choice. Was it a mistake when Homer failed to step up and take responsibility for you? Of course it was, but now he wants to right his wrong.

"It's too late for that."

"We all make bad choices and the wise ones among us ask forgiveness. And those even wiser forgive. It hurts when you call me a fat boy and to fuck off. Why would you do that to me? I've always been on your side. I still am. You know why? Because you're worth it. If you call me a name again or want to fight when I let go, I'll kick your ass all the way down the mountain. I love you, Rudy, like a son. I forgive you for what you said." And with that he lifted me into the air and tossed me sprawling about ten feet up the trail. I came up to go back at him, but he'd turned his back and started down the mountain.

I was angry enough to think I never wanted to see his face again, but after cooling down I realized he'd reminded me that I was worth being loved. Something my family had never done. I felt like an ass.

He'd always had my back. Damn it, what was wrong with me? Why would I take my anger out on Preach of all people?

Darkness had settled in by the time I arrived back at the house. I had to see Preach tonight, to apologize and let him know I was sorry.

Will Jean refused to let me borrow the truck, but an apology couldn't wait. Guilt sent me out the door and down the mountain for the two-mile walk. The orphanage was located at the edge of town and Preach lived in a small cottage on the property.

I knocked, ready with an apology. The door opened and Preach stood smiling. "Come on in, Rudy. I had a feeling you might show up so I'm making salami sandwiches. I remembered you like them." He went behind a counter in the mini kitchen and held up a jar of mustard in one hand and a jar of salad dressing in the other. "I've forgotten which you take."

I stepped inside. "Uh, mustard."

"Mustard it is," he announced. "Do me a favor and push the bed in the wall so we can get to the table."

I stood the bed on end and rolled it into an indented space and then faced him. "Preach, I came here to apologize."

"I thought you would."

"I said some nasty things to you up on the mountain. I'm sorry. You didn't deserve me talking to you that way. You should be mad."

"Mad? No, I forgave you. Didn't I say so?"

"I'd feel better if you were mad. You forgiving me makes me feel like . . . an asshole."

"I'm sorry about that, Rudy. You and you alone are in charge of your feelings and your asshole. Decisions to say or do something is a choice made in one's head. I've accepted your apology. But have

220

you thought that I may have been right about some of the things I said?"

"Yes, sir. I've screwed up as much as the next guy and I'm far from perfect."

"So how do you plan to resolve your problem with Homer? Keep in mind you're the one with a problem and not him."

"I know that now, but I can't be close to him if I don't feel it. I'm willing to talk with him."

"That's a start. Good for you. To forgive Homer would be as beneficial to you as to him."

I didn't think that was possible, but I decided to keep my opinion to myself.

We talked for a couple of hours and I was once again reminded that this man was wise, a truly good man. He offered to drive me home, but I wanted to think over our discussion and decided to walk. Things were right between us and my upswing in mood made the chilly November night stimulating. The moon was out and all seemed well here in my little town, but I couldn't forget that the world was coming apart and no one seemed to have an answer. The My Lai massacre became public a few days earlier. It had protest marches against the war all across the country.

I took a shortcut across campus, passing in front of the chapel alongside the arts building. I recognized Homer's gold Cadillac in the driveway across the street from the college and remembered that he'd moved there after separating from his wife. A light burned in the front window. I stared for a moment, and then moved on a few feet and stopped again. Before I could change my mind, I turned and charged across the street and banged on the door.

The door soon opened. I stepped out of the shadows and Homer's eyes widened. Before he could speak, I blurted, "I don't know why I'm here. It wasn't planned. It just happened."

"Come in, come in. I'm glad you're here regardless of the reason." He backed into the room while motioning me to follow. He turned toward the sofa that was covered in stacks of newspapers. "Sorry about that. Cliff says I'm a lousy housekeeper." He stacked the papers on one end and motioned for me to sit. "I have papers coming from all across the country. Evenings are my time to read them. How about a coke? I could use one."

My mouth felt dry and I nodded.

He disappeared into the kitchen. I looked around the small room. It was a far cry from the large house on the mountain. A recliner sat to the right of the sofa with an ottoman stacked high with more unread papers. Across the room a gallery of 8 x 10 photos of Cliff hung on the wall above the TV. I rose and moved toward them, surprised to find pictures of me among those of Cliff. They were taken at track events over a period of years. There I was getting a trophy, another showing a ribbon being pinned on. The scrawny kid in one was me in grammar school. There were four or five that went back for years.

I didn't know Homer had returned until he spoke. "I've followed your progress over the years. I hope you don't mind."

I returned to the sofa without answering. He handed me a coke and slipped into the recliner. "If you have questions, I'll answer them as honestly as I know how."

"What's with the pictures of me?"

"After you came to live with Will Jean, I collected photos of you. Being in the newspaper business made it easy to send a photographer to cover sports and school events where you were involved. I kept them locked in my office desk until my wife and I separated last year."

"Did you ever think about looking for me?"

"God knows I didn't know where to look. Then time passed. I can offer you reasons that seem like excuses now. You must understand, I had another son that loved me and a wife that would have taken him away. I was afraid."

"So, you had to choose which son was worth keeping."

"I never thought about it like that."

"It's okay. Mama did the same. I came up a loser twice."

"I'm sorry, so sorry. I can imagine what your life has been like."

"I don't think you can. Mama never loved me and Will Jean has never found one good thing to say about me. Then add in Mama's boyfriends who often beat my ass until it stayed blue for weeks. Now can you understand why a part of me wanted to find my dad and the other part hated him at the same time?"

He faced me. "I do understand. I'm guilty of sacrificing one son to keep the other. I always wanted both."

I rose. "You made your choice to keep me in your desk drawer. So, put me back there."

"What?"

"I don't want you to have my pictures."

"Please don't ask me to take them down."

I pulled the ones of me off the wall and smashed them against the floor.

Homer shouted, "Rudy, isn't hating me enough?"

I froze for a moment and then shot out the door. I never stopped running until reaching home. Breathing hard, I dropped down on the steps.

"What did you do, Rudy?" Will Jean asked from the shadows at the end of the porch. I hadn't noticed her being there bundled up in a blanket.

"I saw Homer. Why are you still out here?"

"Did you hurt him?"

"No."

"I didn't think you should ever know. Was I wrong?"

"I don't know. Did he ever pay you money?"

"He offered. I never took it."

"Have you always known?"

"Yeah. Me and Margret was down at the stables when I learned she was carryin' Homer's baby. I slapped her hard. I wished I hadn't done it now. She left not long after that. Homer come lookin' for her, but she was already gone."

"He came looking for her?"

"Yeah, with a suitcase packed. He wanted to know where he could find her, but I didn't know. He wouldn't leave until I threatened to call the law. A week or so later, I saw him comin' up the road again. I met him with a gun. He begged me to tell him where he could find her. I told him I didn't know, 'cause I didn't. I shot up over his head, but he never flinched. He started bawlin' like a baby and refused to leave. I called the sheriff. He said Homer was drunk and took him away."

"Was that the end of it? Did he come back again?"

"No. He left for a few years and then moved back and took over the paper."

"You said he had a suitcase. Do you think he would have gone after Mama if he'd known where to find her?"

"I thought so at the time. But that's enough about old stuff that don't amount to a hill of beans anymore."

"It does to me, Will Jean."

"It shouldn't," she growled. "Don't come buggin' me with questions that I can't answer. That's all I'm gonna say. Besides, it's my bedtime. The temperature is droppin' and I've 'bout froze my ass off waitin' for you to get home."

I slept little that night. My assumption about Homer was wrong. I was surprised, and glad. But what to do about it now?

22

Annie waited at the bus station bundled in a red hooded coat. We exchanged smiles as I stepped off the bus. She slipped into my arms and I held her close with neither saying a word. We didn't need to. This was the moment I'd dreamed about for two weeks. My world felt complete again now that we were together.

Several inches of snow had covered the landscape while I was away and seasonal decorations had transformed the town. We chose to forgo a taxi and celebrate the spirit of the season by walking. The whole scene was like passing through a winter wonderland, with colored lights hanging from lampposts, wreaths on doors, and lighted trees in front windows.

We walked arm in arm and said little. Being together, touching, and a shared glance was a language in itself until I inquired about her vacation.

"Not the most pleasant," she said. "My parents drilled me about you, thinking themselves subtle and clever. I knew better. They're suspicious. I was surprised and puzzled when Dad asked if you were spending Thanksgiving with your grandmother in Barbourville. I wasn't aware he knew where you lived or that you had a grandmother."

"He knew. He learned it when he had me checked out."

"Had you checked out? What do you mean?"

"Oh, it was the time we met at my dorm. Remember? He wanted to check me out to see if I qualified as his little girl's friend."

She giggled. "Oh, now, I remember."

I hurriedly changed the subject by suggesting we grab a sandwich and take it with us. I'd decided that nothing would be gained by telling her he'd tried to bribe me to stop seeing her.

The bar was packed for a weeknight and, as usual, the debate over the war was underway. Positions for and against were more intense, even more frightening than a few weeks before. It reminded me of the vulnerability I once experienced as a kid by being on the side of the mountain with a storm brewing. Mountain air currents were as tricky to read as the rhetoric from speakers who took to the stage. Some begged for peaceful protest while others suggested violence.

We took our sandwiches and left feeling stunned by hearing talk about anarchy. Preach had been right when he suggested the My Lai slaughter would have an explosive effect across the country.

"Let's forget about what we just heard," Annie suggested. "It's too frightening to dwell on. Tell me about your visit home. Where did you get that suitcase? It looks older than my grandmother."

I chuckled. It had little life left now that it took two belts to keep it in one piece. "It belonged to my uncle."

"I didn't know you had an uncle."

"I don't anymore. He killed himself."

"What happened?"

"I guess I'm still a little pissed. He fell in love with this girl. Got her pregnant and walked away."

"Oh, my God. If he walked away he never loved her."

"Actually, he did, but she could never forgive him, and he never forgave himself."

"Oh, how sad. If I were pregnant, you'd never leave me, would you?"

"For God's sake, don't you get pregnant now. It would mess up all our plans." I gave her a quick kiss. "I've told you about my mother leaving me."

She hugged my arm with her face pressed against my shoulder. "I'll never leave you, Rudy. You'd have to shoot me to get rid of me."

"I wouldn't get rid of you, ever. I do have some news. I've learned the identity of my father."

"Did you meet him? He wants a relationship, I hope."

"Yeah."

"Oh, Rudy, I'm going to cry. That's the best Christmas gift ever. Santa came to see you early."

"You think it's good?"

"Why wouldn't it be? I mean . . . he's not a criminal, is he?"

"No, but for a lot of years I needed him and he wasn't there."

"But he wants a relationship now. That's a plus."

"You're right. It would be a plus, wouldn't it?"

"You know the poems you gave me when we first me? I've read them a hundred times or more. It was obvious from them that you missed having a father. Now you have one."

She was right. I couldn't ask for a better Christmas. I chuckled. "I have you . . . and a dad."

Later that evening after we'd had time together, Annie lay in my arms with soft Christmas music in the background. She hadn't mentioned David and I finally asked if she'd seen him.

"Couldn't," she said. "He didn't come home. His time off was short since the English don't celebrate our American holiday."

"I can't imagine why they wouldn't," I teased. "You can break the engagement at Christmas."

"No, I can't. Mom said his parents are going to England for Christmas. He won't be home until spring."

"Then write him a fucking letter."

She pulled away from me and frowned. "I'm not going to do that. You're just jealous."

"I'm not jealous."

"Of course, you are. Your face turns red at the mention of his name."

"It does not."

"Come on, Rudy. Be honest."

She smiled and held my gaze until I finally said, "Maybe a little." I chuckled and pulled her to me for a long kiss and whispered, "I'd die without you."

"I never want to be without you either." She walked her fingers across my bare chest. "Now kiss me again like you just did."

The few weeks between Thanksgiving and Christmas found college students across the nation joining protests after learning about the My Lai massacre. In our own happy little world, we couldn't escape the gruesome headlines about body counts and threats of violence against the government.

The weather went downhill the first week of December. One snowstorm after another forced us to abandon our regular afternoon run in the park. We took to the pool for a swim instead and seldom went out at night. Our routine after dinner was to watch the news and decipher newspaper reports and editorials in every major newspaper available. As journalism students, we felt this would be the best way to remain neutral in our assessment of the war and conditions at home.

The Christmas break was soon upon us. The thought of being apart for two weeks left us both depressed. We vowed never to let that happen again. David's stay in England would end in April. Annie would break their engagement when he returned and we would inform her parents about our relationship. We expected a negative reaction and planned to disappear for a few weeks. I wanted Annie to experience the mountains when they were at their peak. Bear Mountain would be the perfect place to hide away and enjoy nature's splendor during its spring rebirth.

23

Snow banks several feet high flanked the road as the bus made its way slowly down the mountain toward town. Trees on the mountains at higher elevations were coated with ice and glistened like clusters of diamonds. I pictured Annie and me together here for a few weeks during summer break. She would love the mountains. My problem was to convince Will Jean to approve her visit. The best chance to get approval would be to ask before she fell into her usual routine of disagreeing with me about everything.

Preach waited at the station. It was good to be welcomed by the big red-faced smiling Irishman. He gave me a ride up the mountain and, in turn, I committed to help deliver food and toys to needy families before Christmas.

A Christmas tree with colored lights stood in the window as we approached the house. My first Christmas tree ever. I couldn't believe my eyes. Will Jean did it for the same reason she'd cooked and ironed every piece of clothing I'd worn since my first day with her.

Preach pulled into the yard and Will Jean soon appeared in the doorway. She moved to the edge of the porch, squinting until she recognized me.

"What are you doin' here?" she called. "Why didn't you let me know when you was gettin' here? There's not a scrap of food cooked in this house." Without another word, she disappeared inside.

I turned to Preach and winked. "She's glad to see me."

He chuckled. "Yeah, I can see."

I said goodbye to Preach and eased inside the door. She was taking pots and pans from the cupboard and talking to herself about what food should go into which pot. "Will Jean, don't worry about cooking. I wanted to surprise you."

"I don't like surprises," she snapped. "Never have and never will."

"Let me treat you to supper. Is Willie Mae's Home Cooking still in business?"

"I ain't eatin' none of Willie Mae's cookin'. The last time I was there she used enough grease to make the cabbage squeal like a pig."

I chuckled. "Will Jean, I want to talk to you for a minute."

"I ain't got time for talk if we're gonna eat tonight."

"There's this girl . . ."

She jerked around. "Oh, my God! You've knocked her up."

"No, nothing like that. When we finish college, we're getting married. I want you to meet her."

"I ain't got no business meetin' her. I ain't marryin' her."

234

"Will Jean, please. You would like her. She's real special. I want her to come for a visit after school lets out."

"A visit, my ass. I ain't got enough beds and there's to be no sleepin' together under this roof."

"I'll sleep on the porch like old times. I want Annie to experience the mountains. She'll love them as much as I do. It's like I can hear them whisper sometimes."

She turned toward me. "Mountains don't talk. My God, boy, College must have turned you into a nutcase."

"I know they don't talk, but as a kid I thought they did. Anyway, I talked to them and they talked back."

"That's pure nonsense. As for the girl comin' . . . havin' her here might cause a problem. Boys your age don't use the brains God gives 'em when it comes to girls. I ain't wantin' you to mess up like Robert."

"I'm not a boy. I'm a man, Will Jean. And I'm not Robert. I never will be."

A sadness dimmed her eyes for a moment. Then without a word she turned back to the stove.

"Will Jean, that boy grew into a man thanks to you. You provided a roof over his head, gave him healthy food to eat, and provided clean clothes for him to wear. That boy was me. I'm a man now. I love you for all you did for me, Will Jean."

"Don't start no silly talk about lovin'. It makes me sick to my stomach."

"It's not silly. It's the truth. I love you."

She busied herself by adjusting knobs on the stove. I waited, but she said nothing.

"Thanks for the Christmas tree. I love you for that too. I know why you did it."

"Weren't nothin'. Them lights was old. I found 'em in the attic. Robert bought 'em years ago and never used 'em. Now get out of here so I can get somethin' cooked."

I slipped the hood over my head and zipped the coat all the way up before heading across the meadow. Will Jean never said no to Annie coming for a visit, but she gave me little reason to hope. At least she was in a good mood and I was far from ready to give up.

The thought of meeting with Homer had been on my mind since Thanksgiving. I was anxious, yet nervous and unsure about what to say. Hating a man without a face was easy, but not so after learning that Homer was my dad. I'd witnessed his warmth and generosity while trying to deny it. Preach had been right. Homer deserved an apology. I'd blamed him for his teenage mistake when I was far from perfect.

After an hour's walk along the base of the mountain I returned to the house determined to get answers. I'd stated that I was a man, so I had to act like one.

Will Jean had her back toward me as I slipped in the door. "All my life you told me I wasn't wanted or worth a shit."

She froze.

"Why did you take me in?"

She stammered, "I ain't talkin' to you about that."

"Yes, you are."

"I had no choice."

"That's not true. There's an orphanage down the mountain. You could have sent me there. They never turn a child away."

She grabbed a dishtowel and began wiping the stove. I waited. "I'm not a boy any longer. Talk to me. It's time for the truth."

"I don't . . . Maybe I didn't always mean the things I said."

"You didn't mean them? Thanks for that, Will Jean."

She faced me. "Don't misunderstand. You was a pain in the ass, but I come to like you a little. Now, hush your talk and go."

"Just now you wanted to say you've come to love me a lot."

She caught my gaze and held it for an instant, then turned away and mumbled that everything was getting cold. She dished up a plate and motioned toward the table. A glance told me she'd prepared my favorite foods.

I wasn't in the mood to give out compliments, so I began to eat in silence. After a few minutes, she finally spoke. "I've been thinkin' about this girl you have. Are you good to her . . . treat her nice?"

"Yes, I do."

"Have you ever raised a hand to her?"

"No. I would never do that. You try never to hurt people that you really love."

Her eyes widened a little and she stared for a moment before turning away. "Then I reckon it would be okay for her to come, but you're gonna have to sleep on the porch."

"It's a deal." I jumped up and pulled her into a hug.

She struggled to break free, but a smile flickered across her face as I planted a kiss in the center of her forehead.

I'd received a phone call from Annie that night and my spirits couldn't have been higher as I headed out the door to see Homer. There was something beautiful about a still, snow-covered world at night. The moon was full and a dome of twinkling stars made it easy to believe there was a God. He'd decided it was time for me to be blessed with good fortune by bringing Annie into my life.

A timid knock on Homer's door soon brought footsteps. My stomach nerves fluttered and my head was blank. How should I tell him that I wanted to be his son after acting like an ass toward him for years?

Moments later Cliff stood in the doorway smiling. "Welcome, brother from another mother." He pulled me into a quick hug. "It's good to see you."

"Yeah, you too."

Homer's head popped around the kitchen door with a surprised expression that quickly turned into a smile. "Rudy! Welcome and Merry Christmas. Come in, come in."

"When did you get here?" Cliff asked as he ushered me into the room.

"This afternoon."

Homer pointed and chuckled. "Have a seat. The housekeeper was here today, so there's a place on the sofa to sit."

I glanced at the wall of photos and saw five blank spaces. He'd taken my pictures down as I'd asked. "Mr. Kellerman, I need to talk with you."

"Not Mr. Kellerman, please."

"Homer, then," I said, though I had an impulse to call him Dad just to hear how it would sound.

Cliff looked from Homer to me. "I'm not needed here right now, am I? I'll go pick up three giant-sized steaks and give you two a chance to talk." Without waiting for an answer, he grabbed his coat and was out the door in a flash.

"I'm glad you're here, Rudy," Homer said. "I've prayed that you could find reason to come back." I made no comment and he must have sensed that I wasn't sure how to respond. "What is it, Rudy? You look as if you have something on your mind. Spill it."

"This is awkward. I'm ashamed about how I've been with you. I'm here to apologize for the way I've acted."

"You owe me nothing. I could never apologize enough for what you've been through."

"Will Jean said you tried to find Mama after she left."

"That's true. Did she also tell you that I got drunk and could have gotten my ass blown off?"

We both smiled. "She mentioned that."

"Will Jean knows how to use a gun for sure."

"She said you had a suitcase with you. Were you planning to go with Mama?"

He glanced down and then back, catching my eye. "I've got to be honest. I just wanted to bring her back. I wasn't going to be with her. I'd promised to take care of her and the baby when I first found out. She wanted more . . . wanted me to marry her. I refused."

"So, it's like we talked before. You had two sons and made your choice."

"No, Rudy, it's not that simple. The choice was made for me before you were born. I'd seen Cliff come into the world, held him against my chest, changed him, fed him, and watched him fall asleep in my arms. I'd also hurt and disgraced my wife. She didn't deserve it."

"You never intended to be with my mother."

"No, but I would have been with you had Margaret stayed around."

239

"When I was sent here to live with Will Jean I wasn't contacted . . . you never said a word."

"I wanted to. There were times I nearly did. I monitored your grades and watched you become a standout on the track field. You seemed to be doing fine. At your young age, I was afraid of doing more harm than good."

"When did you decide you wanted me around?"

"I always wanted you. The opportunity came when your uncle died. I told Cliff the truth about us. He met you and thought you were a super guy. It was his suggestion that I give you a job at the paper and make it work with your track schedule. For a short time, I enjoyed having my two sons close by. I'd planned to tell you that you were my son when you became more of an adult and knew me better."

"Things would have been so different if I'd only known this years ago."

"Yeah, Rudy, *if only*. Hindsight always gives us something to agonize over at some point in our lives. It also gives us an excuse to blame others. Paraphrasing the Good Book, 'ye without fault cast the first stone.' We're all imperfect creatures."

"I used to worry that my father was some kind of lowlife and that I'd be just like him. I'm honored to have you as my . . . father."

"Oh, thank God, Rudy. I'm the one honored." He tilted his head back and used forefingers to swipe his eyes. "Cliff says I'm a water-spout when my emotions are made raw What you just said made them really raw."

"Perhaps you passed that trait on to me. I cry like a bride left at the altar."

We both chuckled.

"Cliff and I are huggers," Homer said. "May I give you a hug?"

I rose and got a long hug, the one I'd waited twenty years to get. We both had watery eyes when we backed away.

"We can never make up for what we've missed," Homer said, "but we can make the most of our future together."

Will Jean waited up. As I stepped in the door she tossed her knitting aside and turned down the radio that was blaring *Everything is Beautiful* by Ray Stevens.

"Everythin' alright with you?" she asked.

"Yeah."

"You didn't fight with Homer or anythin'?"

"No, Will Jean. Things are fine with us. I'm spending Christmas with you. Then Homer is taking me and Cliff to Florida for a couple of days before I go back to school. I've never seen the ocean. I'm actually going to swim in it. Cliff is going to teach me how to surf."

"I don't see no fun in tryin' to stand on a board and bustin' your ass over and over."

I laughed. "Guess I'll find out."

"I've been thinkin' on somethin' while you was out. Maybe it was a mistake not tellin' you about Homer."

The fact that she questioned her actions was a surprise. The truth about my feelings might have jumped off my tongue a few years back, but not now. "You took great care of me. And I love you for it."

She looked uncomfortable, yet somehow pleased. "Not everybody knows how to show feelin's. Life has a way of makin' people afraid. You was a good boy even when I was hard on you. Maybe too hard."

241

"Not good all the time, Will Jean. I had plenty of faults and still do."

"No, no. You was different."

"Are you saying that I was special and that you loved me?"

She stared for a moment, and then dropped her head. "For some reason, I could never make them kind of words fit my lips very well. Can't figure why."

I kissed her on the forehead without a protest and announced that I was turning in for the night. I stopped at the door and sniffed. "What do I smell?"

"It's the cord on the Christmas lights. It smells when it gets hot."

"That's not good."

"What do you mean not good? It still lights the tree."

I pulled the plug. "Don't use that cord again. It could cause a fire. I'll pick up a new cord tomorrow."

The next few days were spent helping Preach spread Christmas cheer. We packed baskets of fruit, repaired toys, and made deliveries from morning until night. On the second day Cliff joined us. It was great fun to have him along. Even Homer got into the act by sending several bushels of apples and oranges to help the cause.

I spent most evenings going to dinner with Cliff and Homer. Each time we were together I became more relaxed. I knew Cliff was cool and I was pleased to find that Homer could be a lot of fun in the most relaxed way.

I was puzzled that Preach never mentioned us getting together for dinner. He was in a rush to leave after work. I inquired to another volunteer about what was going on with him and learned that Preach had a lady friend. She taught Bible at the college.

Preach in love? I thought that the greatest thing ever. He was such a good guy, he deserved someone to love him. At the end of the day I decided to have some fun and suggested we get together for dinner.

"Tonight?" He paused. "Well this is not, uh . . . not a good night," he stammered. "I'm sorry. But we'll do it before you leave."

"It's okay." I dropped my head. "If you don't want to eat with me, you don't want to eat with me. It's that simple."

"Wait. I've hurt your feelings."

"I'll get over it."

"I have hurt you. I'm sorry. The truth is . . . you see I have this lady friend . . ."

"You mean like a girlfriend?"

"Yeah. We had something planned."

"Oh, that explains everything. Are you two intimate?"

"What? Rudy, I'm forty years old."

"I know, but keep in mind testosterone tends to have a mind of its own. If you're intimate, use a rubber. It could affect your life forever."

"Oh, my God . . . Wait a minute. Have we had this conversation before?"

I laughed. "Sort of, when I was here for Thanksgiving, but we'd played opposite roles. Are you in love with her like I am with Annie?"

Preach chuckled. "You little shithead. Someone told you already."

"Yeah, and I'm proud for you Preach. She's a lucky gal."

243

"I'm the lucky one. I was going to tell you later. We're leaving here to do missionary work for a couple of years at the end of this school term. Maybe we can help some kids that can't help themselves."

"You can. I'm an example. Thanks for all your help."

"I'm glad you connected with Homer."

"Yeah, me too. I've even made progress with Will Jean. Life couldn't be better."

24

Someone shook my shoulder. I awoke to a blinding light from the hallway and a man in silhouette hovered over me.

"It's me, Rudy," Homer said.

It took a moment to remember that I was in his Florida beach house. Still half asleep, I rubbed my eyes and realized it was still dark.

He sat on the edge of the bed. "Rudy, I have some bad news. There was a fire and . . ."

I rose up on an elbow. "A fire? What fire? Where?"

"Back home. Will Jean . . . her house burned."

"What are you saying?"

"I'm sorry. They tried to revive her but couldn't. The structure was fully engulfed before the fire department arrived. It trapped her."

I shivered. "You mean she was burned to death?"

"No, no. They got to her, but she died an hour later from smoke inhalation. Cliff is packing up the gear now. We need to start home."

Too numb to speak, I nodded.

Homer squeezed my shoulder. "I wish I could take this hurt from you, boy." Tears filled his eyes

The trip home was made in silence with Homer and Cliff taking turns driving. My thoughts turned inward, moving back and forth over the years like flipping pages of a thick book. I'd never for one minute given thought to Will Jean dying. She was such an indestructible force. Most people thought her just a crazy old woman, but she was that and more. I wasn't sure what she was to me other than a paradox. All those contradictory qualities. Her presence had always generated a feeling of anxiousness in me, except for the other night when she came close to telling me that she loved me.

The next few days were a repeat of having arranged Uncle Bob's funeral. So many things to do in such a short time kept me on edge. My anxiety was tempered by sneaking booze from Homer's liquor cabinet.

Will Jean had helped make things easier by planning her own funeral. After Robert's death, she'd sold young calves for beef each summer to cover her burial cost. Her plans included a mahogany casket she'd chosen in advance and the purchase of a red dress to wear. It ended with a list of twenty-seven people who were to be barred from the viewing. They had proven to be gossips and would have negative things to say. It was humorous that some names were scratched out and new ones added over the years. As requested, she was buried an hour before sunset between Robert and her babies.

While the grave was being filled, I stared down the hill at the charred remains of the house. Hundreds of thoughts were running through my head until someone patted me on the shoulder. I turned to find the fire chief's hand extended. "Sorry about Will Jean. The general consensus is that the fire started from a defective extension cord that was connected to the tree."

Suddenly I couldn't breathe.

The chief grabbed my arm. "What is it, Rudy?"

"Nothing, nothing," I muttered, though my whole body seemed to be shutting down.

"Homer, get over here," the chief shouted. I pulled away and staggered slightly. He grabbed me. "Come on, Rudy. You need to sit."

"I can't breathe," I gasped. "I've got to get out of here." I started down the hill when Homer grabbed my shoulder. "Wait, Rudy. Let's get you off your feet." He eased me to a sitting position. "Just try to relax. Take deep breaths."

Cliff arrived and dropped down on his knees beside me. "You're having a panic attack."

"Let me up, everyone is looking."

Cliff pushed me back. "No, not yet." He whispered, "Fuck the people who are looking."

I began to cry. No sound, just tears rolling onto my cheeks. "I'm losing my mind."

"No, you're not," Cliff said. "I've been watching you. It's the strain of the last few days. You've held everything inside."

"I thought I heard Will Jean say that I'd forgot the cord."

"What does that mean?"

"The chief said an old extension cord started the fire. I was supposed to get a new one for the Christmas tree. I must have forgotten. So much has happened . . . I can't remember. I thought I got it."

25

I returned to Kent State the next day. Seeing Annie would get me out of the dumps. Guilt about causing the fire had hit hard. There was no way to undo what I'd caused. Will Jean's death was on me. Every thought about her only reminded me of all the many times I'd been angry and wished her dead. I wanted to speak to Preach, but he and his fiancée were out of town visiting her family during the holidays.

I left thinking there was nothing to come back to other than to see the mountains. Preach was getting married and leaving on a two-year missionary trip. Cliff would be away doing his internship, and Homer planned to travel. At dinner on my last night there he told us that he and Virginia had been seeing each other. They hoped to recapture feelings once shared by taking a year-long trip. The culture of Japan and China had always held an interest for them. Homer looked happy at the prospect and Cliff was beside himself with joy by seeing his parents back together. He insisted we toast our dad. One toast led to another, and with each I told myself that I'd swear off booze the minute I was back with Annie.

Annie arrived the day after I'd returned from Christmas vacation. It was wonderful to be back with her, but things didn't feel the same, perhaps because I was haunted by the fire. A smoldering depression settled in and I couldn't shake it. Annie often woke me from nightmares that were usually about Mama or Will Jean. She urged me to talk, but I made excuses, saying I couldn't remember.

Anger flared over little things. I ran more, usually five to ten miles a day. Sometimes that failed to take the edge off and I would drink more, which only depressed me further.

Weeks went by. Where was the sweetness we had shared before Christmas? We had known what the other was thinking, no secrets between us. I began to think it was a mistake not to tell Annie about the fire. But how would she feel to know that my negligence had caused Will Jean's death?

Annie worked more on the school paper in the evenings making it harder to spend time together. I'd always applauded her success, but now I found myself resenting it at times. All kinds of scenarios played out in my head, even with her being with another guy, though I knew better at more rational moments.

The growing unrest over the war and racial tension left no sunshine in anyone's life, including ours. Just as Preach had predicted, the My Lai incident added fuel to campus protests as more college students joined the cause.

My relationship with Annie became tense. Never any big fights, just little negative moments that hung around in my head. Neither of us knew quite how to resolve the freeze between us.

26

Only weeks after the first of the year the president announced that American and South Vietnamese forces had entered Cambodia. Protests increased everywhere, and by late April the anti-war fervor was beginning to be felt on campuses in small towns and universities such as ours.

A few discontented students had tried to get a movement going on campus since early last fall. It was a hot and cold endeavor until Friday, May 1st, the day after the "Cambodian Incursion" was announced. A quickly organized demonstration grew to about five hundred protesters that met on The Commons and announced a push for an all-out rally for Monday, May 4th. With anger surging, several protesters called for the war to be brought home, and a group of history students buried a copy of the Constitution to symbolize that the president had killed it.

Annie came home that evening excited that the editor of the school paper had chosen her to write the lead story on the upcoming demonstration. But her excitement quickly waned after her parents called to say they were coming over on Saturday and that perhaps she should plan to go back with them until things cooled down.

"I'm not leaving," she declared. They still remained unaware of our relationship and, as usual, I packed my things to move back into the dorm during their stay.

On Friday evening, we both wanted to forget about the war for a while and splurged by going downtown for an early dinner and a movie. A comedy-drama called *Mesh* had been released a few weeks earlier with glowing reviews. It put a new spin on the war and offered two hours of great humor. We left the theatre in good spirits and found that trouble had exploded in the street after a few people began throwing beer bottles at police cars and smashing store fronts. An alarm sounded at the bank and more people spilled out from nearby bars and joined the vandalism. They appeared to be a mix of bikers, students, and transients. We watched the crowd of a hundred or more start a bonfire in the street before the police arrived in force.

That evening the Mayor declared a state of emergency and ordered all the bars closed which only increased the size of the angry street crowd. Tear gas was used to disperse the mob from downtown back toward campus.

I said goodbye to Annie and stayed in the dorm that evening. Charles and I listened to the nonstop local news coverage the next day. City officials and business owners had received threats that radical revolutionaries were in town to destroy the city and university. A decision was made between the mayor and governor to send the National Guard onto our campus. They arrived after 10:00 p.m. that evening. A large demonstration was already underway, and the

ROTC building was on fire with more than a thousand protesters cheering its burning.

Urged by citizens and city officials the mayor and governor declared a curfew for Sunday evening. Around 8:00 p.m. another spontaneous rally was held at The Commons. By 8:45 p.m. the guardsmen had used tear gas to disperse the crowd, forcing them outside the campus where they attempted a street sit-in but were forced back into their dorm around 11:00 p.m.

Annie and I had no contact all weekend. We met at the cafeteria on Monday morning as we had planned. She was excited about the assignment and was anxious to cover the protest without a hint of bias in her story. She discussed at length the various points of view under consideration during breakfast.

I noted it was time for me to leave for an early class. Annie faced me. "You're not going to like this, but David is back and accompanied my parents here over the weekend."

"You saw him?"

She nodded.

Anger burned my face. I said nothing, but she noticed my expression and placed her hand on mine. "Don't get upset, Rudy. I'm in love with you, but that doesn't mean I no longer consider David a friend. We've known each other all our lives."

"You broke the engagement, right?"

She looked away and shook her head. "I didn't have a chance. We were never alone."

"Damn it, Annie, you promised to tell him first thing after he returned."

"I know, I know . . . and I will. But not in front of Mom and Dad. They would have taken his side with all three against me."

253

"You sound as if you're having doubts about us."

"Will you stop it, Rudy? You know better."

Our gazes met and held for a moment. "I've got a class." I rose to leave. She followed.

"Wait, Rudy." She hooked her arms around my neck. "Don't be that way. I love you and I don't want us to fight. In spite of all that's happening, I haven't forgotten it's May 4th, your birthday. After the march, I'm free. Would you like for us to spend the afternoon curled up under a blanket at my place eating cake and drinking champagne? We need to talk. I don't like what is happening with us. I know you feel it too."

I nodded. "I'd like that." She'd remembered my birthday. I pulled her close. "I'm sorry. I love you so damn much."

"I know and I love you, too. I'll meet you on The Commons at twelve-thirty." She gave me a quick kiss and then cupped my face with her hands. "Don't worry about David. He's no threat to you." Her eyes teared. "I'll never love anyone but you."

I kissed her on the end of her nose and left her smiling.

My class ended at twelve. I grabbed a coke from a vending machine and headed across campus to meet Annie. A five-minute walk with five or ten left to find her in the crowd would put me there on time.

My thoughts were about us having the afternoon together when a volley of shots rang out. It took an instant to absorb what I'd heard. "Oh, my God," I uttered and started running toward The Commons, screaming Annie's name while threading my way through a stampede of oncoming students trying to escape.

It took only minutes for hundreds of students to flee The Commons, leaving behind a few students and teachers, who tried to administer first aid to those shot. Death had brought mostly silence, except for approaching sirens and guardsmen barking orders somewhere in the distance.

I went from one group to the next, gently elbowing my way past onlookers, sometimes staring down at pain ridden expressions of those wounded and at faces much too young to have died.

How many were dead or wounded? My God, too many to remember. I only knew that Annie wasn't among them.

"Oh, God, let her be okay," I kept repeating while racing from one dorm to the next, screaming her name and asking friends and strangers alike if they'd seen her.

Exhausted, I finally dropped down on the dorm steps, trembling, drenched in sweat and feeling the panic of desperation. My heart pounded. "Oh, God, help me find her." After a few moments of gasping air, I rose and headed to find Charles. My roommate sat at his desk with the Bible open. He looked up as I entered. "Mom heard on the radio and called. She said pray."

"Annie's gone."

"What?"

"I can't find her anywhere." My fear gave way to tears.

"We'll find her," he said. "People were running in all directions to escape. She's probably holed up somewhere still in shock, like us all. Maybe she went to the apartment. Have you looked there?"

"No. She would have been helping with the wounded. I've checked the dorms . . . looked everywhere."

"If she thought you had gone to the apartment, she could be there. It's possible. We should check."

Police cruisers, ambulances, and military vehicles had converged on campus. Guards stationed around the perimeter forced us to work our way around dorms and classroom buildings in order to reach Annie's apartment.

With my key in hand I rushed up the stairs calling for Annie. The door swung wide. My heart sank. The cake and a bottle of champagne on ice sat on the table. The only thing missing was Annie.

PART THREE

27

I opened my eyes and was blinded by the brightness. "What the hell?" I growled and looked around. The room was no more than six by six and looked as sterile as a germ-free lab. A stainless steel john and sink were on one wall, and the bench I sat on was across from them. It was a fucking cell, but I'd never been in one this clean.

My head throbbed and my eyes burned. A tall police officer with a strong, lean face and gray hair stood looking down at me. "Where am I?" I asked.

"In a holding cell for drunks who want to hurt themselves or someone else."

"Then why in the hell am I here? I don't want to hurt anyone."

"You fit a profile that says you're not telling the truth."

"Profile, my ass! I don't hurt people."

"Your record shows you've been picked up a number of times before for fighting and drunkenness. You're a drunk, my friend."

"My friends don't tell me I'm a drunk, so you couldn't be my friend."

"They know it, you know it, and I know it. Maybe that should tell you something."

"You're an asshole."

"No, I'm a drunk that don't drink. Last night you said your name was Rudy Kelly. Is it the same in daylight?"

"Yeah. It's my name. Fucking names don't change when you're drunk."

"We're leaving here now. I have to cuff you."

"Wait a minute, I had too much to drink last night. I'm usually released the next day. What's changed?"

"You've never been caught naked with your feet dangling from a seventh-floor balcony railing before."

"What? I wouldn't do that."

"You did that." He leaned close and looked me in the eye. "You'll succeed in killing yourself if you keep trying. I'd like to convince you not to do that. There's someone that loves you somewhere."

"Bullshit on that. So, why are you here?"

"To take you to the psych ward for an evaluation."

"I'm not crazy."

"You don't prove it by sitting on balcony railings."

"Shit, did I really do that?"

"You really did that. You'll be evaluated. If the doctor likes what he hears, he'll let your friend take you home."

"What friend? I don't have friends."

"Charles Sanders."

"How did he get involved? I never asked anyone to call him."

"I did you a favor and called. You said he was your only friend in Chicago. He'll meet us."

"I don't want him in my shit."

"I can understand why. It's embarrassing, isn't it?"

"No, it's just . . ."

"Embarrassing to remind your friend that you're a drunk."

"Wait a minute, you can't . . ."

"Let's go. It's a five-minute walk. I'm curious, why are you so crazy about mountains?"

"They saved my life."

He stopped and looked me in the eye. "Then go back to the mountains. You're trying to kill yourself now. You'll succeed if something doesn't change. I've been where you are before. I told you I'm a drunk that doesn't drink. Without booze life is a different color. You get me?"

I nodded.

We crossed a catwalk that connected the two buildings and continued down more halls until reaching a door with a sign that read Restricted Area. Once inside he pointed to a row of stainless steel chairs, all with rounded backs and bolted down. There were no sharp edges on anything.

The policeman started to leave, and then turned back. "I bet you're a nice kid under normal conditions. You must be about thirty years old. My son is about your age. I'd tell him what I'm going to tell you. After they got you off the balcony and put you in my car to come here, you cried all the way and talked about a girl named Annie. I don't know what happened between you two, but everything in life has a resolution at some point. An ending happens because you make it happen or it becomes a tragic event that finally kills you. I'm going to ask my wife to light a candle for you over at St. Josephs tonight."

I watched him go. The man hit on a cord of emotion that I didn't know I could still feel. I knew my friends would show that kind of concern, but he was a stranger who cared. I wished I'd asked his name.

I was shown into another sterile room and given a battery of tests. After waiting an hour for the result a doctor appeared. He asked me a number of questions while stroking his chin whiskers and then signed a release.

Charles waited at the door. He shook my hand and pulled me into a hug, looking as embarrassed as I felt. Charles lived across town, married to that beautiful girl whose picture I saw my first day at school. They had a young son.

I'd never called him to rescue me because of mishaps in my social life, which was best described as drinking alone each night and getting laid once or twice a week. I wanted coffee and Charles suggested we stop for lunch.

Little was said on the way there, other than chitchat about his family and my work at the bookstore. He chose a restaurant famous for Chicago's original Italian beef sandwiches. Once we'd placed our orders and coffee had arrived, he looked at me and smiled. It was a sad smile, one that caused me to glance away. His expression showed disappointment and that bothered me.

"Rudy, the policeman told me what happened. Then I spoke with the doctor who administered the tests. We need to have our say and walk out as brothers. Rudy, you're in trouble, big trouble. Having my best friend in trouble concerns me."

"I never intended for you to be brought into this. It's embarrassing."

"How long has it been since Annie disappeared?"

"Eight years yesterday."

"You've spent eight years trying to find her. The Kent police have spent the same amount of time trying to prove you had something to do with her disappearance. Right?"

"Yeah."

"Did you?

"Hell no, you can't be asking me that."

"It's been a long time since we talked about Annie. Bring me up to date."

"I don't know much. I've never been able to get the family to talk. I learned there were three tickets purchased by her mother. She and two other people flew out of the country the next day. I believe Annie was one of them, and I think it was against her will."

"Think, Rudy. Now, it's eight years later. If she wanted to be with you why hasn't she come back by now?"

"Well they . . . I'm sure they forced her to go . . ."

"Do you think she's been locked up for eight years? Is that what you're saying?"

"I don't know."

"Come on, Rudy, think about it. By now she's either dead or has chosen another life. But look at you. You've become a victim. You haven't moved forward with life since the day she disappeared. You're bright and talented. Think back, you started writing *A Girl Named Annie* five, six years ago. Will it ever get finished? You've worked numerous jobs that require little talent or ability. And being a drunk probably got you fired from most of them. Now you sell books during the day, drink yourself to sleep each night, and probably party on weekends. Is that a life?"

"It's mine."

"By choice or circumstances?"

"Fuck you, Charles." He caught my eye. I looked away. He waited. "You're right, I know you're right. Charles, I'm so fucking tired of life."

"You have always had a special attachment to the mountains. Each time you visited and returned, you were invigorated . . . acted like a new person. Did you ever think about going back there to see how it feels? Sometimes it's good to turn over a new leaf."

"It's crossed my mind, and you're right about the mountains. I've always missed them."

"Was I right about just the mountains?"

Reluctant to answer, I looked down.

"Come on, Rudy. Only the truth works for me. Once we were like brothers. Remember?"

"I remember. You're right about everything." I looked at him and chuckled. "I should kick your ass for being so right."

He laughed. "You and what army?"

"My social life of late has made me street savvy."

"The neighborhood where I grew up made me savvy moons ago. Will you get your head around what we've talked about?"

"I'll try, but it's like saying goodbye to Annie forever."

"Maybe it should be. She may have said goodbye to you eight years ago."

"No, no, don't say that. I could never find another girl like Annie."

"Don't you believe you could love someone, and then years later love someone else?"

"Oh, God! Stop saying that. No! It's only Annie for me." I pounded on the table and said, "Son-of-a-bitch!"

"Why? What is it?"

"Why did I never think about this before. I'm just like Uncle Bob. He was a drunk, could only love one woman. He finally killed himself. That's me, and I don't want to end like he did."

"I'm a therapist and you're my best friend. You need professional help. You probably have issues that have nothing to do with Annie being gone. One is about the bear killing your teacher and perhaps your relationship with your grandmother."

Emotion sent tears spilling onto my cheeks. "I killed Will Jean."

His brow moved slightly. "What are you telling me?"

"I forgot to get a new extension cord for the tree after saying I would. Will Jean used the old one and died in the house fire eight years ago."

"You've held onto that guilt for eight years?"

"Yeah. I think about it all the time I wished her dead and often told her so. Not meaning it doesn't make it go away."

"You've taken this guilt on and it doesn't belong to you or anyone else. Do me a favor. If you stay here or go back to the mountains, you've got to get professional help. Will you promise?"

"Maybe."

Depression settled in like a dull headache after I said goodbye to Charles and headed across town to my place. I'd been hit with reality by both Charles and the policeman. I was a drunk and didn't want to die.

My life had stalled the day Annie disappeared. I didn't want to be like Uncle Bob. I made a decision to return home to the mountain at that moment.

I closed down life in Chicago with help from Benny. He spent most of the week with me. I took my books and typewriter. Everything else was sold or donated. I hoped the decision to leave Chicago would be an affirmation that my dreams about a life with Annie had ended.

The weather was perfect for travel. It was also a time for soul searching. I planned to shut myself off from the world until I could manage my drinking. Homer and Virginia had moved to Florida after he retired. I'd spent the holidays with them. Cliff and his wife, Judy, were always there. He'd married a classmate and the two had a practice in the Appalachians north of Barbourville. They had two children now.

28

I stopped on top of Bear Mountain and stared at the town. My feelings were mixed. What would it offer? I planned to buy a tent and pitch it on a mountainside until I wanted something different and no longer needed booze. I was twenty-eight and my body was no longer that of a runner, but I planned to run again. My endurance would be nil, yet I could still picture myself running mountain trails like I once did.

I stopped by the hardware store to see if tents were still sold there. I began looking at the few on display when Sammy, the store owner, headed my way. He'd moved from young to middle age with graying hair and too much belly. His big smile was just as genuine as ever. "You got here in the nick of time," he said. "I was about to close. What can I get you?"

"I was just looking. I'm going to need a tent."

"Got several to choose from." He moved a little closer. "You look familiar. Should I know you?"

"I lived here a few years ago."

"Movin' back or just visitin'?"

"Moving back."

"Dang it, young fellow, I know you. What's your name?"

"Rudy Kelly."

"Of course. I used to watch you run track in high school. You made us all proud."

I made no comment.

"Your grandma was something else. Will Jean took nothin' off of nobody. The last time I saw her was just before she died. Showed up one day a little before Christmas demandin' a refund for an electric cord. Said I overcharged and it had never been used."

I was speechless and struggled to find words to ask him to repeat himself.

He frowned. "Will Jean wanted a refund on an electric cord. She said her old one would do just fine for her Christmas tree."

Emotion pushed me close to tears in front of the man.

He placed a hand on my shoulder. "I never meant to upset you."

"No, I'm not upset. Look, I'm tired from travel and you're about to close. I'll be back tomorrow for supplies and a tent. Without waiting for a response, I shot out the door, climbed in the car, and leaned my face against the steering wheel. "Thank God, thank you, God, for that bit of news." I saw eagles flying in my head and felt as free as they looked. The guilt over Will Jean's death was gone.

The next morning, after purchasing a tent and supplies, I headed up the mountain. Nerves fluttered in my stomach after turning up the lane toward the old home site. The car bumper pushed aside weeds that had taken over the road. Large hardwoods that surrounded the house remained, as did the stone fireplace. The chimney, visible above bushes and vegetation, was the only reminder that a house once stood there.

Neither Cliff nor Preach knew I was back. I planned to keep it that way until my drinking was under control. As I stared at remnants of the past my head was flooded with memories, both good and bad. The only thing I wanted at that moment was a drink.

29

By the third week back spring had arrived on the warm side of the mountain. I'd tried to walk off my need for booze each day with little success. Late one afternoon I noticed a skinny kid stalking me. I'd seen him before. He peeked around bushes or looked down at me with binoculars from higher up the hill. I couldn't pee without him having me in focus. We finally met . . . came face to face on a narrow mountain path. He backed away. His eyes told me he was about to run.

"Don't you dare move," I shouted.

My outburst stopped him. He tugged at pants that hung low on skinny hips as if weighted down. He grinned real big. "I ain't meanin' to bother you, mister. I just wondered why you walk the mountains all day long, every day."

"To keep from drinking myself to death, but it's none of your business."

"Does it work?"

"No."

"Then try somethin' else. Don't it bother you to keep doin' somethin' when it don't work?"

"What bothers me is you sneaking around and watching me."

"Just lookin' for rocks. A geologist pays me." He patted his pockets. "Found some too." He flashed a nervous smile. "They're about to pull my britches off."

"I don't want you on my property. Get off my mountain."

He pulled his shoulders up, thrust his chin forward, and tugged at his pants again. "I ain't afraid of you," he said, though his voice cracked. "Besides, this ain't your mountain. Preach says it belongs to God 'cause he created it."

"Then you know Preach. Have you told him about me?"

"Couldn't tell much. I don't know your name. But he said he'd pray for you anyway."

I looked away and blinked to stop the burning in my eyes. "Please, just go. Don't watch me. Get out of here before I toss your skinny ass down the hillside."

He backed away a few steps. ""People are sayin' you was goin' crazy livin' like a hermit. I ain't seen a person go crazy before. That's why I've been watchin'. What's your name?"

"John Brown."

"I don't think you're crazy. I think you just need a friend. Everybody needs somebody."

"Not me. Now get your ass moving."

He ran, but a few days later I spotted him watching me again. At first, he kept a distance away, but as the weeks passed, he moved a little closer. Then one day I returned to camp after a walk and found a candy bar on a little stool I kept by the fire pit. It was a peanut cluster. How did he know it was my favorite? I always purchased a few each time I went to the local store at the foot of the mountain. I finally realized the kid was determined to watch me, so I let it go.

30

Shadows were waking up in the valley and the lonesome sound of mooing cows floated up from the meadow below as I headed back to camp. I'd walked mountain trails most of the morning. Even did a little running only to realize I was out of shape. It'd been a hot day, but a good one. I swam for a while and lay in the sun naked before finding a cool shady spot to read and take a nap. It was the most restful time of my days since nights were filled with dark dreams. A few drinks were always required before sleep would come. I was anxious to get past that, but it seemed an end was slow in coming. My intentions not to drink seemed attainable during the day, but usually failed to last through the night.

A man sat on the bench beside the fire pit as I neared the camp site. His arms were crossed and his chin lay on his chest as if asleep. He must have heard the rustling of leaves and looked up. Though a little thinner and with more gray, he had the same warm smile and twinkling eyes.

Preach rose and came forward. "You must be Mr. Brown. My friends call me Preach. I hope you'll be able to do the same from now on."

I was touched to hear him use the same introduction he'd used the day we first met. It'd been eight years since I last saw him. I hadn't shaved or cut my hair after returning to the mountains. He didn't recognize me.

"A kid at the orphanage told me you lived up here. I thought perhaps you needed some supplies. Do you have food, soap, toothpaste?"

I swallowed the emotion that crept up in my throat. He'd had such high hopes for me and I'd let him down, let everyone down. I spoke barely above a whisper. "It's me, Preach. Rudy."

His eyes widened and his mouth opened. "Rudy!" With giant steps, he pulled me into a hug. "I'm glad to see you, boy." He kept patting my back and telling me how glad he was that I had come home.

"I let you down, Preach. I'm sorry."

"No, no, none of that now. So, you're the John Brown the kid at the orphanage told me about. He said you'd been here for a few weeks. Why didn't you let me know?"

"I didn't want anyone to know."

He motioned toward the bench. "We ended a long mission stay a few months ago, but I've been trying to chase you down for years. With Homer retired and living somewhere in Florida, and with Ms. Will Jean gone, no one around here knew anything. You want to tell me about yourself?"

"No, not now. Maybe later."

"We'll talk when you're ready, but allow me one question. When I last saw you, you'd met this girl and was in love. What happened with her?"

"She disappeared during a protest march in 1970. For years I've looked for her. Now I'm trying to accept that she's gone for good."

"I'm sorry, Rudy. Perhaps tragedy in our lives is to test our faith and make us stronger. I hope you'll come and stay with us until your life gets sorted out. We have a spare room."

"I knew you'd ask, but no. I'm better here for reasons that I don't want to talk about."

He nodded. "May I come to visit, maybe walk the trails with you? Doc said for me to walk. Can't beat it for exercise."

"You're always welcome, Preach."

He rose and pointed to a paper bag beside the tent entrance. "I brought groceries for John Brown." He chuckled. "He must be a good guy. He won't mind you having them."

I smiled. "Thanks, but you're the good guy, Preach. Not me. The kid from the orphanage thinks so too. Tell me about him."

"You mean Boonie. A good little guy, but no one wants him. Can't get him adopted out. Everyone wants younger kids. I never get used to the hurt in their eyes when the older ones are passed over."

"I can't understand why anyone would pass up that kid."

We stared at each other for a moment.

"Rudy, things happen for reasons that we don't understand at the time." He rose. "I have another stop before dark. If you need anything you know where I live. I'll see you in a couple of days. Just remember that God loves you, boy. And so do I."

I watched him walk away. He was a good man. But how was a good man supposed to feel? I wanted to be a good man. I wanted to feel the kind of love that he talked about.

True to his word, Preach showed up every few days. We took long walks, but I never mentioned my problems and he never asked. A few weeks went by before I met the kid again. I was changing with the mountains. Not drinking less, but feeling better in a spiritual way as if the mountains knew my needs. It was uplifting to experience all the sounds and colors of a mountain spring in the Appalachians. Birds were singing. Green buds hung thick on all the deciduous trees, and mountain wildflowers were popping up everywhere. Painted trilliums were blooming in the low damp areas near the spring where I bathed. It was there that I met the kid again. The tall, thin, thirteen-year-old had ears waiting for him to grow into. But he was blessed with a killer smile that would serve him well with girls in a few years. I was getting a bucket of water from the spring when he appeared out of nowhere. The sight of me should have made anyone run. I still hadn't shaved or had a haircut.

He pulled his shoulders back and came forward. Binoculars hung from his neck and his pants pockets were again filled with something that weighed them down. I assumed it was rocks.

"You still following me, kid?"

"Yeah, a little bit, I guess. I'm Boonie. Preach said you were joking about your name. being John Brown. What's your real name? He wouldn't tell me."

"Rudy. Why are you still following me? I haven't gone crazy yet."

"Maybe not, but you're still livin' like a smelly old cave man."

"Kid, I don't smell. I bathe every day. I just need a shave and a cut."

"You sure do. But there's another reason I'm here. Preach said I should ask your forgiveness for somethin'. Been meanin' to before now."

"What sin would that be?" I pulled a soda from the spring. "Want something cold to drink?"

He shook his head. "Better not. That's what I stole. I took a bottle of orange crush one day when the sun was boiling hot. I was as thirsty as a baby pig with a sunburn."

Pig with a sunburn . . . I laughed. "It's okay, kid. Have a soda on me any time you're up this way. Have you been leaving me a candy bar when I'm away from camp?"

He dropped his head, "Yeah, I guess I have a time or two."

"More than a time or two. Why did you do that?"

"You're sad. I know about being sad. It don't feel good."

"What made you sad?"

"A lot of stuff. My dad leavin'. He didn't care enough about me or my mama to say goodbye. Just left."

I could identify with that.

"Look at that." He pointed at an eagle that rose up from the valley floor and landed on exposed rocks high up. Boonie pulled binoculars from around his neck and handed them to me. "See them naked rocks stickin' out. Focus on that speck of green and look to the right. "There's a mama and daddy eagle buildin' their nest?"

Tears gathered and blurred my vision. I'd watched those same eagles the day Mr. Wells was killed.

"Are you okay, mister?"

"Sure. Just a drop of sweat in my eye."

"The mama would be the one fixin' the nest while the daddy is off gettin' sticks."

"It's good that he helps," I said.

He grinned. "Yeah. I read they both take care of their babies. You'd take care of your babies, wouldn't you?"

"Yeah, I would."

"Preach says we're all under God's care. Bad things just happen. You can't take ownership of every bad thing in the world. Some years the eagles lose all their babies, but they're still tryin' the next season. You ain't even tryin'. You do nothin' but be lazy."

"Hey, I used to work."

"Why did you quit? Don't make sense not to work. Even birds work for what they eat. Maybe you have a reason to be sad, but not to quit on the world. My mama lost three kids not countin' sendin' me away. She goes on livin' with her sadness."

His words were another poignant reminder that I might never find Annie, but with some effort I might be able to live again. The kid gave me things to think about.

Boonie and Preach continued to come around all summer. At one point in late summer, Preach asked if I planned to live in a tent the rest of my life. It made me realize that I hadn't given any thought about my future since the day Annie disappeared. For eight years, I'd lived my life with my energy and focus centered on finding her.

Following his inquiry, thoughts about having my own place took shape. The trust fund that Homer had provided became available on my twenty-fifth birthday. Funds wouldn't be a problem since I hadn't touched a penny.

To have my own house made sense. What didn't make sense was to build on Will Jean's home site. But for some reason I wanted the house there. I told Preach of my decision to build after a local architect had started work on a plan.

It would be a modified A-frame made of logs and covered with cedar boards. A wrap-around porch would offer a clear view of a sunrise or sunset. The old stone fireplace still remained intact. With minor restoration, it would become a part of the great room which included kitchen, living, and dining area, much like Will Jean's old house.

Boonie heard about my plans from Preach and came by with a bigger than ever smile. We celebrated by sharing the candy bar he'd brought and toasted with a couple of lukewarm orange sodas.

With the plans spread on the ground in the shade near the tent, Boonie pulled small stones from his pocket and placed them on each corner to counter the strong mountain breeze. He dropped down and studied the plan on hands and knees. A gust of wind flipped his mop of sun bleached hair over his eyes. He pushed it back with one hand and looked up with large brown eyes. "Three bedrooms don't make sense. Cut cost. You need only one."

"When my dad comes up from Florida to visit, I want a room for him."

"That makes sense. A good thing lookin' out for your dad." He tapped the third bedroom with his finger. "Then get rid of this one unless you plan to have kids. Are you having kids?"

"I don't know, I might."

He stood on his knees and looked up at me. "Then you've got to stop drinkin' and get healthy."

"What are you talking about?"

279

"Right now your sperm is probably like fish dyin' in swamp water."

I laughed. "My sperm? What's with you, Boonie? You're still a kid. What do you know about reproduction?"

"I can read and I love biology."

"Oh, so you know about sex?"

"Of course. Text books tell me a lot. What do you need to know?"

"Me? I mean, I thought you. I don't need to know anything."

He smiled again. "I'm really glad about the house. It means you're ready to live again."

I laughed. Not sure why. Maybe it was because of such positive and forward thinking by the kid. "I want to hire you to help out when the building gets started."

He paused. "We're friends, right?"

"Of course we are." I remembered how I felt about Mr. Wells and added, "You're my *best* friend."

He grinned again and began shaking his head. "Then I couldn't let you pay me. Friends help friends."

Emotion hung in my throat for a moment. "Boonie, you're so damn special. I'm honored to have you as my friend."

He laughed. And with it came a blush.

The kid always made me feel guilty about something or good about something. He was contagious and had an intellect like a sponge. I let it go about the pay, but I planned to make it right. It hit me that I often laughed around him. The kid had taught me how to laugh again.

31

Morning fog hung low along the river as I approached Builders Supply Company. Its name was stretched across the front of the building in giant-sized letters. A few cars were parked under various shade trees out front. I assumed they belonged to employees who wanted to shield them from the hot August sun. It was early and the only activity was a large truck in the drive-through being loaded with lumber.

A short, middle-aged lady, with granny glasses resting on the end of her nose, leaned against the counter reading the morning paper. Her quick smile disappeared after seeing me. Did I look that bad? It had to be the beard and long hair. For a moment, I expected her to scream for a manager. Peeking over the top of her glasses, and sounding suspicious, she asked if she could help me.

"I'm here to see Carl," I said.

She pushed a buzzer without taking her eyes off me. A tall, sandy-haired man soon appeared. He came forwarded with a hand extended and a broad smile. "You must be Mr. Kelly."

"Make it Rudy."

"I'm Carl. We've developed a material list and a cost estimate for the house. I have a conference room just off the loading dock. We can work there without being disturbed."

I followed him between two rows of head-high shelving filled with various kinds of hand tools, assortments of hardware, along with various sized cans of interior and exterior paint. The back door opened onto a loading dock that ran the length of the building. Three ladies were busy behind desks in a glassed-in office that overlooked the dock. The younger one with long, dark hair glanced up as we walked past. She looked familiar, but then so did most everyone I'd seen since getting back.

A long table with chairs stood in the center of the conference room. Oversized wooden filing cabinets lined the back wall. Above them were racks suspended from the ceiling with cotton ropes. Each was filled with rolled up building plans. Some were old, yellowed with frayed edges, while others looked relatively new.

Carl pointed to a coffee urn on a small table near the door. "Help yourself. Lou Ann will get you started on paperwork."

"Lou Ann Warren?" I asked.

"No, Lou Ann Stuart. She'll be right in."

Thinking it was the Lou Ann I knew made for a pleasant moment. I'd only dated her that one time, yet I'd thought about her over the years.

The coffee was hot, strong, and black, just what I needed to get my day going. I was blowing to cool the coffee when someone entered the room. I pushed my hair aside and looked up. It was Lou Ann. She might be a Stuart now, but she was a Warren when I knew her.

She smiled. "Good morning."

She didn't recognize me. I nodded, wishing I'd gotten a shave and a cut before coming. No way was I going to reveal my identity. She was still pretty, though her large aqua colored eyes had lost the excitement that I remembered seeing when she smiled.

She reached across the table and placed papers in front of me. The wedding band she wore took me down a notch. I should have known by the name change.

"Start on these," she said. "Just personal information. Carl will be back in a few minutes."

She'd been the only woman other than Annie who interested me beyond just wanting to get laid. With Annie gone I had nothing real to offer a woman other than friendship and sex. Both with her were probably out of the question now that she was married, but I had to know for sure.

After the meeting with Carl I wasted no time in getting a shave and a cut. I'd left my copy of the cost estimate on the conference table as an excuse to return. The excitement I'd felt the first time I saw her in the hallway at school was back. Even though she was married, I had to know more.

The truck in the drive-through was gone when I returned. I entered by way of the dock and went directly to Lou Ann's office. She was alone. Surprise turned into a smile when she saw me standing in the doorway. "Remember me?"

She stood. "Rudy Kelly!" Her smile brought a sparkle to her eyes as she came toward me. "It's good to see you," she said and gave me a hug.

"Same here. It's been awhile, but you're just as pretty as you were the night we rode every ride at the Daniel Boone festival. Remember?"

"Of course, I do. We had fun." She giggled. "I've thought about that night hundreds of times over the years. I still have the teddy bear."

"You kept the bear?"

"Yeah."

"You know that game was rigged to make me win."

"You rigged it?"

"No, not me. The guy let me win to look good in front of you."

"Oh, how sweet of him. The bear reminds me that there's still fun in the world somewhere. It makes me less sad."

"Why would you ever be sad?"

"I've had my share of trouble. Are you visiting or back to stay?"

"To stay. I have an ongoing love affair with the mountains."

She teased. "Only the mountains?"

I chuckled. "Would it be out of line to take you to lunch? It'd be business."

"Totally appropriate. Let me tell Carl I'm leaving."

Lou Ann suggested we try a new restaurant near the edge of town. The decor was modern, maybe contemporary. I wasn't sure which, but colorful and sterile-looking with chrome everywhere.

We chose a corner booth that offered privacy. Seats were covered in red and white plastic and looked to be well padded for comfortable sitting. "So how did you know I was working for Carl?" Lou Ann asked as we took our seats. "Did you find me by accident?"

I chuckled. "Remember the guy in your place with a beard and long hair? That was me."

"You've got to be kidding. The Rudy Kelly I remember would never . . ."

"He died a few years ago."

She frowned. "Why would you say that? You may have been kidding, but please don't say that anymore."

"Everyone has a bit of sadness in life, some more than others. I've been in Chicago for a few years, but the city had nothing more to offer me. I wanted to get away from everything. I've always loved the mountains and decided to live in the wild for a few months to figure out what I wanted. That was the reason for my mountain man appearance. But I'm building a house with plans to stay here. I need advice about decorating. Would you like to help?"

"That's part of my job."

"Good. I'm helpless when it comes to that kind of thing. You'll have to hold my hand and walk me through it." Our eyes connected for a moment. We both looked away. "Now, tell me what you've been up to other than working for Carl."

"I've also had bumps in the road. To be more accurate, I've had mountains to climb. I've been back nearly four years. Went to work for Carl and started school at Union. I had little money, but the people at school were like angels, and Carl has also helped by letting me stagger my work schedule according to class times. I'll earn my teaching certificate this year."

"So you want to teach?"

"I love children."

"Do you have kids?"

She muttered, "No."

"A husband?"

"No."

She turned away as if the questions were painful. I'd gotten the information I wanted and changed the conversation back to our night at the Daniel Boone festival. We both had kept every moment of that night alive in our memories.

Nearly two hours were spent at lunch. It ended with plans for me to meet her the next morning at eleven o'clock and look at paint and wallpaper samples.

Thoughts about Lou Ann stayed in my head. I had trouble falling asleep that night. Even with booze to help, I kept thinking about her and our first date. I finally moved my sleeping bag out under the stars.

Eager to see her again, I awoke early, did my morning run, and still arrived well before our appointment time. Eleven came and went and she hadn't arrived. After three cups of coffee and the clock hands pushing twelve, Carl stuck his head in the door.

"Sorry, you're being kept here. Lou Ann is usually here by ten. I suspect one of the AA members was in crisis and she went to help."

"What does she have to do with AA?"

"She's belonged since a few years back. Started a year or so after the accident."

"Accident?"

"Yes, a car wreck killed her husband and baby son. She's been dry going on four years."

I must have looked as shocked as I felt. Carl stepped inside the door. "Are you okay?"

"Her whole family?"

"Yeah."

I rose. "Tell her I'll call and set a new time to meet."

"I didn't mean to upset you, Rudy. I'm sure she'll be here soon."

"It's all right." He must have noticed I had the shakes . . . anxiety rising. Annie was gone, but I still had hopes of finding her. Lou Ann would never see her family again. Her loss shook me more than I could have imagined. The alcoholic demon in my head kept telling me that I needed a couple of drinks, though I knew better. When anxiety reached a certain point, I had to have booze. I'd suffered night sweats and had stayed dry for four days prior to last night, but I would get drunk tonight unless I talked with someone.

I headed my car up Bear Mountain and stopped two hours later in front of a building that read Drs. Cliff Kellerman and Rita Kellerman.

Seeing Cliff was just the best. His wife, Rita, agreed to take his patients that afternoon. She insisted that Cliff and I spend the afternoon together preparing for a family cookout that evening.

Rita was a beautiful woman, soft-spoken with an easy smile. The opposite of his choice of blondes a few years earlier.

We laughed, ate man-sized steaks, and talked until near midnight. Their two children crawled in and out of my lap until Rita ushered them off to bed, and only after each gave me a goodnight kiss. It was neat to hear them call me Uncle Rudy.

No alcohol was offered during the evening, which meant Homer had told Cliff that my problem had become severe. In addition to flying me down to Florida each Christmas, Homer made a couple of trips to Chicago each year and had called me once a week until I moved here. Never had he mentioned my drinking or my ongoing search for Annie.

I left shortly after midnight and replayed the evening in my head during the drive home. Cliff lifted my spirits. He was thrilled that I had moved back and was building a house. Seeing him and his family happy made me wonder if such a life would ever be possible for me.

Annie would love the house plan and the mountains. To see the patience Cliff had shown and the love given to the children made me long for the same experience with her.

I slept until near noon the next morning and decided a move into a motel made sense. I was isolated without a phone should the builder need to contact me during construction.

It was late afternoon before I'd finished moving things out of storage and into the motel. I called Lou Ann. She sounded glad to hear from me and apologized over and over for missing our appointment but made no mention of the reason. I suggested that signing the contract to build was reason to celebrate. I knew no one here anymore and couldn't celebrate alone. She agreed to join me for dinner.

We followed a scenic road to a lodge up in the mountains frequented mostly by people who owned summer homes in the area. A rustic décor suggested casual living which included golf, tennis, swimming, hiking, and informal dining.

Lou Ann dressed in jeans and an aqua colored blouse that matched her eyes. Her long, dark, tousled hair framed an oval face.

Heads turned as we entered. She knew how to make a man look good and slipped her arm beneath mine as we were shown to our table. It was difficult to take my eyes off her. As we sat she placed her hand on mine. "Thanks for asking me to dinner. It's my first evening out in years."

The ring was gone from her finger.

She laughed. "You just checked my finger. I finally took it off. Carl said he told you about the accident. It happened nearly six years ago. I can't talk about it much without spoiling the evening. Let me just say my life was turned upside down. I tried to kill the hurt with alcohol. It never worked and I joined AA. My life has been moving up hill ever since."

"I can't imagine how you've survived."

"Faith that God knows more than I do about what path my life should take. So, how did you end up back in Barbourville?"

Her question turned our conversation into talk about the mountains and the house under construction, and what both meant to me.

She didn't need the magic of the harvest moon to be beautiful, but it added a touch of romance, as did her throaty laugh as we chatted about our one and only teenage date while going down the mountain.

She lived in her family's old house. I took her key and unlocked the door. Our eyes met. She was beautiful . . . desirable. I wanted to kiss her, but this was her first date since the tragedy and I was unsure.

She suggested we have coffee and led the way, passing through rooms and flipping on lights until we arrived in the kitchen at the back of the house. It had been updated with new cabinets, harvest gold appliances, gold curtains, and specks of gold in the linoleum floor covering. The newness was obvious when compared to the rest of the house which appeared unchanged, including the furniture.

"And your parents, are they still . . ."

"No. Dad had a heart attack the year after I graduated. Mom passed a year before the accident." She reached to start the coffee-maker and her necklace caught on the button on her blouse. The strand broke, sending white marble-sized beads dancing across the floor.

She gasped and dropped to her knees, grabbing for beads. I took an empty cup she'd set out for coffee and joined her. We scrambled around on hands and knees, laughing and bumping into each other. It turned into a game about who could grab the most beads. We sat up and scanned the floor. There seemed to be none left until we both spotted one in the far corner where the bar joined the wall cabinets. Laughing, we both went for it at the same time, crashing together. The impact sent her rolling across the floor.

Afraid she might be hurt I crawled over and grabbed her up. "Are you okay?" I asked, cradling her in my arms. She nodded and looked up laughing, her face inches from mine.

My lips touched hers, lightly at first. She responded. Moments later she pushed against my chest. "No. Please let me up."

I moved away. She rolled to her knees and rose.

I waited.

She leaned her head on the counter. "I'm sorry. I thought I was ready, but I'm not."

I flashed back to my own hopeless journey when searching for Annie. Lou Ann was having trouble moving on. Perhaps, like me, she never would.

"I understand. I'm still in love with Annie after eight years. I could never fall in love with another woman in a traditional sense, yet I get lonely and want a woman's company. You're beautiful and desirable, a woman any man would treasure as a wife or lover. I'd like to be more than a friend to you. An arrangement like that wouldn't work for some people, but it does in my screwed-up world."

"I'm not sure I'm ready for that."

"I want your friendship, regardless. Until or if you decide differently, we're just friends." I rose. "The light on the coffeemaker is blinking. Let's have a cup."

32

The builder offered congratulations and presented me with the key to the house as Lou Ann, Preach, and Boonie applauded. I designated Boonie as tour guide since he had watched every inch of the house go up.

We followed him from room to room and stopped often to hear his explanation about how something was constructed. At the third bedroom door, he backed away and stared for a moment. Attached to the door was a hand carved sign that read Boonie's Room. "I don't know why this is here."

"Why do you think it's there, Boonie?" I asked.

"Maybe you're wantin' me to be a part of your family, but it would hurt Mama for me to be adopted. I love Mama and she loves me."

"I understand. Nothing changes except your address. You would have a place to call home."

"Nobody has ever been this nice before. Why would you want me?"

"Because you're the coolest kid I've ever known. I wish I could have been like you at your age."

"Rudy, you, you . . ." His voice crumbled. He pushed past everyone in the hall and went out the front door. We all spilled out onto the porch and watched as he raced across the meadow.

"Will he be all right?" Lou Ann asked.

"He'll be fine. I've done the same thing hundreds of times when I didn't want anyone to see me cry. I'm a crier. I'd cry if the wind blew a bird nest out of a tree."

"I love you for what you're doing for Boonie," Lou Ann whispered.

I raised a questioning brow and caught her eye. She laughed and added, "Like a sister, I love you."

After everyone left, I sat at the kitchen table and stared at the fireplace. I could only imagine the meal Will Jean could cook with the latest appliances. I knew she'd be happy that I'd kept the fireplace.

Preach had blessed the house before he left. If all that he prayed for would come true, my life was on a new course. I walked out on the porch and knew this was where I'd spend my time writing next spring.

Boonie returned a couple of hours later. His eyes were red as he stuck out a hand to shake. "I can't figure why you'd be doin' this, but you're my friend 'till the day I die."

I took his hand. "I'd like to be your big brother or substitute dad, whichever works for you if it's okay?"

He pulled himself up straight. "I'm fine with that. Maybe I could call you Pop."

"I'd love it. You know about me and alcohol. When I get edgy something inside tells me the only solution is booze. I know better, but until now I've been unable to solve my problem."

"Maybe I can help."

"No, you're not to be my caretaker. You're to live your own life and be happy. That's more important to me than you'll ever realize."

"You and Lou Ann have been as thick as cold molasses since startin' the house. Are you two serious or is it just . . . you know?"

"We're just friends. There may be nights I don't come home, but don't worry about me. It's probably because I met a lady friend."

"If you married Lou Ann you wouldn't have to go looking for . . . you know."

"That would be unfair to her. I know it's not normal in most people's thinking, but I can't get past being in love with Annie."

"Why not? I loved my daddy. Then after he left us, it got easy not to keep lovin' him."

"With Annie, it's different."

"I really like Lou Ann. I hope she keeps on bein' your friend."

"She will. One other thing. This is our house. We both will respect each other and share chores. Are you good with that?"

He grinned. "Yeah, I'm good."

"We need to move you in. Let's go to the orphanage and get your things."

Not long after moving into the house, winter unleashed its fury of wind and snow, leaving depths of two to three feet at higher elevations. We received about a foot in the valley with a texture perfect for sledding. Once the storm passed I suggested to Boonie that we

295

check out the sled. It'd been stored in the barn loft for years. He was excited and we took to the hill that ran from the house down to the edge of the meadow. A few spills occurred, but that only added to our fun.

More snow fell the next week and our world became a snow-covered fairyland. Signs of Christmas sprang up everywhere. Students gathered in front of the chapel at Union and sang Christmas carols most evenings. Streets and storefronts were decorated and Christmas music floated up from the town when air currents were right.

Two weeks before Christmas Boonie and I waded through knee-deep snow until finding the perfect tree. That night we invited Lou Ann over to help decorate. Leftover spaghetti was in the fridge for our supper until she brought a pot of vegetable soup, cornbread sticks, and a tray of Christmas cookies.

Once we'd eaten and trimmed the tree, the three of us sat on the floor beneath the tree and enjoyed hot chocolate with Christmas music in the background. Without a word Boonie rose and put another log on the fire, and then began lighting candles and placing them around the room.

With no place left for candles I asked him what he was doing.

"Addin' Christmas spirit," he answered.

"Why so many candles?"

"Can't get too much Christmas spirit." He flipped off the lights. "See how good the tree looks."

I got it. He was playing matchmaker. Not only did the tree look good, he'd probably noticed that I hadn't been able to take my eyes off Lou Ann. She was beautiful in a Christmas green dress. We'd been inseparable during the weeks it took to complete the house. It was becoming more difficult to maintain a friends-only policy. Lou

Ann would kick me off the mountain if she knew the thoughts that bounced around in my head.

"Penny for your thoughts," she said.

"You wouldn't want to hear them."

"Are you thinking about her tonight?"

"You mean, Annie? I think about her all the time."

"Are you ever going to tell me about her?"

"Maybe." Boonie started to leave the room. "Hey, where are you going?"

"Got lessons to get."

"You told me you were caught up. That's why I agreed to play in the snow after school."

"I'm caught up, but it never hurts to study a little extra."

I chuckled. The kid was crazy about Lou Ann and the candles were to enhance romance. I didn't need candles, only for Lou Ann to say the word.

"Why are you staring?" she asked.

"Can't help myself. You're so damn beautiful. I need to tell you something. True friends shouldn't have secrets. I'm an alcoholic, a secret drinker."

"I know, but I'm glad that you told me."

"It doesn't matter to you?"

"It matters, but it has nothing to do with the way I feel . . . I mean about our friendship."

"I need to be drunk when bad thoughts come home to roost at times."

"What bad thoughts?"

"That Annie will never come back."

"Have you ever talked to anyone, a professional?"

"No, never. My buddy, Charles, advised me to. I've thought about it."

"Why not do it?"

"Seeing a shrink feels like a weakness."

"Not being able to stop drinking might be called one also. Everyone needs help at some point, about something. Superman is not real. He's only in comic books."

33

The week in Florida with Homer, Virginia, and Cliff's family was fantastic. To have a family who loved me was over the top. I couldn't believe I was the same kid who hit Virginia with a shoe. She was the most giving person that I'd ever met. When Cliff and I were together, she introduced us by saying, "These are our sons, Cliff and Rudy."

I arrived back home three days after Christmas with a tan and feeling relaxed. I knew something was missing the minute I stepped inside the house. It was Boonie. He was such a great kid. It was selfish to wish he was back from spending the holidays with his mother. He would be gone until after the first of the year.

There was no one to talk to. Preach and his wife were out of town. Even Lou Ann was unavailable. Her deceased husband's parents had invited her to spend Christmas with them in Lexington.

I fried a couple of eggs and ate in front of the TV, but I was soon restless, bothered by thoughts of Annie, especially memories of our one Christmas together.

I climbed up into the loft and took down the cardboard box that held all the many attempts to write A Girl Named Annie. It was obvious after skimming over a few that I was drunk when writing. I pitched them back into the box and put them back on the shelf.

I wasn't ready to write yet. To do so would make me feel like I never expected to see Annie again. I had to believe she would come back. I sometimes doubted and it made me crazy.

The doorbell brought me hurrying down the ladder. Who could be at the door this time of night? I opened the door and light fell on a beautiful, smiling face. Lou Ann held a small overnight bag. I stared.

"You told me to let you know. I'm letting you know."

I pulled her into my arms and held her for a moment, kissed her, and locked the door.

We spent the next few days together. I felt more alive than I'd felt in years. We were lovers. We were kids playing in the snow. We were two adults discussing uncertain futures. I was surprised at her reaction when I mentioned plans for her to move in with me. She said no, and insisted on keeping her place. Her parents had raised her to have certain moral boundaries, and being with me unmarried would be a big jump for her. She didn't want to be thought of as a kept woman.

"But it's 1980. Couples live together," I argued.

"Rudy, you don't know about women. Even nice women can be vicious."

"I know a woman expects a man to be kind, to be loyal, to be loving, and supportive. I would be all those things to you."

"I know that, Rudy. That's why I'm here. I wish I didn't care what people said or thought. But I do. I have to. It's what my mother taught me and it's a part of me. Women have made advances, but in

300

many areas they still don't get a fair shake. Until they do, I'm keeping my place. Don't misunderstand, I'm happy with my decision to be with you, regardless of what people call me."

It was a wonderful few days and I hated to see Lou Ann go back to her place. Boonie returned the next morning. He came toward me with his hand extended and wore an ear-to-ear smile. Instead of shaking hands, I pulled him into a hug just as Homer always did to me. Perhaps he'd never had enough hugs in his life. I could tell he was glad to get the hug and to be back.

He brought with him a big bag of laundry and began separating the colors from the whites as I left for my morning run.

When I returned, the washer was still going. I came in the door, picked up a dishtowel, and wiped perspiration from my face and upper body.

"I've still got a load of whites to do," he said. "Do you have anythin' other than that contaminated dishtowel you just used for a sweat rag? It can never be used in the kitchen again."

I laughed and threw the towel at him. "All my other laundry is in the washer."

He chuckled. "Which leads to a question." He held up a pair of panties. "When did you start wearing undies with lace?"

"Oh, God," I muttered and felt my face turn red.

"It's none of my business, but I hope they belong to Lou Ann and not you." He laughed. "Look at your red face. So, they do belong to her. Why don't you ask her to marry you? Is it because of me?"

"No, it's not because of you. Lou Ann and I have an understanding. I can't marry anyone until I know what happened to Annie."

"That doesn't make sense to me. Lou Ann is crazy about you. She's real cool and I don't want her to get hurt."

"She's not going to get hurt. Like I said, we have an understanding. Besides, our personal life is personal."

A month later, family and friends attended a surprise birthday party for Boonie. Preach and his wife were there as his godparents. Homer and Virginia flew in and surprised us all, including Cliff and his wife who drove down for the occasion.

This time Boonie didn't run off into the mountains to hide his tears. They rolled freely down his face. This was the first time he'd ever had a birthday party. His attempt to thank everyone for coming touched us all. We all felt the emotion of the moment and, at some point, had watery eyes.

Homer suggested that Boonie call him Grandpa and promised, for him and a friend, plane tickets for a two-week stay in Florida next summer.

At the end of the ceremony I made a surprise announcement. The room went silent with all eyes on me. "I've been Rudy Kelly all my life, but I'm actually Rudy Kellerman by birth. I've had my name changed."

Both Homer and Cliff had watery eyes as polite applause filled the room. It was then that I realized everyone had expected the announcement to be about me and Lou Ann.

Lou Ann had arranged quite a spread. Included were all of Boonies' favorite foods. He had chosen his favorite music and played it so loud that some, including myself, escaped to the porch to carry on a conversation. It was there that Preach approached and gave me a hug. "I'm sure you'll be blessed by what you're doing for Boonie. He's a fine boy and you're giving him a chance to be a fine man."

"I'm blessed to have him."

"Me and several others in the room thought you might be making another kind of announcement." Preach chuckled. "You and Lou Ann. It's obvious that you two are crazy about each other."

"We're just friends. I'm not in love with her. We have an understanding."

He frowned. "What kind of understanding? She's crazy about you."

"As a friend, yes. It doesn't go beyond friendship. I'm in love with Annie."

"Aw, Rudy, what are you saying? You've got to let go sometime. Don't break this girl's heart."

"Preach, you're making me angry and I don't like being pissed off at you. We'd better drop this now."

He stared for a moment and then nodded. "I love you, Rudy." He walked away.

I suddenly felt angry and confused. Maybe challenged was the right word. Everyone wanted me to break up with Annie. Oh, my God, what was wrong with me? I couldn't break up with someone that'd been gone for years.

I heard my name and turned. Homer came forward. "I called your name a couple of times. Are you okay?"

"Yeah, I'm fine."

"You've got a good kid in there. I've just had a long talk with him. He's bright. I'm going to set up a trust fund for his college if you approve."

"Thanks, Dad. That's nice of you."

"Rudy, you seem happy, yet not happy. What's wrong? You want to talk about it?"

I took a moment. "Dad, did you ever reach a place in your life when you didn't know how to handle a problem by yourself?"

"Yes, I have. I felt a lot of guilt and couldn't figure out a way to make you see the truth about what happened with you and me. I had two years of therapy."

"You saw a shrink?"

"None of us are supermen, Rudy. Thoughts and feelings sometimes rule our thinking, thus our actions. Thoughts in our heads can often become cloudy, but to see them on paper or hear then spoken often paints a clearer picture. Think about talking to someone."

PART FOUR

34

I finished a five-mile run and dropped into my deck chair to cool down. Dark, low hanging clouds were moving up from the southwest. The morning forecast warned of a freak storm with freezing rain in higher elevations by tomorrow evening. For such an occurrence in late April went back more than fourteen years. My right knee called for a liniment rubdown after the run. I'd like to blame it on changing weather patterns, but I knew better. I was nearing forty and stress on the knee from years of running was revealing itself.

Lou Ann left the morning paper on the kitchen table before leaving for work. She knew I enjoyed having a cup of coffee and reading the paper after a run. The headlines declared the Cold War was drawing to an end after forty years. Thank God for that.

Lou Ann and I had been together for nine years. Just as she made clear at the beginning of our relationship, she'd continued to keep her own place, but spent less time there as each year passed. She was a second mother to Boonie and he was like a son to her.

Boonie was twenty now, a college senior with his eyes on medical school, no doubt influenced by his Uncle Cliff. He had dated a Union transfer for several months now. We didn't know how serious their relationship was, only that he described her as cool, smart, and pretty.

Homer had celebrated my birthday with me each year since I returned to the mountains, but he passed away last fall. Thanks to therapy, I'd learned to focus on what I had instead of what I didn't have. The few years with Homer couldn't have been better. He was a great dad. I would always miss him.

I shared a secret with him last summer when he was here for a visit. I'd purchased a ring for Lou Ann and planned to give it to her on my next birthday. I chose that date so the stigma of May 4th would end and become one of the happiest days of my life.

I'd accepted that Annie was not coming back, but even now there were times when I connected with old feelings. My shrink explained it as a fixation, an attachment that could often occur early in life, persisting in immature and neurotic behavior into adulthood. For whatever that meant, I'd take it. With AA and therapy my life had evened out.

"Hey, there. Anyone home?"

I reached for my glasses and stepped out onto the porch. A tall, slim female with brownish-red hair stood at the bottom of the steps. She wore jeans and a green jacket with a handbag hanging from her shoulder.

"You must be Rudy Kellerman," she said.

"I am. And who are you?"

"I'm Kathryn Reed, but my friends call me Katie. I'm a student at Union. I recently read your book *A Girl Named Annie.*"

"Oh. Come on up. Are you just reading it now? It's been out three years."

"I didn't know about you or the book until last summer."

I motioned her inside. "So, how did you hear about the book?"

"I found it in my mother's things after she died."

"Oh, I'm sorry. I hope you're doing okay."

"Thank you, I'm fine. I'm a journalism student. Maybe that's why I've connected with Annie in your book. I feel there's a bond between us." Tears rolled out onto her cheeks.

"Are you okay?"

"I'm sorry. I didn't mean to get emotional. It's just that the love you two had was so pure, so real. I can't sleep at night thinking about it."

Assuming she was here to have me sign the book, I reached for my pen. "So, you liked my book and you want me to sign it."

"Actually, I would like to interview you about your book for a column I'm writing."

"That would be wonderful."

"I didn't like the book. The ending sucked."

I was speechless and felt my face grow red.

"Where was the happy ending?" she asked. "Your book ended like a heart attack. It just stopped."

I forced a smile. This girl had insulted me in my own house. I took a breath. "It had no ending, no conclusion. Annie disappeared."

"Don't you see what a stupid ending that is for a book of fiction? Love stories have happy endings. A writer can make stories end the way the writer wants if it's fiction. You failed to do that. Your book is not fiction."

"It's what it is, young lady. I have things to do." I rose and started for the door. She followed.

"You were Annie's lover."

I froze for an instant and then turned and faced her. "No, young lady. He was a fictional character like all the rest. Now, please go, I have things to do."

"Annie was a real person. Your book ended the way it did because it happened. You promoted it as fiction, but it wasn't fiction."

A chill crawled up my back. What could she want from me? "Why are you here . . . the real reason?"

"I have to know why you and Annie broke up. Did she leave you? Is she dead? Did you hurt Annie? You were her lover."

"No, no, you're wrong. Why is the ending of the book so important to you?"

"I've told you that already. I want to know why you and Annie aren't together. I read *A Girl Named Annie* and couldn't stop thinking about it. You two were so much in love. I couldn't sleep, couldn't let go of it. So, I transferred to Union to meet you."

I took a breath. This girl was sick. "You moving here makes no sense. Don't you understand that you're obsessed? You're letting characters in a book control your life. You've got to stop it. You're still young, just beginning your life."

"I know it doesn't make sense to you, but it does to me now that I know you and Annie were lovers." She turned away for a moment.

Was she crying again?

She turned back. Tears rolled down her cheeks. "Did you try to find her?"

"I have no idea what happened to her. Please let it go."

"I wanted you and Annie together. Is that so bad?"

"Young lady, listen to me. The book couldn't have ended any other way."

She wiped her eyes. "I'm sorry for crying." She looked at me. "Talking to you has confused me more."

"I'm sorry. The truth shouldn't confuse you. Sometimes things happen that can't be changed. Go home to your family."

"No, I'm happy here at Union. I'm going to stay. I like the mountains. Besides, I've met the man I'm going to marry someday. All the guys in my life have been duds until now. But this one, Boonie, is the sweetest, most wonderful guy in the world."

A chill shot through me. "Did you say, Boonie?"

She laughed, "I did. I feel bad now that I tricked him into dating me. Dropped my books in front of him so he'd have to pick them up. After that I had him. But he's a sweetheart."

I was so angry that I could hardly speak. "Boonie is a good guy. I'd hate to see him hurt."

"I'll never hurt Boonie, I promise. Did you love his mother as much as you loved Annie?"

"Did I love . . . What are you asking me? Boonie calls me Pop, but I'm not his dad.

I'm just giving him a home." Her expression changed. She looked pleased. "You seem happy to hear that."

"You gave him a home for no reason."

"No, there was a reason. He's a nice kid who needed a home and a chance to be happy. Kids are special. They need to be loved. You're also special, Katie."

She looked away. "Please, don't say that, you'll make me cry again and I'll be sorry for all the mean things I said about your book. Do you have a girlfriend?"

"What? Why do you ask that? Yes, I have a girlfriend."

"You can't marry her if you are going to be with Annie."

This girl was crazy and not just odd. I didn't know what to say or think.

"I said bad things about your book. May I give you a hug?"

I hesitated, knowing I should say no, but nodded instead.

She hugged me and held on until I gently pushed her away.

"I hope Boonie won't hate me for coming to see you. Don't tell him, please."

"Boonie could never hate anyone. But he could be hurt. I hope you won't do that. We don't keep secrets from each other. I have to tell him about meeting you."

"I would never hurt, Boonie. I'm crazy about the guy. He's my reason for staying at Union." She headed for the door. "Got to go."

I watched her hurry down the lane, still wiping her eyes. What had just happened with this girl? Was she obsessed over me or the book.

For the remainder of the day my thoughts kept going back to Katie. I knew what it was like to be a kid with problems. They multiplied if not attended to. This girl was pretty. I could see why Boonie would like her, but the thought that she might hurt him left me worried. She needed professional help.

310

Katie's surprise visit ended all hope of getting any work done in spite of my many attempts to concentrate. This girl could cause Boonie a lot of unhappiness. I hoped he wasn't serious about her. We had to talk about their involvement. I couldn't imagine him not seeing that she had problems. His astuteness in reading people had always been sound, yet he'd described this troubled girl as being cool, smart, and pretty. She was pretty for sure. Perhaps that had blinded him from seeing her flaws.

The morning dragged on as if in slow motion. I checked the time every few minutes and often thought the hands on my watch had stopped.

I assumed this girl could be called a groupie, obsessed with a character in a book. But what was her motivation? She never mentioned a search to find Annie. Did that mean she knew where to find her? I hadn't thought of that.

It was nearing two o'clock and I'd given up hope that Boonie was coming home when his red Mustang shot up the driveway. Homer had given him the car for his eighteenth birthday. I stood and watched him climb out. He raked light brown hair away from his face, swung his backpack over one shoulder, and came up the steps smiling. He pretended to belly punch me with his free hand. "Pop, I'll have to shoot you for taking my girl."

"What do you mean?"

"Katie told me she visited you this morning. She couldn't stop talking about you. I teased her about having a thing for my old man."

"We need to talk about her."

He laughed. "We certainly do. I can't let you take my girl without a fight."

"Please, Boonie, this is not the time for teasing. She's got problems. She's disturbed."

He frowned. "Pop, everyone's got problems to a degree. She's passionate about the things she cares about."

"Don't you find it strange that she transferred to Union because a book didn't end like she wanted? The girl needs professional help."

"Come on, Pop, ease off some. I don't understand what you're talking about."

"Boonie, she's got real emotional problems. She wanted me and Annie together. Couldn't accept that we weren't. A person like that might do anything."

"Come on, she told me about having a meltdown. You're reading her wrong."

"She said you're the guy she's going to marry."

He smiled. "Really. That's interesting."

"The girl knows things about Annie."

"Why do you think that?"

"Think about it. She spent months looking for me. Why not look for Annie? I think she knows where to find her."

"Come on, you've got to stop this. You're overthinking what happened this morning. She's nothing like you're projecting her to be. I'll admit she's a romantic that sees drama in situations others might ignore."

"Boonie, listen to me. This girl could be dangerous. I'm telling you to stop seeing her. It's not good. You're getting too close."

"Come on Pop. I'm a big boy now and I can take care of myself."

"Is she the friend you've been camping with since last summer? You've given me a weekly update about you and a friend going camping. I had assumed it was a guy friend. Now, I'm thinking it's her."

His face grew red and he stared for a moment. "Pop, I've tried never to disappoint you, never to give you reason to be sorry one minute for taking me in. I'm nearly twenty-one. I'm a responsible guy. It hurts that you asked . . . no, that you've demanded that I drop Kate. I refuse to do that. Let it go, Pop. We're done here."

He disappeared inside. All I could do was to throw my hands in the air. He was right. I had treated him like a kid when he was a man. Now, I did what I'd always done when problems appeared unsolvable. I dropped off the end of the porch and headed across the meadow, running at full speed.

I returned an hour later with my energy spent. I wanted to apologize to Boonie, but his car was gone. He must have eaten and then left. It depressed me that things weren't right between us.

Lou Ann soon arrived home from school. She placed a small package, along with a handful of mail, on the table beside the deck chair as she slipped onto my lap and snuggled her face against my shoulder. "They were talking about a freak storm brewing in the mountains at school today. It's like spring and the weather report predicts an ice storm coming our way."

"Yeah, that's what I heard." She looked tired. I kissed her cheek. "Welcome home. Have a rough day?"

"My little sweet peas were full of energy. Those kiddies kept me jumping all day. I'd like to stay right here, but I have a meeting at school tonight that may run late. How about cranking up the grill and tossing a couple of steaks on. You cook. I'll make a green salad and get a baked potato going."

I nuzzled her neck. "How about staying right where you are forever?"

She giggled. "How about going easy on the nuzzling. You haven't shaved today."

I patted her on the butt as she crawled out of my lap. She giggled again. "Did you finish the last read through of the proof of your new book?"

"Still some to go," I answered. With her tired and a meeting tonight, the Katie matter could be discussed later. The quibbling between Boonie and me would cause her concern. Why trouble her since I would apologize and it would be over after I saw him?

Lou Ann told me she might stay at her place tonight as she left for her meeting. Feeling a little down with her not coming and Boonie away, I pulled on a sweater and slipped into the deck chair. Black clouds had moved closer, taking the sunshine and returning our world to the gray of winter. I began working my way through the pile of mail stacked on the table. My system was simple. I created three stacks on my lap. One for those that should be thrown away, another for those to consider, and the third for the ones that needed immediate attention.

I finished the letters and picked up the package. It had a Chicago postmark and no return address. "That's odd." I tore into it and seconds later came up out of the chair, dumping the contents from my lap onto the floor.

"My God," I cried. "Annie's alive."

35

The package contained love letters I'd written to Annie, along with a note. They were stacked on the kitchen table. Preach sat across from me. I handed him the note. He laid it aside and wiped his glasses on the tail of his shirt, and then held the note at arm's length to catch the light. He read aloud,

> I know where to find Annie. You said you loved her, then why hurt her? She nearly died. Would you be ashamed for your friends to know the way you left her? I'll be at your birthday party.

Preach muttered, "A strange note. It's not blackmail. Whoever wrote it wasn't asking for money. It's demanding a confession about why and how you hurt Annie before your birthday party two days away. Any idea what this is about?"

"Not a clue. I've never hurt her. I loved her."

"Maybe cheated on her?"

"No, never. I wouldn't do that."

"I didn't think so, but I had to ask. After nearly twenty years who would be sending this to you? And why? Friends would never play such tricks. You mentioned on the phone that a strange-acting girl visited you this morning. Do you think there could be a connection?"

"There's got to be. Both had to do with Annie. I can't think of any other possibility."

Preach took a moment and studied the letter. "It's printed in small box letters, each one neat and precise. It could be a female writer because of its neatness. The pen was pressed hard enough to nearly cut through the paper. People who do that are tense or angry."

"Or crazy like the girl this morning."

"The sentence *I know where to find Annie*. What does that say to you, Rudy?"

"That Annie's alive."

Preach shook his head. "Not necessarily."

"No. I don't want to think she's . . . not alive."

"Nor do I, but we have to consider all possibilities. The next line reads *You said you loved her, but then why hurt her?* You either hurt her or you didn't."

"Damn it, I just told you I never hurt her."

"I know, Rudy. That was a statement, not a question. There's a fine line between a disagreement and a fight. On the phone to me you said you two had words that Friday night. Did it reach a stage where anger ruled your words and actions?"

"No, it was a discussion about her not breaking her engagement to David. Everything was made positive at breakfast before I left for class Monday morning. She called me back when I started to leave and told me she would never love anyone but me. She'd planned for us to celebrate my birthday with cake and champagne at her place that afternoon. I never saw her again."

"If she felt that way about you, it's strange that she still had a fiancé. You two had been together a few months. Why do you think Annie was reluctant to break her engagement to this David fellow?"

"It's complicated. She never found an opportune time. She'd planned to break it off with him that weekend."

"But she didn't."

"No."

"How did you feel about that?"

"I was pissed. That's what we had a *discussion* about."

"And things got fixed between you two at breakfast on Monday morning. You had no contact with her over the weekend?"

"No, not even by phone." Preach continued to stare. "What is it, Preach? Where're you going with this? I never hit Annie, not once during our time together."

"I know that, Rudy, but we don't know where this is going. You could face questions like these if there are reasons for the law to become involved."

"Yeah, I know."

"The last line indicates that the person who wrote this note will be at your birthday party unless you confess before. Does that mean anything to you?"

"Only that my birthday always turned out to be a shitty day. It was bad in 1960 and 1970. So why the fuck should I think 1988 should be a *good* day? I now know Lou Ann had planned to surprise me with a party. I didn't know about it until this note came."

Car lights sprayed across the back wall. Preach looked at me. "Expecting someone?"

"It's Boonie. That sounds like his Mustang."

He soon popped in the door and stopped. He looked from one to the other. "Something wrong?" he asked.

"This came in today's mail," I said.

He took the note, spun a chair around, and straddle it. A frown crawled across his face. "What does this mean, Pop? Did you and Annie have a fight before she disappeared?"

"Yes. Well, no. We had words that night, but it wasn't a fight. She was supposed to break her engagement to this guy and had put off telling him again."

"Telling him again? Pop, think about what you just said. Are you saying she'd put off telling him multiple times before? As much as you don't want to believe it, she walked out on you."

"No, no, Annie would never do that. This letter is somehow connected to Katie."

"Come on, Pop, don't go there, please. I can't listen." He rose.

"Wait, Boonie," Preach called. "Why not get a cup of coffee and the three of us figure this out together? Your girl may not have a connection to the note, but the letters and note were about Annie. They arrived on the same day. We can't dismiss the possibility of a connection. Think about it. The idea is for us to get to the truth."

After a moment, he settled back into the chair. "You're right, Preach. I'll bring Kate back here in the next half hour and prove she had no connection." He started toward the door.

I rose. "Wait, Boonie, I'm sorry for . . ."

"Pop, don't. You'll never have anything to be sorry about where I'm concerned. I understand your take on this whole thing. Your concern has always been about what's best for me. I love you for that, Pop." He shot out the door.

I dropped back into the chair.

Preach muttered, "Wow! We just witnessed a beautiful moment."

My eyes moistened. "Yeah, Boonie has a beautiful, forgiving spirit. I wish mine was as good."

The phone ringing broke the silence.

"That's probably Lou Ann calling to tell me she's not staying at her place tonight." I rose and shoved the phone against my ear. "Hey, Sweetie, I'm lonesome for you. I hope you're calling to tell me you're coming home . . . say that again . . . Annie?"

Preach came to his feet and moved a few steps toward me.

"Yes, Annie. I understand. Of course, I will. Tell me quick . . ."

Preach whispered, "Is that your Annie?"

I nodded. "I'll be waiting." I replaced the receiver and faced Preach. "Annie's coming here."

"Thank God she's alive," Preach said, "but why would she come here? What does she want?"

"I'm not sure. She had no time to explain. Her plane was boarding when she called. She'll be in Knoxville in less than three hours and wants me to meet her. She said our local airport is closed to lightweight flights because of the storm."

"She wants you to meet her tonight?" Preach asked.

"In about three hours."

"Rudy, the rain just started. Roads at higher elevations will be freezing. It'll take hours for crews to salt down those steep mountain passes and eliminate the black ice."

"That's why I'm leaving now. I should have a small window of time to make it across those steep passes. Please call Lou Ann and . . . No, don't call her, don't tell her anything. She's staying at her place. She was dead tired. No need to worry her. I'll call her early in the morning. Tell Boonie where I've gone and for him not to tell Lou Ann should he talk with her."

36

A windblast of sleet peppered the windshield with a bang and brought me back to the present. Visibility had become more difficult, making it important that I stop thinking about Annie and focus on the road.

Trees had bowed to the weight of winter and stood silent beneath a coat of white. Large snowflakes crashed against the windshield and the wipers soon strained against the melting slush. I had to be sensitive to the slightest loss of traction, so I gripped the steering wheel with both hands as the car crawled up the mountain. Chains on the rear tires helped, but the bed of ice beneath the snow still caused the car to slip and slide.

After three hours of squinting against the white glare my eyes burned and my arms and shoulders ached. "Thank you, God," I muttered as snowflakes turned into raindrops after descending into the Knoxville area where a blanket of fog had spread over the city. It was well after midnight and the airport appeared deserted on the approach to the main terminal. Luggage check-in stations at each concourse entrance had closed for the night. Only Concourse A appeared open if the amount of lights was an indication. An airport policeman sat on a stool inside the doorway. He rose and asked with a sleepy smile if I was there to meet someone. The last incoming flight had arrived from New York some time ago, and all planes were grounded until tomorrow.

"I'm meeting the New York flight," I said.

"Your flight docked at the last concourse terminal to your left. Your party would most likely be in the lounge area."

I nodded and turned to leave. Then he added, "If you traveled over the mountains you can't go back tonight. Mountain passes are closed until daybreak. Black ice. Road crews will be working all night. Better grab a motel if there are rooms left. If the storm doesn't stop travel, the fog will."

I thanked the officer and found that a scattering of people had remained inside the concourse. A few were reading and others slept in chairs and on sofas, with their legs drawn in fetal positions and covered with coats.

Silence, mixed with shadows of all shapes and sizes, gave off a cold and eerie feeling as I made my way toward a lighted area the length of a football field away. My stomach nerves worked themselves into a frenzy during the walk. My mouth felt dry. Would I be able to speak when I saw Annie? What would I say? Once words weren't necessary—a light touch, a quick glance, and the hint of a smile had said so much. Now I'd finally learn what happened on that day and where she'd been for eighteen years.

A female dressed in a long red coat sat beside a floor lamp with her head laid back against the sofa. Her eyes were closed. It was Annie. To protect against the chill her hands clutched together the coat collar. A large, green wool scarf draped her lap.

For a moment, I stared. She was just as beautiful as ever, looked much the same, except her hair was cut short in a current style. A rush of memories came and went. How many times had I stared at that beautiful face sleeping on my shoulder? Our lovemaking, the dreams we shared about careers and children. Why did they go? Perhaps to make room for new dreams. That seemed to be the way life works.

"Annie . . . Annie, wake up, it's me, Rudy."

She opened her eyes, looked up, and smiled. "Thank God you're here. I was told the roads were closed." She rose and looked me up and down. "You're still a runner, aren't you? You look wonderful. May I have a hug?"

Without waiting for an answer, she came into my arms. I held her for a moment, but felt uncomfortable and backed away. "I've got to know. Where have you been and what happened on the day you disappeared?"

She frowned. "Why would you want to talk about that day? I've tried to forget."

"Have you succeeded?"

Her expression told me she was surprised by my response. After an impatient sigh, she said, "I haven't forgotten, but I've survived."

"Okay, first things first. Why did you call me?"

"It's about my daughter. She . . ."

"You have a daughter?"

"Yes." She chuckled. "Why are you surprised? Don't you remember? I always wanted children."

"I don't know . . . it, uh surprised me for some reason. I just never thought about you . . . having a child. So, you're married."

"No. Two times married. Two times divorced."

323

"Why contact me? I know nothing about your daughter."

"I believe you do. You've met her. She told me she visited you yesterday."

"You can't mean Katie?"

She nodded.

"That's my son's girlfriend. She said her mother had died."

Anguish moved across Annie's face. She paused briefly. "To her I have. She's really a sweet child. I'm the bad mother."

"Why would you say that?"

"For a lot of reasons. My career, bad marriages, and the worst part, neglect of my daughter. Kathryn was raised by my mother for most of her life. Don't ask me to give the reasons."

"Then you got what you dreamed about, didn't you?"

Her bottom lip quivered. She whispered, "No, Rudy, not even close."

"You were more ambitious than me. Did you ever really love me?"

She looked away for a moment. Tears rolled onto her cheeks as she turned back. "God, Rudy, how can you ask me that? Please, let's not get into what happened with us."

"I've got to know what happened. That last morning you said you'd never love anyone but—"

She grabbed my arm and slapped her hand over my mouth. "Stop it, Rudy," she cried. "I know what I said, but I married David."

I jerked her hand away, turned and circled back. "For years, you owned me heart and soul. I was unable to get on with life. You owned me."

"I owned you?" Her face grew red. "Was it because of guilt, Rudy?"

"Guilt? About what? Are you crazy?"

"Please." She bowed her head and inhaled. "Forget I said that. I need your help with Katie."

"I don't see how I could help."

"You can. I'm not sure she loves me. And maybe with good reason."

"Does she love David?"

"She did, but after I divorced him he wanted nothing to do with me. Time passed and he saw less of Katie, until he wasn't seeing her at all. You of all people can understand how not being wanted would make her feel. She read your book and found your letters to me. Katie has this fantasy that you and I should be together now. You wrote as if our love affair was perfect. Life is not like a love story in a novel, but she thinks it can be."

"Love story in a novel, you say. Is that what you think we had? It was real, Annie."

She looked away. "I'm here for my daughter."

"Your daughter mailed me the love letters you mentioned, along with a note that accused me of *hurting* you. She threatened to tell my friends how I had *hurt* you."

"It was probably Katie. She sent mail to her Chicago girlfriend who forwarded letters to me. I assume that's what she did to you. I wasn't aware she'd transferred to Union College months ago until recently."

"Why would she accuse me of hurting you? Annie, you walked out on me and married David."

"Rudy, please. Don't force me to talk about what you did to me just because you have regrets."

"Regrets about what? One of us has lost our mind, and it's not me."

"Okay, Rudy. I'll talk about what happened if you answer one question. What did you buy with the money?"

"What money?"

"The five thousand dollars that Dad paid you to drop me. And don't deny he paid you. It was a three-part cashier's check. I still have the pink copy he gave me. He said you took the check and left town. I took pills and wanted to die because of what you did."

I couldn't speak, couldn't breathe for a moment. Anger surged until I pumped my fists in the air and screamed like a madman. "The son-of-a-bitch lied. I never took a penny."

She cried out, "Oh, God, no. He tried to bribe you?" She dropped down on the sofa covered her ears, and looked up at me. "Please don't tell me you never took the money."

"No, not a penny," I whispered.

She covered her face and began to cry.

"You believed him," I said. "Why didn't you trust in my love?"

"I didn't believe him at first. But he showed me the pink cashier check receipt made out to you. I screamed and tried to run, but they forced me into the car. I cried all the way to Chicago. I was upset and confused. I couldn't think, couldn't remember."

"Couldn't remember that you were supposed to be in love with me?"

She looked up at me. "Oh, God, help me, I did love you, Rudy. I married David, but I never loved him. I married again. Never loved him. I meant what I said to you that last morning. It's never changed, Rudy. I still love only you."

326

37

Sunshine and a blue sky favored a spring-like day when we awoke the next morning. On the drive home crews were still salting roads at higher elevations. It caused one-lane stops and starts, but even with short interruptions we arrived back in Barbourville before noon.

We'd talked most of the night. By morning I hoped she knew something I'd known for a couple of years. Our time had passed. It left a touch of sadness that would be felt when our thoughts floated back to our time together. I would treasure the good memories, but I had no appetite to go back. Does love last forever? No. Just the memories of having loved.

I'd lived with loneliness as a kid and knew the feeling of not being wanted. Katie was the one left with the most scars. Something compelled me to help the girl. In view of my own childhood, I couldn't walk away.

I dropped Annie at the hotel to rest with plans to meet later in the day, perhaps contact Katie and the three of us spend time together, maybe have dinner. Perhaps we could convince her that we wouldn't be getting back together.

When I arrived home, Boonies' car sat in the driveway. He stepped out onto the porch as I arrived. Something was on his mind. No smile from the guy who invariably lit up a room with his pearly whites, except when worried. "Are you okay, Boonie?"

"What's going on, Pop? Preach said you went to meet Annie."

"Yeah, I just now left her at the hotel." He followed me into the house.

"Lou Ann didn't stay at her place last night, she came home. I had to tell her where you'd gone. I told her you'd call this morning. You didn't call."

"Couldn't get through last night, lines were down." Tired and in need of a shower, I emptied the contents of my pockets onto the kitchen table. "I need to talk to Lou Ann about Annie. Didn't try this morning. Had stuff on my mind and left early for home. Is she coming here after school?"

"Yeah, between four and five."

"Aw, rats, I'll miss her again. I'm to meet Annie about that time." I slipped off my shirt, stepped out of my jeans and tossed them into the laundry room. A shower and a few winks was what I needed before meeting anyone.

"Why is *she* here?" Boonie asked. "What business does *she* have here? What about Lou Ann?"

"Relax, Boonie, I'm going to talk to Lou Ann. Everything will be fine. Lou Ann and I understand each other. But I have something to tell you that's going to shock you. Annie is here because your girlfriend is her daughter."

His mouth fell open.

"Yeah, she is." He continued to stare. "Katie had a difficult time growing up. She can't forgive her mother for a number of issues. She

328

has this fantasy that her life would be perfect if Annie and I were back together."

"That doesn't sound like the Katie I know. Though she does question me about you all the time. Maybe it wasn't me she was interested in, it was you. She just used me."

"No, Boonie, I don't think so. She said you're the reason she wants to stay at Union. Because of you she's ready to fight her mother to stay."

"She wants to stay because of me?"

"Yeah, she does."

He stared for a moment and nodded. "I like her a lot too."

"I thought you did."

"What are you going to do, Pop?"

"I thought about Katie on the way home. There's something about the girl. It'd be tragic if she fails to work things out with her mother. Life is about forgiveness. I hope I can help her forgive her mother. Annie loves the girl in spite of all that's happened."

"Thanks, Pop, for having an interest in Katie. She feels like she's fighting the world."

I gave him a thumbs-up and headed into the bathroom. Standing in the shower with water running full force, I thought about what to say to Katie when we faced each other at dinner. She ended up liking me when she visited a few days ago, but she'd lied about her mother being dead, so who knew?

Preach always said if you couldn't find an answer it never hurt to pray. I was concerned about the end results of this tug-of-war between mother and daughter, especially where it might leave Boonie. I knelt in the shower and prayed for answers. I couldn't explain why, but I felt better after having done so. All things were possible with God. I needed more forgiveness in my own life. I thought of Will Jean and the things that were never said.

It would be muddy after the winter storm. I slipped on knee-high rubber boots and climbed the hill to Will Jean's grave. I wasn't sure why I needed to go there. Tears flowed down my face as I began pulling dead weeds from all the graves. It'd been two summers, maybe three, since I'd cleared them away. I couldn't explain the tears until I heard myself say aloud, "I forgive you, Will Jean, for everything." I dropped down and sat on my heels until a cloud moved past the sun and spread light across the hillside.

When I returned to the house Boonie had left. I had only time for a short nap before leaving to meet Annie. I nearly overslept and arrived at the hotel a little after four. She was waiting, dressed in a black pant suit with a floral blouse. She would always be beautiful, regardless of age.

It took only minutes to reach the Union campus four blocks away. Katie's dorm was relatively new. Decorated in neutral tones with splashes of color made it a perfect home for lively young girls. Katie wasn't in her room and a girl across the hall didn't expect her back before curfew. She had left in a red car with a guy. That had to be Boonie. I assured Annie that Katie was safe with him and suggested we postpone until tomorrow.

I offered to take Annie to dinner, but she declined, preferring to have room service and get some real sleep. I was pleased that she'd declined. That would give me time to find Lou Ann. It had only been two days, but it felt like a week since I'd last seen her.

On the way home, I swung by her place. Her car was gone and no lights were on. She'd be at the house. My excitement began to build as I approached the house, only to be disappointed when her car wasn't in the driveway. "Crap," I muttered. I wanted to talk with her, tell her for the first time *ever* that I loved her and then ask her to marry me.

Boonie rose and faced me as I entered. I started to ask about Lou Ann but noticed the scowl he wore. Something had happened since we last talked. "Okay, Boonie, let's have it. Something's going on?"

"Lou Ann knows about you and Annie. The hotel receipt was on the kitchen table. Two people occupied that room."

I chuckled. "I can explain. Nothing happened."

"You've never lied to me before."

"And I'm not lying now." He was a peacemaker, but I saw anger in his eyes and knew that he was ready to fight me. Even his fists were balled. He was a man in every respect, and I had to approach him like one. "Okay, Boonie, I deserve time to explain."

He nodded. "I'm listenin'."

"Hotels were full because of the storm. We found one room. I slept in a chair. Annie slept on the bed in her clothes. I promised Lou Ann never to cheat nine years ago. I've kept that promise."

"How do I know that? I'm aware of your abnormal history with Annie."

"Abnormal?" I threw up my hands and circled around. "That hurts coming from you. Wait here." I went into the bedroom and pulled a small bag from the toe of an old cowboy boot that I wore as a teenager. I returned and handed him the bag. "Take a look."

He took a small box from the bag, flipped the top open, looked at me, and then back at the box. "For Annie?"

"No. That was hurtful. You're being a smart ass with that comment. It's a ring I purchased for Lou Ann last August when Dad was here. I'd planned to give it to her tomorrow on my birthday. Now I'll be giving it to her tonight if I can find her."

"Aw, Pop." He took a step toward me. "I'm sorry I didn't believe you." He stuck out his chin. "You want to hit me? Go ahead."

I chuckled. "No, Boonie, I don't want to hit you."

"I doubted you and I've never had reason. I'm ashamed."

"It's okay. I've learned that forgiveness is about loving. And I love you, Boonie, like a son.

"Pop, don't say that now. You should kick my ass. But I do love you, Pop."

"I know you do."

"I don't like myself right now."

"It's okay. I like you. Everything is cool between us. It's always going be that way."

"Yeah, cool. Lou Ann said tell you she was spendin' the night with an AA friend."

"Oh, my God, I'm glad she's doing that. Do you remember when she took me to my first AA meeting? That sweet woman is the reason I'm not drinking. She's taught me how to love again. Did she say who she's with?"

"No. She just said to tell you . . . here, I've made notes. She's with an AA friend until the party tomorrow night. She doesn't want to talk to you or see you until then. She said to tell you not to embarrass her by tellin' your friends that you're back with Annie until after she leaves."

"Until after she leaves? She's not going anywhere. She's coming home with me. Damn, I screwed up. I've hurt her, Boonie. I should have known better. Let this be a lesson, never take someone you love for granted. And I do love Lou Ann." Boonie beamed. "Now, tell me what happened with you and Katie."

"Nothin'." When answering, he looked away and shifted his weight from one foot to the other. The question bothered him.

"What do you mean, nothing? She was picked up by a guy in a red car about four this afternoon. I assumed that was you."

He sighed. "Yeah, it was me."

"Talk to me."

"Okay, here's the deal. She's upset that her mother is here. Pop, I'm worried about her. She's got this crazy idea that she's your daughter."

"What? She's more delusional than I thought. She needs professional help."

"We had a fight about her sayin' it."

"You can rest assured that I'm not her father. Annie told me David was a good father until their divorce. Katie was five. She turned bitter in later years. Then after reading my book and the letters, she apparently lost touch with what's real. Does she plan to attend the party like she threatened?"

"I don't know. I left the fight and drove around. After coolin' down, I went back. She was gone." He looked at his watch. "I need a distraction. Get my mind off of things. Some of the guy are shootin' hoops over at the gym. I'm goin' to join them."

I watched him pull away thinking he'd left me with another reason to worry tonight.

I flipped on Johnny Carson and flopped down on the sofa.

The knocking awoke me. I turned off the snowy television screen and hurried to the door. Katie stood shivering as she clutched a lightweight sweater together. I reached for her arm. "Get in here, girl, before you freeze."

She stepped inside. "It was colder than I thought."

I glanced at my watch. "It's after midnight. What are you doing here?"

"I need to see Boonie."

"He went to shoot hoops with some friends." I jerked a blanket from the top shelf of the coat closet and draped her shoulders. It was Will Jean's lap blanket that had survived the fire. She'd used it on winter nights while knitting and listening to country music.

"Will Boonie soon be here?" she asked.

"I would think so." I motioned to a chair near the fireplace, punched up the smoldering coals, and pitched on a log. The flames blazed up. She kicked off her shoes and held her feet toward the blaze. She was at ease with her surroundings, projecting a confidence unlike her visit yesterday when she was noticeably nervous.

"Sorry to be so much trouble," she said, "but I really need to see Boonie."

"You're not trouble to me. How about coffee? It should warm you up." I moved to the kitchen counter. The coffeemaker had been preset for in the morning. I hit the "on" button and then checked the cookie jar. Empty. It was half full earlier in the day. Boonies' sweet tooth must have won out over his effort to cut back on sweets. I glanced at Katie a number of times. Her thinking that she might be my daughter scared me a little. In some ways, we looked alike. Her thin build, hair color, and eyes were the same as mine, but that didn't prove anything. Her facial bone structure was like Annie's.

She pulled her feet up, hugged her knees, and pulled the blanket snug around her legs. And then in a casual, off-handed way, she asked if I knew she was Annie's daughter. I assured her I did and told her she was beautiful like her mother. That seemed to excite her. She put her feet on the floor, sat up straight, and wanted to know if Annie was as pretty now as when we were together. Her sudden excitement worried me. Had I sparked a renewed effort for her to get Annie and me back together? I quickly stated that Annie would be considered a beautiful woman, then and now, by anyone's standards.

She looked at her watch again. "I wish Boonie would get here."

"You're anxious to see Boonie. Is there a problem?"

"The problem is with me. We had a fight. He said you always told the truth and never lied. I challenged him and he was furious. Have you ever lied to Boonie?"

"No, I'm sure I never have. I would never lie to him just like your mom would never lie to you."

"I'm not so sure about her."

"What did your mother lie about?"

With a smirk, she said, "Why not ask her."

"Okay, I will."

She looked doubtful. "You really mean it?"

"Yes, I mean it."

"Would you lie to me if I asked why you left Mom pregnant and she had to marry David?"

I hesitated. Was she here to see Boonie or to spar with me? It was like a game of chess by deciding what move to make next. Preach always said telling the truth ends up being the right move. "My answer is, no, I did not leave your mother pregnant. I knew nothing about her marrying David or you being born until yesterday."

Without comment she rose and reached for a small framed photograph of Will Jean that sat on the mantle. "Who's that? She doesn't look friendly."

"She wasn't. That's my grandmother."

"Did she love you?"

"I think so in her own way. But she never said she did."

"She never told you one time that she loved you?"

"Not one time." Her eyes teared. What was going on with this girl? Her empathy was too much. She truly cared about what had happened to me, or else she could cry on cue like a good actress.

"It's sad to think you're not loved," she said.

"It's the worst thing ever. Thank God I have a lot of people who love me now."

"Boonie loves you. We argued. He said you're the greatest pop ever. After he was gone, I asked myself how Boonie could be so nice if you weren't." She eased back into the chair. "I came here never intending to like you, but I do."

"I like you, too, Katie. I think we could be great friends."

"Maybe. Do you remember the date you last saw Mom?"

Was she back to chess playing again? "I do. How could I forget? It was my birthday, May 4, 1970. I never heard from her again until yesterday."

"I'm an October baby."

The buzzer announced that coffee was ready. I suggested we move to the kitchen table. She took a chair across from me. I poured two mugs and sat. "So, you were born in October?" I always loved that month. Daniel Boone's fall festival is an October event. An October baby. "That would be what, sixteen months after I last saw Annie."

336

Her face had held such a sweet smile moments before it changed. "October 1970." She stared without blinking.

The date left me stunned. Was she lying? She sounded so sincere about things that couldn't be faked. I took a sip of coffee. "Could you have been less than a full-term baby?"

"I weighed over eight pounds."

My God, she was saying I was her father. I couldn't find words.

Her bottom lip quivered. "I can't stay here." She started toward the door.

I jumped up and called out, "Wait! I believe you."

She turned back. "Would you say that again?"

"I believe you, Katie." She took a step toward me and stopped. It was then that I realized she wanted me to initiate the next move. I opened my arms. She came into them. I squeezed her tight and we both cried together.

38

My watch said 1:35 a.m. when I knocked. On the second attempt Annie responded. I identified myself and she opened the door. "What is it? Is something wrong?"

"We need to talk." I stepped inside and closed the door. "How old is Katie, and what was her birth date?"

Her eyes widened. She turned and reached for a robe. "Katie's been to see you."

"Yes, tonight. She said she's my daughter. Should I believe otherwise?"

"No. It's true."

"Damn you, Annie. Why?"

"You'll hate me for what I've done."

"No, I've learned that hate never works for me. But I'm pissed that you've denied me knowing my daughter."

"Let me explain. I should have known you never took money. I was in a bad place, mentally, for a lot of reasons. One being that I was pregnant. After Christmas break, you weren't quite the same.

339

I couldn't talk to you like before. You had changed and you would never tell me why."

"I was guilty of that. I was depressed. I thought the fire that killed my grandmother was my fault. It'd been an accident."

"You never told me that before. Or perhaps I was focused on my own problems and didn't listen. I do recall convincing myself that the pregnancy was all my fault. Young girls were too quick to take all the blame in those days. I'd gathered my courage and was going to tell you after the march. Remember, we'd planned to celebrate at my place."

"Yes, I remember . . . cake and champagne to celebrate my birthday."

"Yes, and for you to learn you were going to be a father." Tears rolled onto her cheeks. "I'd memorized what I was going to say about us and our baby. Then my parents showed up at the march with that pink receipt. I went crazy. They took me back to Chicago and we left for Europe the next day. I had Katie in October. It was five years later, after my divorce from David, before I returned home again."

"I've missed out on a lot with Katie."

"We've missed a lot by not having each other. But we both know it's too late . . . don't we?"

I let silence answer. After a few counts she reached for her purse, took out an envelope and handed it to me. "It's Katie's birth certificate. She saw it at some point in the last couple of years and that's what changed her."

I unfolded the paper. The name Kelly jumped out at me. Born to Rudy Thomas Kelly and Annie Louise Edmond, a daughter, Kathryn Louise Kelly, born October 16, 1970. "You had my name put here. Why? You'd married David."

"Yes. No one knew about the change except me and a sweet little French nun who made it happen. During my pregnancy, I had time to think about us. When Katie was born, I was haunted with doubts that you had taken the money, but I couldn't be sure. Even if you'd taken the money, I wanted Katie to have your name."

"Thank you for that."

"I've thought about a lot of things since being here. It would be good if Katie continued at Union. The two of you could get acquainted. You would learn that she's a sweet girl, worth loving."

"I've learned that already and I'd like for her to be here. What did she hope to gain by the letters and threatening note?"

"We had arguments. For a while, she referred to herself as my bastard child. The love letters contradicted all the venomous lies my parents had fed her. Remember, they mostly raised her. My mistake was teaching her that David was her father for most of her life. The birth certificate proved that I'd lied to my own daughter for years. She came looking for you to confirm what was true and what were lies."

"Lies on top of lies. I'll ask Boonie to bring her to the party tomorrow. You'll go with me. I'll pick you up about seven."

"I'm not sure I should go."

"You have to be there for Katie."

"I'll stay only a short time. My plane is scheduled out at ten o'clock, but I'd like to come back in a couple of months and spend time with Katie. I've never forgotten how we'd planned to spend those weeks in the mountains that spring. Maybe I can see the wildflowers with her."

39

Laughter and a band rocking it out grew louder as we approached the ballroom door. Annie whispered that she was nervous and asked me to hold her hand. The room was packed. Some were dancing and others stood chatting. I saw Boonie and Katie at a table near the band. He gave me a thumb's up, our signal that all was well with Katie. Annie slipped away and joined them. I scanned the room for Lou Ann. She was standing in a doorway at the far end of the room. I started toward her, but the band broke into a rendition of happy birthday. A swarm of people surrounded me, offering birthday wishes. When I looked again, Lou Ann was gone.

My closest friends, who knew my history with Annie, wore less than happy faces after seeing us together. Preach leaned to hug me and whispered, "Boy, have you lost your mind?"

I whispered back, "Have you seen Lou Ann?"

"I saw her grab a bottle of wine and go out the door. And the results of that will be on you, boy."

"Preach, I'm not a boy. I haven't been in years. Believe me, I'm sure about what I'm going to do. Do me a favor, go talk to Boonie. He'll tell you what's going on. See the girl he's with?"

"Yeah, his girlfriend."

"She's my daughter."

"Wait a minute . . ."

"Don't have time. Talk to Boonie. I love you, Preach."

40

Memories from all the years with Lou Ann had my heart humming by the time I reached her place. I was going to marry the prettiest girl in school. That girl loved me and I loved her. It couldn't get better than what we had.

I knocked and the door soon opened. Lou Ann glared up at me. She wore a faded blue floor-length housecoat, and a pair of bunny house-shoes that Boonie had given her as a joke. A row of hair rollers was perched across the top of her head. "We need to talk," I said.

"Maybe you need to talk, but I don't."   She tried to close the door, but I blocked it with my foot.

"Come on, Lou Ann, we've got to talk."

She let go of the door, and headed toward the kitchen. I followed, slipped upon a barstool, and pointed at the bottle of wine that sat on the bar. "What's that?"

"It's nothing. I thought I needed it, but I don't."

"Honey, I'm sorry. I know I've hurt you. Nothing happened with Annie. I can explain everything."

"I saw the motel receipt. I saw you holding hands tonight. If you start lying to me now, I'll hate you." Her voice cracked, "I don't want to hate you." She covered her mouth and turned away. "Please go."

"No, Lou Ann, I'm going nowhere. I didn't know until recently, but I've been searching for you since that night at the Daniel Boone festival. The fortuneteller was right, we're soul mates."

"That wasn't real."

"What's real has been the last nine years." I took the ring from my pocket and held it out toward her. "Nothing happened with Annie. The snowstorm caused us to share the same room. I slept in a chair. I've been your guy since that night ten years ago when you appeared at the door with an overnight case. I love you. I want you in my life forever."

"Why were you holding her hand tonight?"

"She was nervous about meeting our friends and ask me to hold her hand. I purchased the ring for you last August. The receipt is in the box. What Annie and I had was special at that time, but we're different people now. Those months with her served its purpose for whatever reason. And you should know that we have a child together."

"So, Katie's your daughter. She's a sweet girl."

"Yes, she is. Our son is crazy about her and I'm crazy about you. I'm not in love with Annie. I don't know if it's destiny or choice that pulls people together. We're soul mates. We've proved that to be true during our time together." I dropped to one knee. "Lou Ann, I love you now and I'll love you forever. Will you marry me?"

She paused for a second then dropped to her knees and grabbed me around the neck, sending us both backward. We lay sprawled on the floor, laughing and kissing. She pulled away. "Before this goes any further, I should remind you that you're missing your own party."

I slipped the ring on her finger. "You're my girl, Lou Ann. Let's go tell Boonie and all our friends. This party will be an all-nighter once they see the ring on your finger. I'd like a short engagement. Some other guy might go after you and I'd have to shoot him.

She laughed and reached to push her hair away from her eyes. "The curlers! Oh, my Lord, my hair. I look—"

"Beautiful," I said. "Start thinking about a wedding gift. Choose something you've wanted for a long time."

She laughed and her eyes flooded when she said, "Your baby."

THE END

About the Author

Dwain L. Herndon grew up in western Kentucky, earning his undergraduate degree at Murray State University and a graduate degree in drama from Southern Illinois University. He taught at colleges and universities before joining the corporate world for several years before he and his wife started their own art business. They live in Grayson, Georgia and have three children, Kim, Myles, and Devin, as well as three grandchildren, Amanda, Maya, and Mason.

Dwain became a writer after retiring. His first novel, *Beyond the Next Hill*, was published in 2013, followed by *When the Birds Stop Singing* in 2014. He writes most every day and finds pleasure in pulling characters from the rural South, hardworking, patriotic, and fun-loving Americans who are the heartbeat of this nation in bad times and good times.

Dwain would love to hear from you. Let him know if you like his stories at herndondwain@yahoo.com.